Before Anne Boleyn stole the heart of a king and demanded marriage, another woman strove to wed an already married king of England. This is the story of Elfrida, who would become the first crowned queen of England.

CONTENTS

Dedication   1

The First Queen of England   2

Prologue   3

Chapter 1   7

Chapter 2   16

Chapter 3   29

Chapter 4   35

Chapter 5   52

Chapter 6   71

Chapter 7   82

Chapter 8   89

Chapter 9   117

Chapter 10   128

Chapter 11   141

Chapter 12   162

Chapter 13   167

Chapter 14   176

Chapter 15   184

Chapter 16   188

Chapter 17   193

Chapter 18   200

Chapter 19   204

Chapter 20   209

Chapter 21   223

Cast of Characters   226

Historical Notes   230

About the Author   233

The First Queen of England Part 2   235

The Lady of Mercia's Daughter   236

DEDICATION

This novel is dedicated to all Anglo-Saxon women, both named and nameless, who were the equal of their men in all things. If only the Norman Conquest had never occurred.

THE FIRST QUEEN
OF ENGLAND

PROLOGUE

I gaze upon the decaying body of my husband, seeing not the wreck before me but rather the man I came to love and desire, despite my best intentions not to.

His breathing is shallow and his body too warm as he tries to fight whatever infection saps the strength and the life from him.

The callouses of his war mongering are long since healed, as his hand rests in my own. These are hands that have caressed me, stirred me to the greatest passion I've known, made me pant with desire and need, but no more. Now they're simply the only part of him that I can still reach.

He barely even opens his eyes to look at me, let alone stirs himself to take the sips of water I offer him. I don't even think he hears my soft murmuring as I try to ensure I tell him everything he needs to know before he leaves, or that of the priest in constant attention upon him, who prays for his soul without ceasing.

This man, my husband, heir to a great dynasty, beloved by his King, his young children, and by me, slips away, moment by moment, into the everlasting afterlife, and I'm denied the opportunity to go with him, even though I desire nothing more.

I don't wish to be left behind by the man who made me the woman I am today. No, if I could, I'd follow him on his journey and take pride and pleasure in doing so.

With his death, I will be bereft. Our marriage was not one built on passion, but it became one. Our marriage was crafted through his powerful father's need to retire from public life to become a monk. He didn't wish his family to suffer from his retirement, so he made his recently widowed son secure through our marriage. My father is a reasonably powerful man in his own right, with just the one daughter to gift to another man in marriage. My father's greatest triumph is the longevity of our dynasty and the great respect he's held within by all who live near our family home in Tavistock.

He might not yet be a man of the King's Court, but he will be. In time.

When my father arranged my marriage I was unhappy, almost demanding to be allowed to retire to the nearest nunnery instead, but, like my father, I understood the importance of the alliance, and so I allowed myself to marry, to bed the man who was my husband, and slowly, in the short space of time we had together, I came to care for Æthelwald, Ealdorman of East Anglia, more than I cared for myself.

He treated me like a queen from the old legends initially. I still smile to remember it now. He knew of my beauty and my wit, but when he first glimpsed it, I know he temporarily lost his ability to breathe. He told me later, when we lay coiled in each other's arms, sweating from our exertions, how he never expected to be with a woman as beautiful as I. I'm not one to remark on my own beauty. Others tell me that I'm blessed to be so tall and thin, with a face clear of all scars. I hope it will always remain the same.

His hand moves briefly beneath my own, snapping me from my less than holy thoughts, and I lean forward, into the gloom of the night, to see if he wakes or if he just trembles in his sleep.

Cloudy eyes meet my own, and I see some humour there. Even in his death, he stays in good spirits.

"My love," he gasps, and I nod, a tear falling from my eye. Æthelwald's voice is so light, almost a wisp, gone before I can truly hear it.

"Darling husband," I manage to utter, the words sounding harsh because of my constricted throat.

4

"I am sorry," he manages to wheeze, and now tears leak from my eyes and down my cheeks, as he struggles to speak each word separately as if to stress how much he means them. I know he's sorry. He didn't plan on his illness causing his death when he was so young; his father only dead a year or two. At its beginning, he thought it was a small thing, something that would pass with the better weather, but instead, he only deteriorated, and now I know his breaths are as numbered as the days before winter once more stalks our land and turns everything as crisp and lifeless as I feel now.

"You have nothing to be sorry for," I respond. I've spoken the words many times before but at that moment, his dying eyes fixated on my face, tracing the tears with his own, I mean them wholeheartedly. I don't want him to die surrounded by sorrow for those he leaves behind.

This time he seems to finally hears my words, his chest rising a little higher, and I almost wish it meant he had more air to gasp, but it doesn't. Time is no longer his ally but only his enemy.

"My children?" he manages to mumble, although his eyes have closed and stayed closed.

"I'll care for them my love," and I mean it. I've not always enjoyed being his second wife, the barren one, or so it seems, for he has two sons from his previous marriage, but I'll not let them suffer and do all I can for them, even if it does mean giving them into the care of his brother, the man who'll be ealdorman of his dead father's empire in his place.

"The King?" he also mutters, and I look at him, surprised to hear Edgar being mentioned on his deathbed.

"My love?" I ask. I don't know why he speaks of the King. Does he wish me to tell him of his death, or his children, or his wishes for the future? I simply don't know.

"The King and you," he sighs, and I look at him in shock, and at the priest praying by his side, but we've both heard the words, and my shocked inhalation masks his final exhalation, and before I can recover, his hand is still on my own, his pulse fluttered away to nothing and I know my husband is dead.

Tears leak from my eyes, my grief pronounced. What will I be without him? Who will love me and excite me as he once did? How will I continue to breathe in the wake of his loss?

Only it seems he's given me the wherewithal to want to live another day, another year.

The King. Why did he commend me to the King? He already has a wife and women fall at his knees, desperate to be in his bed. What has he arranged with the King in their one brief meeting since our marriage that I know nothing about?

But now is not the time to consider the words of my dead husband.

No, I bow low over his still body, thinking of our time together, the love we shared, and how, for all that I told him it wasn't his fault that he was leaving me, I feel his passing bitterly, and if I could, I'd blame him, for leaving me, not alone, but at the mercy of my father's wishes, and Æthelwald's own family, when I've become used to his gentle ways and kindest regard for me.

There was never any great love between us all, and now there's likely to be even less. Marriages forged from politics are not supposed to erupt into the passion we shared; the mutual respect, the desire to be better people so that the other would prosper from the union.

My shoulders shake, anguish at what I've lost and what I'm going to lose now making me wish that I could only lay on the bed beside him and go with him. But I'm a young woman, not yet into my twentieth year.

Surely there is more for me in this life?

Surely?

CHAPTER 1

I smooth my beautiful dress over my flat stomach, and as I do so, I feel once more the tang of having birthed no children. I pray that one day I'll be a mother, but I don't yet see how. I once felt the first faint stirrings of life within there, but it slipped from me, just as my husband did.

My husband has been dead too short a space of time for me to think of anything but him and yet my craving for children doesn't leave me, even though it's impossible. I could no sooner take a man to my bed than I could ascend to Heaven while still alive.

No, I must grieve and hope that in time, as my body matures, I'm able to both forget my husband's stirring touch and my longing to be a mother.

I'm a young woman, barely old enough to have been married and widowed both, but I have been. Other women my age will have had children, more than one child no doubt, and be safely ensconced in their marriage bed, with a home to order, slaves and servants to manage and a husband to keep them safe, their household keys proudly showing on their girdle.

Not I, though. No. My husband is dead, and I'm a widow, once more something for men to barter with. But I desire more than that for my future.

Once I let my father marry me as he would, and while it was a huge success, in the end, apart from my husband's death and my lack of children, I'll not take the risk again. No, I've felt the hot touch on my skin of a man who genuinely desires me, and I mean to have that again, even if it means defying my father, my brothers and the family I once belonged to.

My husband's final words to me have haunted me throughout the long, dark winter when none could comfort me and the only enjoyment I had was in tending to my husband's children, taken from me now with the turning of the season and gone to live with their uncle. Now, with nothing to wrench my thoughts away from those few words, I find myself at the royal court, desperate to meet with Edgar, to see if I can tell just from looking at him why my husband commanded me to come to the King.

It has taken guile to be invited here, to have my father allow me to journey with him to the King's Court. He's been disgruntled at my unhappiness, not that I blame him. He thought he'd made a great match for me, and for the rest of the family, but now he finds himself having to redo all the political maneuvering he's already done so that he can gain as much as possible from his widowed daughter. I don't tell him of my husband's final words to me. Not yet. I wish to see for myself first.

The King, Edgar, is a young man, barely older than I am. He seems to hold his kingdom firmly for all that he's been a King for a short period, or so my father tells me. My father gave me a good education as a child, far better than most women would ever gain. He ensured that monks from the local monastery taught my two brothers and me, and he made nothing of having me taught. He thought it a frivolous argument whenever anyone questioned him. Why wouldn't he educate me?

I've only met Edgar briefly in the past and from a shadowed recess in my husband's sickroom, for they were foster brothers, Edgar being raised by Æthelwald's mother after the death of his mother shortly after his birth. Edgar perhaps knows Æthelwald's family better than I ever came to know them; for all that I was married to him for nearly five years before his death.

Those five years were a difficult time for my husband's family as Edgar and his older brother, Eadwig, fought for the kingship over England. Eadwig was deeply unpopular in the Mercian heartlands, where Edgar held his greatest power, in part due to his personality, or so my husband told me fondly, eyeing Edgar with a brother's love, and partly because his foster father, Athelstan, known as the half-king for he was such a powerful man, also held the affections and the alliance of the men there and men and women looked at Edgar only to see Athelstan's firm but fair ways.

It was a sorry state of affairs that led to the English kingdom once more having two kings, a situation that was only brought under control by Eadwig's sudden and unexpected death when he was only twenty years old. He'd been an impetuous youth, perhaps more scarred by his father's grisly murder when he was two years old than anyone realised but his sudden death was no reward, no matter how difficult he'd been to manage once he became King. I pity him. I'm the age he was when he died, and I wouldn't want to die yet. Not at all. There is still too much I wish to accomplish.

But now England is whole once more, under Edgar, and for all his love of women and the trouble that brings him with the bishops and Archbishops, the majority of his nobles think little of it. They are content to have a strong king as opposed to an insecure one, and one who will lead them against their enemies and be victorious.

But on the only occasion that I met Edgar, he came stumbling into my husband's sick room, his grief already etched all over his face. They were perhaps closer to each other than Edgar had ever been to his own brother, and I don't think he even knew I was there.

At that moment, I realised my grief was not only mine to carry; at that moment, for all he didn't see me, I knew that he'd loved Æthelwald as fiercely as I had, and for longer. Worse, to see his foster brother die must have reminded him of his mortality. Already his blood brother Eadwig was dead, and now his foster brother, Æthelwald, faltered. Like me, Edgar must have believed his world suddenly wobbled unsteadily, everything that had been so certain no longer to be relied upon. The realisation of his mortality must have pressed on his mind.

The King and his foster-brother spent a brief amount of time together, but I didn't look at the King or hear what they spoke of, content only to have a moment to myself when my sick husband was being cared for by others who loved him as much as I did.

Within the King's Hall, there's a flurry of activity, and I turn to watch him enter ceremoniously. It's the Easter festival, a time of great rejoicing. It's also an occasion when the King deigns to wear his crown, the same one used at his coronation, or rather, it would have been, only Edgar has yet to be crowned, a matter of some confusion amongst the ealdormen and the Archbishops but one which Æthelwald thought nothing of.

"He means to be a different sort of King," was all he ever said, with a wry smirk. A single tear falls from my eye at the thought of my tender lover, his arms around me, his chin resting on my head. I miss him with every beat of my heart.

He told me to seek out the King, and so I do just as he said. He guided my steps throughout our marriage, and I was pleased to let him. He was a gentle husband, a wonderful lover and he was an attentive father to his small children.

Edgar wears the crown of his uncle, Athelstan, fashioned to be a ceremonial crown and not a warrior's helm, as in the past when Alfred, his great grandfather and Edward, his grandfather were kings who travelled everywhere with a troupe of warriors and fought to keep England whole against the ravaging of the Viking menace.

I watch the crown rather than Edgar, as the King makes his way to the front of the hall for the feast he's organised while his ealdormen and thegns are in attendance upon him for the Easter Witan. He walks with a lady on his arm, his wife and the mother of his very young daughter, but despite the beautiful clothes she wears, the purple of royalty offsetting the golden jewels that shine in Edgar's crown, her stance is unhappy, or so I imagine it to be.

I'd heard rumours of this. It seems that Edgar has an unwilling wife, a reluctant mother to his daughter, and definitely, a grudging consort for the King of England.

I think this is why Æthelwald told me to seek out the King. Or at least, during my winter of grieving, this is all I've managed to decipher from the cryptic references to the wedding and the birth of the King's daughter that I've heard on the lips of my father and my previous brother-in-laws, when they came to take charge of Æthelwald's children and bid me back home with my father.

It seems they had no use for me once my husband was dead, and yet I don't think too severely of them. What use am I to any of them anyway? The purpose of the alliance, to assist my husband with a strong political base supplied by my father within Wessex, has been accomplished, but because no children were born to the marriage, there's nothing to hold that alliance together. Not anymore.

Finally, I turn my gaze from his crown and watch the King carefully. He steps lightly, a slight man, with only some bulk from his time spent training with his sword and shield to fill out his frame. He steps nimbly, fluidly, as he expertly guides his unhappy wife to her place at the front of the hall. Rumour has it that she'd rather be a nun than a wife, and I understand her reasoning. I hear that being a nun is an easier life than being a wife, the demands of our God easier to accommodate than those of a man. I once wished the same, before I knew what it was to love a man and feel passion and desire for him.

Only when his wife is settled on her seat does Edgar finally turn his full face toward the assembled mass, indicating that people should sit and partake of his feast by extending his arms to either side of him. His actions are effortless, as though he were born to be a king and has always had such a persona about him. I can only imagine how much he's schooled himself to behave in such a way.

My gaze stays on him as he surveys those before him, as I look at his firm mouth, his moustache elegantly groomed, his hair, beneath the crown of his uncle, blonde and almost as golden as the crown he wears. He has gentle eyes; for all that they are sharp enough to absorb everything within his hall with his sweeping glance.

He makes eye contact with some of his ealdormen, Byrthnoth of Essex especially, and then he must feel the force of my gaze for he turns toward me and it's all I can do to cast my eyes down, to pretend I wasn't intently studying him. For all that, I audibly hear his gasp of delight as his gaze takes me in.

I've chosen what I'll wear carefully. I don't wish to appear in any guise other than the one I can lay claim to. I'm a widow, a beautiful one for all that, or so my father tells me, yet I only have my father's riches to call my own, and some from my dead husband. My clothes are well made, stylish even, and the faint blue blush of my gown accentuates my complexion, bringing warmth to my face, unlike many who would look white and washed out in such an arrangement.

It's the best gown I own. Should I need to come into the King's presence often, he'll soon realise the scarcity of my wardrobe. My husband had been ill for a long time before his death, and my concerns had been for greater things than what I might wear should I ever attend the King's Court.

I make up for my lack of clothing with the few jewels I own, all worth a great deal, but family heirlooms that can never be sold or bartered away. I wear a golden comb in my hair, rimmed with a flashing sapphire, and around my neck I display a small but delicate golden cross that catches the sunlight and candlelight, leaving a warm imprint on my skin.

Around my left wrist, I wear a silver arm ring. My father tells me it's passed down our family line since before we were Christian, and its surface is certainly old and dulled in places, the twin twists of the metal showing signs of rubbing, and yet for all that, it's a heavy piece of jewellery. Its weight is a constant reminder of my family's great endurance, rarely matched in any other noble family, perhaps only by the King himself and a few others.

Most families only last a scant few generations before disease or misfortune decimates them. My father's family has been lucky, as has the King's own. It remains to be seen how my dead husband's family will ultimately fare. His father fell out of favour with the King and retired whereas his son, my husband, is dead. The other brothers say they hold sway with their foster-brother, but I'm too little acquainted with the King's Council to know if they speak the truth or not. Other than Ælfwold, the youngest brother, who I know is essentially the King's closest ally and friend.

Certainly, my husband only attended upon the King when he had to. He said he didn't enjoy the politics of the court. I always believed his words in the past but the whispers I hear when I pass other people make me think that he might not have been honest with me about his reasoning and that their falling out might have been more monumental than he ever implied to me.

Raising my head, I still feel the King's heated gaze and offer him a faint dip of my head, a smile to my cheeks. It could never be said that it was a particularly welcoming smile, but at that moment I realize what I'm doing, and although I've thought of little but being here since my husband's death, I now feel as though the grief of his leaving me behind has squeezed my heart so tightly that it almost can't beat anymore.

I'd set myself the task of making my way into the King's presence, other than that I'd not considered my future options. What will I do tomorrow? What future is there for me now that I'm a widower?

Edgar still watches me, his wife oblivious to the look that passes between us, as he beckons for one of his ealdormen, Byrthnoth, and no doubt asks for confirmation of who I am. I watch him, my heart almost frozen in grief and fear combined, and yet the softening on his face whatever he's told pleases him, and a gentle smile greets my own. The King is already well disposed toward me and that means that my sudden fear should dissipate, only it doesn't.

What was my husband thinking of when he told me to seek out his foster-brother? Edgar is married, he has a baby daughter that he acknowledges, and perhaps more sons and daughters that he doesn't. He's a man who likes women, that's a surety, but he can't very well take another wife when he already has one. Neither can he simply cast her aside. Not unless his church men find some impediment to the legality of the marriage, as they did not too long ago with his older brother's marriage, forcing him to divorce because he was too closely related to his wife, or so they said.

His smile is hesitant and inviting, all at the same time, but I have no idea what shows on my face. I think the smile is still half in place, but I'm no longer conscious of anything other than my fear and my loss, and also, and this almost undoes me, a fierce longing in my body to hold the man I see before me, to have him make me feel the way my husband once did.

My body tingles with longing and desire, and I could almost cry out with my yearning and need but I can't. Not here. My father would never forgive me if I embarrassed him in such a way.

All too soon the King's attention is taken from me, and I find that I've been holding my breath under his scrutiny. At my side, my father is watching me with a puzzled face, his expression showing some understanding. He's not a stupid man, educated just as well as I've been. It'll take him little time to realise what I've been tasked with and then he'll either help or hinder my ambitions. After all, what father wouldn't want his daughter to make a marriage as advantageous as the one that my husband seems to have planned for me?

All I need to do is have the King fall in love with me or desire me enough to think he loves me, either will work and then have him cast aside his wife. Both of those tasks, or so it seems, might be easy to accomplish. I know the King loves women. I could taunt him with my smile, my beauty. I just need to ensure that I'm in his presence as often as I can be.

But there's also one other factor I need to consider, one I've not thought about since my husband's death, do I even want to be married to the King, even without the complication of his current marriage, wife and daughter?

CHAPTER 2

My dreams that night are filled with longing for my husband, and I stir, sweaty and unhappy. Will I ever stop waking to expect to find him beside me? Those few moments when I first realise that I'm truly alone are crushing when I reach for him in my bed and find it cold to my touch.

I miss all those things that once annoyed me. I miss his leaving me in my bed, making it creak as he used to rise early to check on his children and allow his hound to escape from our room, before sliding back into my bed, with cold feet and reaching hands. I miss the feel of his rough beard on my face and the scampering of his children as they came to rouse him from his slumber when our lovemaking was done.

Stray tears fall down my cheeks as I let my grief take me to the dark places of desolation and loss that have been my own to inhabit since his death. I only allow myself this time to grieve, forcing myself to activity throughout the rest of the day. But the morning, when the gentle sunlight wakes me is the time that the spectre of his presence visits me, and so I give into it. Better to mourn now than later and better that no one knows just how deep our regard for each other ran.

This morning my musings are disturbed by a knock at the front door of the hall we're sheltering in while we visit the King. I think nothing of it until a servant comes to seek me out, my tears still wet on my cheeks.

The girl is a pretty thing and hesitant around me. She's seen my tears in the morning and is somewhat scared of my anger, and yet I've done nothing to worry her. I must imagine that my grief upsets her because it never seems to abates.

"My Lady Elfrida," she apologises as she comes within my sleeping space. I smile through my tears, and she swallows quickly, and bobs rapidly, somehow finding the courage to speak to me.

"A messenger has come from the King. He requests your presence this morning."

Abruptly I sit upright, surprised to feel a faint stirring of excitement. Could it really have been that easy?

"At the palace?" I ask, but she's shaking her head.

"No, my lady, he says he'll meet with you at the Minster."

Ah, it seems that he wishes to share our anguish for my husband. My exhilaration immediately dims. I don't want him to see my grief. How could he ever be interested in a woman who still keens for her dead husband?

"My thanks. Please let the messenger know that I'll be there."

The girl quickly leaves, and I slump back onto my bed, my tears a drying trace on my face. I need time to consider my actions, but I know I don't have it. What should I do? How should I face him? Should I entice him with my appearance, as I managed yesterday, or should I go as a grieving widow?

If he only wishes to discuss his dead foster brother, I should go somberly. I can't go as a vixen trying to tempt him from his wife, even if that's what I am. At the moment I have no idea.

Worry has me gnawing at my lip. I still don't know what I want from the King, my shocking realisation of yesterday has plagued me through the long night, and although I've slept a little, I feel the shadows of my fear and worries chasing me. What will I do now that I've carried out my husband's final wish for me?

Why did I heed my husband's words and present myself before the Court?

That thought wrenches a bark of agony and pain from me as I swing my legs from my bed and ready myself to prepare for my meeting with the King.

Why indeed? Because he was my husband, and he cared for me, and I'd become so used to following his wishes that even now, with him dead in the ground for nearly half a year, I find I still do the same. It's his wishes from beyond the land of the living that have brought me to this moment.

Without those final words, I would have allowed myself to wither away to nothingness. My sorrow would have run riot across my soul and I would simply have allowed my father to marry me as he saw fit, and found no joy or passion in that union, only a desire to be what I should have been to my dead husband, a faithful wife but not an object of fierce love and longing, perhaps a mother as well, but certainly not this wild creature of thwarted desire and infatuation.

So, I look at my dress of the day before, noting the delicate embroidery on the cuffs and also down its length and around the rim of the deep skirt, and I shake my head. That was a dress for being amongst the King and his noblemen and women. Today, I'll go as a widow, and a heartbroken one at that, but I'll lighten my appearance a little.

Nervously I twirl the ancient silver armband that hangs near my wrist loosely from having slept with it on. Its ancient burnish gives me an idea, and I stand and rifle through my clothes chest. The contents are good and serviceable, showing my dead husband's wealth, but at the very bottom, I have something older, from my time when I was merely the daughter of a well-thought of, and respected Wessex thegn. It shares its shading with my armband and is soft and well worn beneath my hands. It is in this dress that I met my first husband.

I hope it brings me the same sort of luck today, and if not, then at least I've given myself as much as a chance with the King as I feel I deserve.

I spend time arranging my hair as well. Yesterday, I allowed it to hang loosely around my shoulders, the colour to complement that of my overdress. Today I twirl it between my fingers before tying it in a loose plait that twists all the way down my back. My hair is my vanity, and the one thing about myself that I know and accept is truly beautiful.

I step from my private room and meet the gaze of my father. The servant must have told him of the King's wishes. He's wearing similar clothing to my own, not quite as regal as yesterday but still good enough to stand before a King. He smirks as he sees me. My sadness has worried him and angered him in equal measure. Now it seems he's considered my actions and decided to assist me in doing whatever it is that I'm trying to do.

I nod to him, a sad smile on my face for the memories of the dress I wear and he walks to embrace me. For all his roughness, he's always treated me softly, aware that I was his daughter, not one of his sons. I've not always seen the same sort of care from other fathers but, then, my father has rarely been like other fathers.

We eat and drink quickly and then step outside into the slightly chilly air. It will be a warm day, but with Easter having come so early this year, there's the hint of a frost in the air, unexpected for those so used to living in the slightly warmer climate to the west, as I am.

At the doorway, I shiver and step back inside to retrieve one of my cloaks, one with a rich fur lining around the top. It masks my carefully chosen dress when I pull it tightly around me, but then, I don't plan on keeping so well wrapped when I meet the king.

We walk in silence, while around us there's much activity, and behind us, I know that two of my father's warriors accompany us. I've never been one to speak too much, holding my thoughts tight to my chest, and so as we walk, I think instead of talk, and only when we come within sight of the Old Minster does my father reach out and grab my hand, squeezing it tightly as he does so. Whether it's meant to be supportive or not, I take it as support and thickly swallow as I note that the King is already waiting for me within the grounds of the Old Minster, almost bare apart from the renewed growth of the grass. It's been a long, cold winter and it'll take some weeks yet before the plants and flowers, herbs even, begin to bud and bloom.

The King stands alone, not even looking my way, gazing out into the distance at something only he can see. He's smothered in a thick fur cloak, trimmed with white fur at the top in contrast to the brown of the rest of it. He's dressed for warmth and comfort and immediately I know I've made the correct decision in my clothing.

I take a deep breath and begin a slow walk toward him, my father and his men going to mingle with the king's small contingent of household troops who follow him everywhere.

Whatever conversation I'm about to have with the king, it's to be done in privacy.

I keep my gaze on the ground, ensuring I don't trip as I walk toward Edgar along the small paved walkway that runs to the door of the Old Minster. So many emotions are flooding my body that I genuinely don't know how I feel. A touch of grief and sorrow still wallows inside me, the thought that my dead husband has brought me to this moment, but there is also that same stirring of desire, need and want. I need to want my second husband, but I also need a second husband to give me the children I so wish to bear.

He must hear my step and his gaze swivels toward me, his hand hovering where he might expect to wear his short dagger although today he doesn't have it on him. He sees the understanding in my eyes and offers me an apologetic smile at being caught in such a defensive posture.

"My Lady Elfrida," he offers, his voice deep and well intentioned. I've not been called 'my lady' by anyone but my father and our servants, since before Christmas when my step-children were taken from me, and I returned to my father's home. I thrill at the words. It seems that Edgar is determined to offer me every respect throughout our meeting.

"My Lord King," I respond, pleased when my voice is soft and gentle, the words spoken clearly, for all that I've not spoken much that morning.

"You must wonder why I've called you to me?" he asks, his

words conveying that he's curious to see what cast I've applied to his demand.

"I do my lord, yes." I almost say more, but he seems to want to explain himself to me, and so I say nothing further. Whether he wishes to speak of my dead husband, or of other matters, I find I suddenly don't mind. It's just pleasant to be in the company of a man my age, and one who's hale and hearty and not about to breathe his last.

"I pondered," and here he stops and swallows nervously, and I realise that he's as uneasy as I am. What has my husband done to us both?

"Well, I, well I saw you yesterday and appreciated that we'd never met before to speak, for all that you were married to my foster-brother, and I deliberated, well, I wondered if there were a reason you'd come to my court?" His words trail off helplessly, and I appreciate that it's curiosity that drives our meeting today, just as it was my inquisitiveness that led me to the King's Court in the first place.

"I came to your court because my husband told me to, with his dying breath." Standing before him I find that all attempts at evading the truth of my presence have fled from me. I've barely had time to honestly look at the man, and already I'm telling him of a conversation I've shared with no one since my husband's death. Not even my father knows the truth because I couldn't reveal it to anyone. Not before now, and even the monk who sat with me when my husband took his last breath has sworn to tell no one, thinking it the idle wonderings of a man too close to his death.

"Ah," is all he says, his face softening, and his entire body relaxing. I'm not sure what he anticipated me saying, but this might have been it. I'm curious now. What did my husband say to his foster-brother when they last met?

"Shall we walk a little?" he offers, nodding to show the way he means, and I nod to show I'd like to. This is all such new territory to me. Before today I'd never even spoken to the King, and now it seems he wishes to walk with me as though we're old friends.

Silence hangs between us as we turn to amble around the grounds of the Old Minster. I've been here before. It's a place of stillness and silence until the monks, and the priests raise their voices toward their God. The tranquillity contrasts with the busy-ness outside the gates of the Old Minster, in Winchester itself.

I find my eyes straying back to the King as we walk. His face is young and intelligent, his eyes keen, his nose very straight and his lips just the right sort of thickness that I think kissing them might be pleasant. I don't much like men with thin lips, and certainly not women. It makes them look mean and pinched, even when they're not.

Shocked by my thoughts, I try to think of other matters, of putting one step in front of the other, but time and again, I turn to gaze at him.

"Did you enjoy the feast?" he finally thinks to ask, and I respond as I know I must, in the affirmative, but silence immediately falls between us again, and I feel that this is as hard for Edgar as it is for myself.

I feel confident walking with him, but what should I say to a man I only know by reputation?

"I think I remember meeting you ... before," he offers apologetically and softly. He's speaking of when my husband was dying, and he came to visit him to say goodbye. Æthelwald was almost so far gone that he barely knew who anyone was, and yet I know that the King and his foster-brother spoke for some time, only I couldn't hear what they were saying. I wonder if the King will tell me now.

"The room was dark, I remember only voices and shadows," I apologise and he nods, and silence descends once more between us. This is the most awkward, comfortable conversation I've ever had.

I assume he knows that my husband sent me to him. What more should I do? Does he know what my husband's intentions were?

Eventually, he stops walking, and I mirror his actions. There's a small brook to the rear of the Old Minster grounds, and the sound of the water has filled the void of our conversation. It's a pretty place, just as calm and serene as the rest of the church.

When Edgar speaks, I jump a little, almost forgetting that I don't stand alone, swept up in happy thoughts of absolute nothingness. It feels wonderful to just 'be' and not think, about anything.

"Your husband," he starts and then stops and starts again. "This is difficult for me to say to you." I nod with an understanding I don't feel, hoping he'll speak clearly, only the words seem to be struggling to get past his throat.

"When I visited Æthelwald," he tries again and this time I think he may be able to say a complete sentence, but he stops once more and turns his back on the stream, as though it's that which makes his words so hard to say.

"Your husband and I were like brothers. We never fell out, we never argued. I loved him as brothers should love each other. His mother was so kind to me when my father died. His father treated me as though I were his son, and when I was small, I believed I was one of his children. People spoke to me of my uncle, the King, and it made no sense to me. I was just one of Athelstan's son. Only with the passing of years, and the help of my grandmother, did I come to accept that I wasn't one of Athelstan's son and that I wouldn't have the same freedoms that they enjoyed."

He stops and takes a breath. I'm trying to follow his rambling thoughts, but they are just that.

"But there was something that came between us, something you won't even be aware of, and it's the reason that this is the first time we've met properly."

I don't understand what he's trying to say, not until he grasps my cold hands in his warm ones and lifts them to his lips.

"You," he gusts, his words almost taken by the gentle breeze so that I wonder if I've heard them and then when I meet his eyes and see the truth in them, I feel as though the world is swirling out of control. What's he trying to tell me?

Now his words come in a rush, and I struggle to keep up with them.

"When I was first told to marry, many names were suggested to me, but you know, well, I think you know that I enjoy the company of women." He sounds as though he's trying to apologise for his actions without really meaning it and I'm not interested in that, only in what he's trying to tell me.

"I needed a good marriage, one to unite the Mercian and the Wessex kingdoms. Your name was mentioned, and so were many others. I sent my 'brothers' to seek out these women for me, to return with the one that was the most beautiful. They knew the sort of women that I lusted after and they knew that I'd need a woman with wit and intelligence as well. I trusted them, Æthelwald perhaps more than the rest because he was my older brother, the man who replaced Athelstan at the court, and yet."

"Well, there our friendship was tested, and it never really recovered until just before his death. It seems such a foolish thing now, to drag me away from my friend and the man who was almost closer to me than my brother, but there you have it. We quarrelled, and I vowed I'd not forgive him."

He pauses there and takes another deep breath, but I still have no idea of what he speaks about. All the same, I hold my tongue and wait for more of his mixed up words to spill from his mouth.

"His father had already made many mistakes at court, won himself too many enemies to make it easy for me to keep him at court. He'd decided to retire and had likewise set his son the task of finding a good wife to bolster his popularity at court, as his first wife had died so suddenly. Ealdorman Athelstan hoped that if his son came to court with a new wife, the problems he'd caused would be forgotten about. It was, I admit, a good plan, but it caused a problem for Æthelwald and myself."

"I don't understand," I say, but the King is caught up in his story, and he's not even looking at me anymore as he tells me something deeply personal and private.

"It was Æthelwald, if you remember, who first visited you at your father's home. He came on my instructions, but he never told you as such, and instead, your father soon received an offer of marriage from his family."

I'm still not sure what the King is trying to tell me, but I do remember the first day I met Æthelwald. My father had asked me to dress well because he'd had warning of the visit by a royal official. Knowing my father's mind had often been preoccupied with whom I'd marry, I'd known what he wanted from me, and I'd grumbled all through the process of dressing. As much as my father had allowed me to be educated with my brothers, he'd made no secret of his desire that I make a good marriage. I wanted no such thing. I would have been content with a life in a nunnery, but my father would hear none of it.

I'd presented myself to my father in a surly mood, and I'd been difficult all day. When the 'official' had arrived, I'd been surprised to find the man was little older than myself and that he was reasonably pleasant to look upon but that hadn't made me feel any less like a cow on show at the market.

The man, Æthelwald, had spoken at great length to my father and I'd barely said more than hello and goodbye, although I had watched him from beneath hooded eyes. I'd decided that the man was pleasant to look at and that he had a kind and gentle manner, for all that he expected to be listened to and obeyed.

Yet only three days later my father had received a request for my marriage to the young Ealdorman Æthelwald and he'd agreed to it without even consulting me, overwhelmed by the proposal from the son of Athelstan, Half-King, the man who'd been the greatest advisor of King Edmund, King Eadred and even King Athelstan before them.

"He never told me of his meeting with you until after he was married to you, and he kept it all a secret for one very good reason." The King's voice brings me back to the here and now and not the past.

If only I could go back to the past I'd have only the joy that

25

was to come, and none of the pain.

The King has still not looked at me, and I'm beginning to tire of his long story.

"Because I'd have wanted to marry you. You were exactly the sort of woman that I was searching for." The words actually force me to look at the King, and I glare at him to test the truth of what he says to me.

"Why would you have wanted to marry me?" I ask, and he nods as though he's expecting the question.

He smiles sadly, as though he doesn't wish to admit the truth, but knows he must.

"I told Æthelwald that I wanted to marry the most beautiful woman in England and that my lady, is you."

"But Æthelwald married me," I say, still perplexed, and then I remember that the King spoke of a falling out with my husband.

"So you fell out with my husband because he married me?" I ask into an embarrassed silence and Edgar nods instead of speaking.

"And why does this matter now?"

"It matters now because your husband is dead."

"But you're married now. I can't marry you in place of him. Is that what my husband meant when he sent me to you?"

"I can only assume so."

"Then he was unaware that you were already married?"

"Oh no, he knew of my marriage and my child. He was only too conscious that in place of you I'd married another beautiful woman."

"Then I don't understand any of this," I sigh with frustration.

Now the King looks uncomfortable again as he turns to stare at me, and I think that I can't be the most beautiful woman in all of England. It's a strange thing for men to say.

"I think he hoped that you'd become my concubine and that I'd keep you safe and provide for you, as he knew his family wouldn't."

I feel my blood run cold at those words. I'm sure my husband thought no such thing. He wouldn't have wanted me to live a life of dishonour. But before I can deny them, the King has grabbed my hands and is looking into my eyes.

I feel drawn to his gaze, and although I want to wrench my eyes away from his, I find I'm immobilised. Where I felt a chill at his initial words, I now feel only heat and it's the sort of heat I remember from the bed I shared with my husband.

My face begins to flame, and still, I can't pull myself away and then the King is leaning closer and closer to me. I can feel his breath on my face, and hear him panting. He must feel the same sort of sudden passion that I do, but I can't allow this to happen. Not now. It would be …. It would be shocking for me to become the King's concubine willingly, and I refuse to do so. Only, only, the King has me locked in his gaze, and it's all I can do to simply breathe as he bends his head and comes closer to me, so close we're almost touching.

But I can't, not here, and not now. I can't allow such a precedent to be set.

I close my eyes, as though to welcome the kiss that's coming, only for an image of my dead husband to appear before my eyes and the thought of him is like standing in a freezing river in spate.

With that realisation, I manage to force my feet to move, and instead of the King kissing me, he almost overbalances as I'm no longer standing where I was.

Breathing deeply, I try to compose myself, and not notice the look of hunger and hurt on the King's face.

"My Lord King," I say curtly to him, and rush away from him. I don't want to be alone with him ever again. I can't believe that he thought he could just kiss me in such a way, make such a claim on my affections that could be viewed with dishonour by so many people within our society.

I know rage as well. I'm angry with my husband. How dare he put me in this situation?

I'm also grateful to him. The thought of him allowed me to move away from the king and remove myself from the danger of his presence.

I can feel my breath is ragged in my chest as I rush toward my father. I thought we'd only walked a short distance as the King, and I talked, but it seems as though I've been running for a long time when I finally find my father. He looks at me in shock as I rush toward him, scarcely able to catch my breath and all I can do is indicate with my hands that I wish to be gone.

But the King's household troops are looking around in worry, and I realise they think something has happened to the king.

I manage to gasp, "the King is fine, but I wish to go home, quickly," before the king comes into view, and then I'm left with no choice but to tug on my father's hand and ask him desperately to take me away.

Finally sensing my distress he bobs his head at the warriors looking for their King, and takes firm hold of my hand, before leading me away.

"What is it?" he asks but I only have breath to walk, not to talk and so I escape to my personal sanctuary in silence, not speaking to my father as I rush through the door of the hall we're staying within and head straight for my small piece of privacy.

I need to be alone. I need to think about what just happened. But worse, oh so much worse, I need to stop thinking about the look of desire on the King's face, and my reciprocal reaction. I need not to feel this way.

I simply can't be the King's concubine, and my feelings of desire are so intimately mingled with renewed grief at the loss of my husband that I feel tears falling without ceasing down my face.

I can hear my father calling to me, but I'm too bereft.

I can no more speak to my father than I can bring my husband back from the dead. I cry, and I howl and finally, I sleep once more, but my dreams are filled with sorrow and desire and give me no comfort at all.

CHAPTER 3

When the morning comes once more, I'm still confused and unsure of what yesterday was all about, but I know that if I tell my father of the King's intentions toward me, he will remove me from the King's vicinity and I'm not sure if I want to go away.

I always worried that I'd never feel the same sort of passion Æthelwald had excited in me. It seems that I was wrong, but neither should I feel that way about a man who's married to another woman. I'm conflicted beyond belief.

No, I must tell my father and allow him to be angry toward the King, provided he takes me home. Now.

So resolved, I finally rise from my bed and dress once more. I've spent all night asleep in the clothes from yesterday and now I feel a fool as I look at them. I'd wanted to find myself a new husband and had made myself as appealing as I could while still appearing in my role as a widow, and yet what I'd received was an offer of being a concubine.

I still don't believe that my husband intended the King to behave as he did. Æthelwald knew of my wish to be a nun before I married. He would have expected the King to marry me, although as he was already married then, I'm once more confused by Æthelwald's instruction to me.

I can't help thinking that I wish he'd stayed silent, and then I worry that I just misheard his words and have brought this whole situation onto myself. And yet. Well, the King did say that he and my husband had spoken about me.

Angrily, I stand and call for my servant to help me dress. This time I opt for warm travelling clothes. I want my father to believe my intention to leave.

In the great hall, I can hear my father's low voice as he speaks to someone, and when I step into the room, he looks at me with a guilty expression. I hope the King hasn't made his intentions clear to my father. I would be dismayed to know that the King had spoken with him before I had, but my father is attentive, walking to greet me and take my hands.

It's so reminiscent of yesterday's meeting with the King that I shake his hands from me awkwardly. I wish to banish that memory forever.

"My child," he begins, but I speak over him.

"I should like to go home, today," I say, forcing the words through my tight lips. It seems my body doesn't want me to leave, but I'm determined to say the words out loud as opposed to having them circle round and round in my head. "I made a mistake in asking to come to the King's Court. It's too soon for me. I'm, I still need time to grieve for my husband." There, I've said the words in a sudden rush.

Unexpected sympathy shrouds my father's face, and I feel traitorous for speaking to him so, but I know that it's the only way he'll let me leave with few questions. After all my begging to come to court, and my meddling and cajoling, it's no wonder he's confused by my sudden change of heart, but the mention of my grief means that he's quick to feel sympathy for me and already he's ordering that our clothes be packed away in the travelling chests and that the horses be made ready.

He doesn't even ask what happened with the King the day before. He might already suspect. He might even have watched our meeting but I'm not going to speak to him about it, and I'm confident that if I stay away from the King, I'll never be tempted by the thought of him again. I doubt the King will pursue me when I've made my intentions so clear. He's a married man, and I won't disgrace myself by putting myself in any situation where we'll ever be alone again.

The journey home lasts two days, and throughout them all, I purposefully turn my thoughts away from the King. Yet, they are treacherous and time and time again I see his eyes staring at me, his lips so near my own that I can feel the heat of his breath, and every time my need for him stirs afresh and color streaks my face, and I almost turn my horse around and ride into his arms and his bed.

It would be so very easy, but I can't allow myself the joy of such a union, not when I know that it's so very wrong in the eyes of the Church. It's the Church who guards all widows, and I must act in accordance with their teachings if I'm to remain under the protection of the Church.

With relief, I see my childhood home before me, and I slide from my horse and rush to my room and my sanctuary. I plan on staying there forever, allowing my co-mingled desire and grief to play itself out and then when I can trust myself, I'll ask my father to find a suitable husband for me, and if he can't, then I'll demand he allow me to retire to a nunnery.

It might mean that I never become a mother, but it'll be better for me in the long run. I'd rather be barren than live in sin.

So my life adopts the familiar routine that I knew after my husband's death, of living in the past when I sleep and waking to the harsh reality of grief, and for the space of a week I believe that I've overcome my temptation and that I can live in such a way until my heart heals and I'm able to think straight without my desire rising for the King.

My father is supportive, my brothers as well and we speak and act as though I never went to the court, and as though I were never married and knew that happiness either.

Only then a messenger comes once more from the court, and my fears rise. Surely the King wouldn't chase me? Why would he? What would he have to gain from having another unwilling woman in his life? Only, I'm not unwilling, am I? I wish to be held by him, kissed by him and ravaged by him; brought to the most exquisite pleasure by him and held, sweating and exhausted by him afterwards.

The royal messenger speaks with my father, and I try and ignore whatever is happening between the two men by taking myself for a walk around my father's property. I grew up here, and I know the area intimately. There are places I know I can hide, where I did once hide as a child, and there are places where everyone on the settlement, from the slaves to the blacksmith, can see what I'm doing. I opt for that approach. It would be better than hiding myself away as though I'm ashamed of myself. Although for what, I don't know. In fact, I should be proud of my forbearance.

But my decision plays into my father's hand, and he comes to me, a quizzical expression on his face, and in the bright daylight I notice the lines and shadows on his face. I always thought my father was a handsome man, but now he just seems old to my younger eyes. I swallow quickly, nervous. Why does my father need me? Surely the King hasn't made any complaint about my behaviour or bid me return to him? I hope he has more honour than that.

"Father?" I say his name, but it's a question.

"Daughter," he replies, a smile making the years lift from his face. He must have looked very much like my brother when he was a younger man. I can see why my mother would have been attracted to him. Quickly I stifle the thought. I don't wish to think of the spark of attraction that exists between some men and women.

"The King has sent a messenger to me. He seems to be worried that you or I were taken ill during our visit to the court. He's invited me to attend the court again, in my position as King's thegn for this area."

The news heartens me, and I feel my first genuine smile since my meeting with the King touch my face. It's such a rare feature to me now that I feel my cheeks tug with the exertion of it all. It's a strange feeling to be so infrequently happy, but perhaps that's all I can hope for now.

"Then you think we'll go?" he asks hopefully, and my smile

immediately drops from my face.

"We, father, why would we go when the King asks for you?"

"Well, he's also extended his invitation to you. I thought you wished to be more friendly with him, that you hoped to be important to him." My father is watching me closely, and I don't know what emotion covers my face, but he turns away, perhaps in embarrassment at seeing such a raw need reflected there.

"I would not like to be friendly with the King anymore," I manage to utter through my cold expression. All the heat from the sun has deserted me as I think of the King and what he would have me do with him. My father only nods and moves away.

"Very well daughter. I'll travel alone and meet with the King. I'm sure he'll understand that you still grieve. I'll explain it to him when I'm at Winchester."

I curtsy prettily to my father and thank him, but the chill has extended all its way through my body. Would the King speak to my father of his desire for me? Would he be so bold, and would my father agree to his demands? What might the King offer my father to have me in his bed?

I watch my father's retreating back, and I wonder if I can trust him. He's always loved me and cared for me as any father must, but, well if the King wants me my father could extract a great deal from him and perhaps think little of doing it. He forced me to my marriage with Æthelwald, what would he accept to make me the King's concubine?

I chew my finger nervously, as my mind runs amok with my fears and my worries.

I will have to go with my father, ensure that he and the King are never left alone.

The thought of returning to the court fills me with worry and to me revulsion, longing, a deep-seated need to have the King lying naked beside me, his skin against my own.

I swallow away my desire and longing, realising that I'm practically panting at the very thought of the King and I'm miles and miles away from him.

There's no way I can return to the King's Court. I can't very well involuntarily gasp in his presence when I burn for his touch.

Hot tears of frustration scorch my cheeks, and I think of Æthelwald, dead and gone.

Why has he put me in this situation? What good can it ever do me?

What would he tell me to do if he were still alive?

CHAPTER 4

In the end, I escort my father when he travels to the Witan. I debate it with myself for the three days it takes him to ready himself for the journey, but in the end, I know that I can't allow my father to speak for me before the King.

I must once more muster my resolve and face the King. I must ensure that the King knows my mind and that I'm set on never succumbing to his wishes to bed me unless I'm his wife.

I do hold out a small hope that my father's invitation has nothing to do with me, but I know it's only that, a small hope.

I've seen the way my husband looked at me; I know what it means, and if the King did happen to tell me the truth, then I must appreciate that my husband risked losing the friendship of no lesser man than the King, his own foster brother, just to marry me.

That makes me both sad and fearful.

If my husband, a man who wasn't the King, would risk so much, then what would a man who was the King do to dominate me?

My father is pleased that I've chosen to accompany him. He thinks it means that the return of my grief was only temporary and I know I won't be able to use the same excuse again, but I know that my grief stalks me still, as does my twin desire for the King.

I'll need to hold both of those emotions close to my chest when I return to the King's Court at Winchester. I need to show the King that I'm immune to his charms and that I don't desire him. Not that I think that will be enough but still, I'd rather speak for myself than allow my father to do so on my behalf.

Once more, the journey takes a few days only, and I spend that time considering what I'll wear and how I'll present myself before the King. I don't wish to appear attractive to him, but neither do I wish to disgrace my father or my husband.

I feel as though I have little choice in my actions and yet I must do what I can to stop this madness from preceding any further.

Within sight of Winchester, I finally manage to ask my father what I've been delaying ever since the King's messenger arrived.

"What do you know of the King's wife?" I ask, riding my horse close to his and speaking quietly. He jumps at the sound of my voice, and I don't interpret his perplexed and pleased expression. There's no need to. He does, however, consider what I'm asking him.

"I know little but rumours and what others have said. As you know, the King had been linked with another woman, Æthelflæd, when he was King of the Northern Territories. Their union was barren, and when he became King of all England as opposed to just the Northern Territories, he was advised to make a match with another woman. I hear that he sent his foster-brothers far and wide in search of the most beautiful woman in England." Here he pauses, as though struck by a memory.

"You know, I had thought that was why Æthelwald sought you out. You must know that you're the most beautiful woman in Wessex, although that of course, might be a father's prejudice. But no, Æthelwald came to find himself a new bride and the next I knew the King had settled on a royal woman known as Lady Wulfthryth."

He stops again and looks at me, his forehead creased.

"I would expect you to know all this. Didn't Ealdorman Æthelwald and the King speak of such matters?"

My mouth falls open in shock. How is it possible that my father was unaware that Æthelwald and the King had fallen out?

It seems that while I was being married against my will, all sorts of secrets and lies were being woven to conceal the truth of that marriage and that few knew of the King's feud with Æthelwald.

"The King and my husband little spoke," I mutter, and my father accepts that without further questioning, although he still looks perplexed, but begins to ramble away once more in his deep voice, where almost every word is considered before it's spoken.

"Lady Wulfthryth is the daughter of a good Wessex family, just like yourself, but she wasn't keen to marry, even though he was the King. There are rumours that he stole her away from her nunnery, but they're just stories. There'd be no need for the King to take a woman when he can have any that he wanted." My father's good humour at the story has turned my blood to ice, and I shiver. I should have asked the question before I was within sight of Winchester and its twin Minsters.

I wish I'd known this before.

It seems that there could be nothing I can do to prevent the King taking me against my will. I wonder why I didn't know this. I wonder what my husband thought of his foster-brother's alleged actions, or whether he was even aware of them, or whether he just dismissed them as silly rumours whispered about by those who meant the King harm.

King Edgar's accession to the throne of England wasn't a peaceful event, and it was only brought about in the end by the death of his older brother. Before that, they were both set to rule a divided England, just as in the past before the Viking raiders, and only King Eadwig's early death prevented the calamity that might have occurred. This, at least, I am aware of from discussions with my husband.

He was always a firm supporter of Edgar, but it was Eadwig who became King first, as was his right as the older brother. His reign was characterised by bitterness and infighting between those who the King saw as allies, and those he did not, and some would say, he was ill-advised by those who stood to gain from their close association with him. A bitter smile twists my face.

If the rumor is to be trusted, Eadwig was also fond of women and had his marriage to Lady Ælfgifu annulled by his Archbishops for being too closely related to each other, but he never truly gave her up, waiting for the Archbishops to relent and allow the marriage to resume. He kept her at his side, and more than likely in his bed for the rest of his short life. He died before he could reconcile with his Archbishops.

I almost wish I could use that excuse, but I know that I'm no more related to the King than I am to the King of the Franks.

"Yet the woman, Lady Wulfthryth, is clearly unhappy with her position. I imagine that she'd rather be a nun, just as you've said in the past." He leans over then to touch my cheek with the back of his hand. "I wish I could grant you your wish to remain unwed, but you know you must marry again, don't you?"

I nod, but I can feel tears forming in the corner of my eye, and I look away from him so that he doesn't see my sadness. I do know that I must marry again, but I vow to be married, not used by the King, while he keeps another wife.

Yet, the story of the King's brother and his marriage has made me consider an alternative, and as the horses make their own way along the streets of Winchester back to the small hall we stayed in last time, I can see that there might be a way for me to keep my faith in myself, and still achieve what I want.

Some might see it as an audacious move, but I think it might just be the only way for the King and me to both have what we want, and my father too.

The King has a wife and a daughter.

But his brother had a wife too, and still the Archbishops managed to annul the marriage.

Surely they can do the same if only I can convince him of the necessity, and then? Well then I would be the queen, and he'd be the king.

The thought fills me with a hope that I might yet salvage my virtue from this terrible situation.

For all that my father has been invited to the court when he first presents himself to the King, he's told he's away, visiting another of the royal residences. My father is perplexed by the situation, but I find it amusing. It seems that the King was convinced that I'd accompany my father, and has now decided to pretend that he little cares for me, or so I tell myself.

Only then the few days turns into a week, and a week to two, and still the King is away from Winchester, and now my longing for him to look at me in the way he once did when he stepped close to me to kiss my lips, absorbs me. I can barely breathe without thinking of his hot touch on my face, and I know that the King is winning this little charade, and I find I don't much care. I simply want to see him again, and my need grows greater with the passing of each lonely day.

I spend my days trying to fill my time, praying and walking in the gardens of the twin Minsters, visiting the traders, and then one night, my father bids me come with him to a feast at the house of a man he knows. I agree, just because it gives me something to do, and I dress carefully that night. I half convince myself that the King might make an appearance as well.

As before, I use my best blue dress and my family's heirlooms; my hair brushed to a high shine. I feel as beautiful as people say I am, for once.

But on entering the man's hall, I realise that we're not alone. Not at all. This small feast is more a great court social gathering, and the guest of honor is none other than the King's wife, sitting proudly with her back rigid, her hands crossed demurely on her knees, and her small daughter prominent at her side, sleeping in a cradle that must have been carried here from the women's hall in the King's Palace.

I watch her from my place on the wooden floor. She speaks quietly to those who've come to the meal, and I notice, and I berate myself for not realising that someone who wants to be a nun, is more than likely already a strong ally of the Archbishops and abbots who keep close to her.

She's a beautiful woman. Even I can't find it in myself to be cruel enough to say that she isn't. She's shy and soft in her ways, but that's not necessarily a bad attribute in the wife of the King.

I curse my father for not telling me who the feast was honouring. I'd not have come. I don't wish to know the woman that the King is currently married to and that I must force him to abandon. Neither do I wish to see the child she has with the King. The presence of that child makes my hopes of an annulment difficult. When Eadwig and his wife were separated, there was no child to show for their union, and neither was there between the King and his first wife, Lady Æthelflæd. But there is one for the King and Wulthfryth. The fact it's a girl might help my cause. But it's a small 'might'.

Angrily, I turn to leave the hall. I can't be here. Not now, not when the King's wife is here, and I want nothing more than to steal her husband, in any way I can, and become Queen.

But my father's hand is firm on my back, a smile on his face as he leads me through the throng of people toward the King's wife. He greets people as we flow through those who part to allow us access, and I freeze in the press of so many people. My last trip to the King's Court resulted in us visiting the King's hall and then leaving. I've not been surrounded by so many people for years. I find the press of bodies and the high and loud voices of others chaffs on ears grown used to silence and the quiet studiousness that's all I've allowed myself since my husband's death.

My breath begins to grow ragged, and I feel a sense of panic start to swamp me as people fix their eyes on me, as though I'm an item in the market to be bartered with.

I know that a thin sheen of sweat sheets my face, and I wish my father would release me from his grip, but it seems he's determined for me to meet someone. I fear it's the king's wife, but then, mere steps from where she sits on the dais, seeming to watch everyone but no one at all, only a trace of a smile occasionally turning her lips upwards, a man steps into my path.

For a moment I think it's the king, but then I focus on the man and realise he's a good few years older than the king. His name hovers in my mind, but it's my father who supplies it as he greets him. He's finally stepped from behind me, and I feel my back relax without his touch, and with my view blocked of the king's wife by the man before me.

"Ealdorman Ælfhere," my father, says, a little too loudly for such proximity, but I think he perhaps does it so that I know who he is and not because he's a brash individual.

My eyes are considering the man carefully. I'm assuming that my father has an intention here concerning my future husband. It seems he's unaware that I have my own plans to formulate on that score, but I allow him his moment. Nothing has been decided, and I could still be forced to my father's will instead of my own.

I was unaware he even knew Ealdorman Ælfhere, but I certainly know of him. He was not an ally to my dead husband's family. Too often they almost shared spheres of influence, and that made it difficult for them to be more than grudging acquaintances. Powerful neighbours can never be allies.

I know he's an influential man, though.

It seems my father has decided that if I could marry one of the King's ealdormen once, I should be able to once more. I try to remember if Ealdorman Ælfhere is married or not, or whether he has been, or whether he has children but my mind is too filled with the King.

With great effort, I banish all thoughts of the King from my mind and allow a smile briefly to touch my lips. Ealdorman Ælfhere's face glows with the recognition I give him, and I think that it would be all too easy to make this man marry me, provided he isn't already married.

"My Lord Ordgar," Ealdorman Ælfhere rejoins. "It's good to see you, and this, I assume, must be your daughter?" There's not really a question there, but I let it go. It seems that news of my need for a new husband is far from a closely guarded secret. Not that a widower in the noble society of our kingdom is ever left alone for long, especially one with my ancient pedigree.

"Ealdorman Ælfhere," I offer in reply, bobbing a small curtsey as befits his rank. I turn slightly then to face my father so that I purposefully stand between the two men. This is how it's always been for me. Even with a father as loving and caring as my own, I've continuously been a piece to be played on a board game. How can I help my father now? How can I assist my husband? One day the same will be asked of me if I should be blessed to have a son. It is always the will of parents to use their children to their best advantage, even when they love and care for them as much as my father does me.

If I were to have a daughter, I'd have little control over her marriage, but it would, as always, have to benefit the family in some way, and I can only hope that she would find the love and care I was fortunate enough to share with my first husband.

Ealdorman Ælfhere is a good-looking man, for all that's he probably a decade older than I am. Perhaps if I hadn't allowed myself to desire the King so much, I would have been content with him as my partner in life. Ælfhere grows more and more dominant, and many call him a counter to the threat that my first husband's family present to the King. I don't know if that's true or not. I'm unsure why the King would find my brother by marriage, to be a threat to him, but then, I know so little about Court politics. I was married to an Ealdorman, but I never travelled to Court. Not once.

The bond my husband had with the King was melded in their shared childhood. My father-by-marriage was the King's foster-father, my mother-by-marriage the only mother King Edgar ever knew after his own mother's untimely death when he was first born.

It's the curse of a woman to be wed and bedded and expected to bring forth healthy children to rule after them, but it's a fraught and perilous time. Not all women can carry children well and survive to live the tale. The King had a mother, but only for the briefest of times. He had a father too, but that lasted little longer as he was assassinated, some say on the orders of the old, dead, Scots King, Constantine the Ancient, so known for he lived through so many English Kings – King Edward, King Athelstan, King Edmund and some of King Eadred's time.

I think all this as I smile at Ealdorman Ælfhere. He returns my smile with a slight grimace on his broad face and quick eyes, and I follow where he looks to see him staring at the King's wife. I fix my smile in place. It seems I'm to be forced to speak to the woman, despite my desire to be gone from this location.

Ealdorman Ælfhere quickly turns his attention back to my father and focuses on my face once more, with a slight wink. I think it's an apology and again, I believe that I could like the man very much if I hadn't already decided on the King as my next husband.

"It's good to see you at the Court, again," Ealdorman Ælfhere smiles. I assume he's referring to my brief time at the King's palace before the King tried to make me his concubine.

I nod, words beyond me for the time being as anger fills my soul, and my father must realise my problem as he quickly fills the gap with conversation.

I feel emotionally wrung out. I stand here, adorned with finery as my father, and my husband before him, would have expected, and yet inside I'm torn apart by doubts and grief. If people could see into my soul, what would they think of a woman who mourns her husband's touch still, and yet who hungers to be bedded by the King and made his queen? Would they see me as a bitch, a wanton, or would they understand that grief and desire are two entirely separate emotions and that I have no control over either of them?

It is my desire to usurp the King's wife that worries me most of all. What would people think of that fierce desire that thuds around my body with each beat of my heart? Would they understand that I need to be a legal wife before I give my body to a man who's touch would set my skin afire? Would they even understand that passion?

I feel my face flush at the thought. Slowly, my rapidly beating heart fades, and I begin to comprehend my father's conversation with Ealdorman Ælfhere. It's not what I expect men to speak of unless they're priests or Archbishops, and it quirks my interest.

"The King wishes it to be known that he looks for monasteries and nunneries to reestablish themselves, along the lines that the Archbishop speaks about," my father says, his eyes on Ælfhere, although the ealdorman looks everywhere but at my father, as though he wishes they weren't talking about the King or his religious wishes.

"The King requests we give away more of our land so that he can satisfy the needs of his Archbishop," Ealdorman Ælfhere finally mutters, and I really can't tell whether he approves or not. His words make me think he doesn't, but there's something behind those words. Perhaps he sees this as an opportunity for him to ingratiate himself with the King, even if he doesn't want to.

"It would help if he stopped despoiling the nunneries for all the pretty women," Ealdorman Ælfhere continues, and I feel my spine stiffen at both the insult to his King and the reminder that Edgar is already married, to the very woman this event is supposed to honour.

"The King needed a wife," my father offers as a bland statement. I still don't know if he understands all of my intent, but I'm pleased that he, at least, can speak about the King without his face flushing red, and without his heartbeat rising to an uneven pattern.

"The King could have had any woman. He need not have taken one who wished to be a nun." I'm pleased that Ealdorman Ælfhere's voice has at last fallen to a mere whisper. It would be embarrassing if the King's wife overheard our conversation and we are close to where she sits at the front of the hall, so it's not impossible that his voice might carry to her.

"The Archbishop is keen to explain away the king's marriage. He's at pains to explain that Wilton is a royal nunnery, run by the women of the Wessex royal house, with the express intention of providing practical women for continuing the family line."

"So he doesn't plan to practice what he preaches then?" Ealdorman Ælfhere continues to taunt mockingly, and I can feel a stirring of unhappiness, and I see a faint look of unease cross my father's face as well. I hadn't realised he'd come to talk about monasteries and the King's marriage affairs. But then, until now I'd perhaps not appreciated that these matters were not just for those intimately involved.

I'm beginning to consider the possibility that my father is here with a far greater intention than I'd at first thought.

Only then, the conversation ends abruptly, and all eyes are once more on where I'm aware the King's wife is sitting. I don't wish to be caught in a compromising position, and so I take a calming breath and slowly turn to cast my eyes over the small raised area.

At first, I see nothing but a swirl of cloth and a man I don't recognise making some speech to the assembled crowd. Only, I don't hear the words because at the moment it feels as though the roar of the foaming sea has filled my ears as my eyes finally focus on the woman who, according to rumours, unwillingly shares the bed of the man I wish to share a bed with.

She's a small woman, dark haired with flashing green eyes and a pert mouth that shows neither fear nor disdain. Whether she likes being married to the King or not, I can't tell from just that look, but she certainly appears serene and calm as the man continues to speak, and all eyes in the room are on her.

If she hated her position as much as I've heard she did, I'd expect her to shy away from such events as this, for her to hide away with her daughter and do nothing but pray to God and hope for forgiveness for her sin of lying with a man.

But none of those beliefs, in that flashing moment of despair, appear to be correct and I feel my resolve, which has kept me in Winchester for the last two weeks, begin to evaporate.

I need to leave the room. I know that. Whatever my father had hoped to accomplish here, he's done little but show me that my dreams are foolish. There might be powerful men that my father could ally himself with, but when the King is already married, with a daughter to prove the truth of the union, I see no way that I could ever legally become his wife, and if I weren't recognized as his wife, then any children we had wouldn't be recognized as kings in the future. And that concerns me, but not as much as the realisation that my hopes and dreams have been foolish.

Somehow I manage to evade my father and his close watch on me and make my way through the crowded hall as the conversation resumes in a welter of noise that breaks through the rushing surf in my ear. I've not heard a single word that's been spoken by whichever distant member of the Wessex royal dynasty is hosting this gathering and honouring the daughter of their house.

I walk from the hall into the darkening sky, pleased that my steps are measured and that others barely notice my passing. If I'd run from the room, everyone would have noticed and commented. But instead I've managed to slip and slide my way through the rapidly reforming knots of people gathered in conversation, through the other ladies with their fashionable clothing and exquisite jewels adorning their clothing and their hair, through the press of men with their war belts devoid of weapons, for England lies at peace now that King Edgar's brother is dead and through the few servants and even occasional slaves who present drink and food to the revelers.

Outside I take the time to steady myself, pleased that I don't judder or shake with my grief and my anger and my suppressed desire but in my relief I fail to notice events before me and stumble straight into a stationary horse that's in the process of allowing its rider to dismount, in the spreading gloom of the night.

I utter an apology as I steady myself on the horse's flank only for a voice to say my name. A voice I've been hoping to hear for over two weeks, and one I very much don't want to see here and now, not when I'm angry and emotional and I know that all of my carefully worded arguments about having to marry him, and not simply bed him, have fled from my head, with the warmth of his touch on my arm as he also seeks to steady my interrupted dash for freedom.

"Lady Elfrida," the King says again in his warm voice, humour running through it with delicious delight as he reaches out to steady me with his other arm, for now, I wobble on my feet for different reasons. The belief that he sounds pleased to see me quickly rushes through my faithless thoughts, and I already know that I'll do anything he asks of me, no matter what it might be.

"I didn't expect to see you here. I thought this feast had been arranged for my wife." He sounds perplexed but pleased. I mustn't forget that he sounds happy as well.

I can't speak. I know I can't. Already as I glance at his eyes in the growing dusk, I can feel myself desperately wanting him to try to kiss me as he did before, and I would allow him to on this occasion, and then I would want more.

My legs feel unsteady beneath me, and my yearning for him is so intense that I can barely think.

He steps promptly away from me, his hand dropping from my arm, and the loss of the warmth of his touch somehow brings me back to my senses, and I finally manage to speak.

"My father is here. He brought me with him." I mean to the hall, but the King misinterprets my vague reply as a guilty look crosses his face at my words.

"I forgot that I invited your father to meet with me. Have you been in Winchester long?" he asks, and all of my dreams and hopes of the last two weeks fade away to nothing. I feel cold and small, and coupled with the understanding that the King's wife is a much-loved woman, otherwise, why would he be here after his two weeks absence, I find myself answering in a tiny voice.

"Two weeks, my Lord King." The King has the decency to look contrite, and he turns to leave.

"Excuse me," he says, turning to glance at me as he does so. "I must go and apologise for my terrible memory." He flashes me a cheeky smile and waves aside the squire who comes to take his horse from him. I watch him intently, as though I can't quite believe that he actually stands before me and he returns my gaze and slowly the cheekiness fades, and even I see his sobriety hit him, as he too begins to appreciate that our meeting, although unplanned, has been destined to happen ever since he sent his

47

messenger to my father.

He swallows hard.

"I owe you an apology," he whispers, as though hoping no one will see or hear us. I don't see how they could, with the horse shielding us from the door of the grand hall. I want to hear the words far louder, but first I need to know why he said them.

"For what?" I ask. At his words, I instantly feel fearless before him. Now that I believe he stands before me, this is a conversation I've had by myself for much of the past two weeks. I'm curious to see if he knows why I'm angry with him and why I ran away from him.

"I didn't think when last we spoke," he continues to whisper, almost taking a step toward me, but deciding better of it. Our brief touch was just that. He caught me by surprise, and now I intend to do the same to him. He needs to understand the inappropriateness of his stance toward me.

"In what way?" I persist coldly, and his face turns even more severe. I wonder if others have ever spoken to him in such a manner before.

"My suggestion. It was inappropriate and ill-thought of. I should have allowed myself far more time to think about the implications of your arrival, and my final conversation with your husband."

"So he didn't recommend I become your concubine then?" I whisper, harshly. This has tormented me for the last few weeks. The disbelief that my husband could have done as the King suggested has made my days long and without resolve.

"Ealdorman Æthelwald was unaware of my second marriage when he spoke with me. In all honesty, I think he was delirious."

"Well, he believed in his words enough to tell me them on his death bed. So what did you agree with him."

"I agreed to make you my wife," Edgar says the words even more harshly than I do, as though I've rung them from him against his will, and it appears that I have. His gaze sweeps the yard we stand within, but other than ourselves, and his very well behaved horse, there is no one to overhear us. The squire has long since departed, bored of waiting while our argument rages.

The admittance of his lie gives me pause for thought.

"I didn't have the heart to tell him of my marriage," he shrugs a little helplessly, as though that excuses his actions in offering to make me his concubine and throwing all thoughts of my husband into disarray.

"And what? When you saw me, you thought you'd be able to have the best of both worlds?" The savagery that's trying to burst out of me is almost too much for me to contain.

"To be honest My Lady Elfrida, I saw you, and I thought of nothing but having you in my bed."

His sincerity shocks me, but it so closely mimics my own reaction that I bark a sharp laugh. He looks at me without understanding, and I enjoy that little moment of power over him.

"And now that you've had time to think, what do you propose to do now? Why have you called me back to you?"

"I called your father back," he adds, some of his assurance returning to his tone, but my withering glance quickly clears the smirk from his face.

"I needed to know your intentions; I have some ideas on how I can resolve the ... problem." I hope he's referring to his wife as the problem and not me. I wouldn't want to be his problem.

"As do I," I offer immediately, testing him, and his eyebrow rises and his mouth makes a firm 'O'. I plan on offering him no more insight into my way of thinking, but I would be interested to know if his thoughts have turned to the same slant as my own.

"Then I will pursue those ideas," he offers, a small half-smile of satisfaction on his face, as though daring me to contradict him. I don't, but I offer no assurance either.

But it seems I don't need to.

He steps closer to me, the hand that doesn't hold his horse is pulling me to his side. Immediately, my world shrinks to just him, and I know he hears my gasp of shocked delight.

"My Lady Elfrida," he lowers his head so that it's level with my own, and he positions our bodies so that they lie against each other. It's a shockingly intimate stance to take, but it thrills me.

"My Lord King," I retort, the flash of desire through my body shows itself by my jaunty words.

"I would like to apologise once more," his lips are level with my own, his eyes watching me keenly. He might well enjoy being with women and know how to tempt them to his bed with all the swagger of his youth and his arrogance, but even I can't deny the sincerity in his eyes as he speaks to me. Our conversation has gone from angry to intimate, and even I don't know when the change happened.

"Then please do so," I exhale, giving him permission to do exactly what I resented the last time we met.

When his lips touch mine, hesitant at first, and then deeply probing, our twin desire mingling in the chilly air of early summer, I can think of nothing but being with him, of spending all my life with him, and more urgently, of finding anywhere where I can strip him naked and delight in his body.

The kiss is long and slow and luxurious. I think I could spend the whole night there, but shakily the King ends the kiss and takes a small step away from me.

"Then we're friends again," he whispers, and I nod, words beyond me.

"I would rather be more than friends," I acknowledge, my hand reaching out to steady myself against him by resting on his shoulder. The familiarity of the movement is alarming, and instantly I try to snatch my hand back, but he places his hand on my hand and holds it there.

"Then we should be more than friends, and not just lovers," he replies. Whether the words shock him or not, I don't know, but he seems content with them.

He picks up my hand and kisses the inside of my wrist, the movement intimate as is the fierce desire in his eyes.

"I will make you my Queen," he utters.

"Then I will see you soon," I retort, not unhappy at the thrill that runs through my body at his words. I should ask for specifics, but at that moment, someone else exits the hall and I turn away, keen to avoid my father and Ealdorman Ælfhere, and also to end my conversation with the King before I say or act even more improperly with him.

I'm sure my father will miss me and search for me, but he'll find me at home, in my bed, alone and fast asleep. I'll tell him I felt unwell.

Seeing the King in the flesh once more has reignited my desire for him and that night my dreams are filled with memories of my husband and me when we pleasured each other. Only this time, my husband wears the face of the King, and I know that I'm ruined, completely.

I will allow the King to make the first move, but if it fails to give me what I want, I will use my own guile to gain it. I have no illusions about my intentions now. I will make the King my husband, and then, he will make me his Queen.

CHAPTER 5

I never have the time to speak with my father the next morning, for I'm woken by a noise outside the hall I'm sleeping within, and the rush of my servant to my side.

She seems a little frantic, and as she forces me from my bed, I begin to understand why. The King has finally come to speak with my father, and while I've been sleeping the morning away, keen to never wake from the dreams of my fantasy lover, my father and the King have been speaking, and my attendance upon them both is now demanded.

I feel wrung out and half asleep. My dreams have been filled with the joy of a happy coupling, and I feel as though I've been loved all night long, and my limbs are slow with the joy of a man on my skin, and I know that when I'm finally ready to confront the King and my father, I'll look sleep deprived and grey. It's not the way I wished to face either of them, and it's not helped by the flash of heat that spreads across my washed out face at seeing the King and remembering how he touched me in my dreams and outside the hall last night.

I smile without faltering, though, and go to stand beside my father. He and the King are stood before the fire at the centre of the hall; its smoky tendrils leaching away through the small hole in the croft above our head. They look as though they might have spent much of the morning together as they both have the flushed faces of men who've been hunting or riding, or perhaps both. I don't understand how I could have slept through such a gathering in the first place, only to be woken by its return, but my father seems pleased, and the King offers me an engaging smile as I provide both a dip of my head and a belated good morning.

I kiss my father on his cold cheek, and for my efforts, I'm rewarded with what feels like a bruising on my lips, as though I have genuinely withstood a long night of bedding with the King who stalked my dreams.

My blush grows deeper at the thoughts, but I try to focus on the King's words, and when that fails, I watch the beat of his pulse on his exposed neck. I fancy that it beats a little too quickly and that he's as affected by my presence as I am by his. My heart races and I struggle to hear the words he says as my blood rushes through my ears, almost drowning out all sound.

Only when he looks at me questioningly, a half-hopeful look on his handsome face, do I realise that I've failed to hear something and that both my father and the King are waiting for me to respond in some way.

I feel a moment of utter panic. How can I explain away my failure to respond, to even acknowledge that I'm being spoken to? I falter, too embarrassed to ask the King to repeat himself, and my eyes fasten on my servant, her head nodding empathically at me. I hope she's trying to help me out of my awkward predicament. After all, she woke me from my dreams, and I'm convinced she knows who appears so prominently in the dreams that left me sweating and feverish.

"It would be my honour, my Lord King," I dip my head once more, hoping that I'm supposed to be agreeing to something and that I've not just made a fool of myself.

The King's face, a little pensive at my slow response, breaks into a great smile and I know that I've done the right thing. He holds his arm out to me as if I should loop my own between his to be escorted to .... somewhere, and I look around a little frantically. I think I should probably have my cloak with me, but perhaps the King is only escorting me away from the heat of the fire and that we're not going anywhere at all.

Only then one of the main doors into the steading opens, and a blast of chill air forces an involuntary shiver to run through my flesh. At that, many things happen at once as my father and the King both realize I'm inappropriately dressed, and my servant arrives, a little flustered, but with my beautiful fur cloak draped over her arms and a small hat in her hand, and gloves for my own.

I nod to her with thanks, and the King releases my arm, the only part of my body to remain warm, and I manage to step away from him for just long enough to be helped into my clothes. My servant wears a concerned look on her face. I imagine she's unused to my distracted state, but she takes pity on me all the same. I will have to thank her later.

"To the Old Minster," she mutters, and I blink in recognition of the words and nod my head quickly in thanks. I wonder why the King wants me to see the Old Minster? I hope it's not for a re-run of the events at Easter. Or do I wish that? It would be nice to be alone with him once more, to determine more about his plans to ensure we marry.

Once I'm correctly dressed, even my shoes changed from my softer indoor ones to sturdier leather ones fit for outside, I return to the King, with a grateful squeeze of the hand for my servant. I will have to thank her more vocally later.

"My Lady Elfrida," he offers, a moment of gallantry overtaking him, and I turn once more and kiss my father's cheek, my eyes downcast, although his are keen and watching me carefully. I hope he's not already gifted me away to the King, given his blessing to whatever this is but I have no time to ask him because I've slept my way through their initial meeting.

The door still stands open, the King's household warriors standing to attention, waiting for his commands, so although I shiver once more as the cold air blasts my skin, it's the feel of his white hot arm threaded through my own that burns as I walk outside and quickly mount a horse that's been made available for my use.

The King helps me onto the horse, the touch of him beneath

my cloak almost making me fall before I can mount the dopey animal. Indeed, I gasp at the intimate contact, the sound far too loud for my ears, as I grasp the reins of the horse and settle myself in the saddle. Luckily, my stead is very placid, and simply stands, waiting for me to sort myself out. If we were in a less public place, I would berate the King.

The King doesn't speak to me, but neither does he take his eyes from me as he mounts his horse and brings it promptly to my side. I want to be able to say that I see my father and my servant through the open door, watching my every movement before the King, but in all honesty, I see nothing but the King. I think the world could end here and I'd never even notice.

Edgar looks handsome that day. His face is ruddy from his time hunting with my father. I can see now that's where they've been for a deer is being strung out by the servants of the house. His clothing is so finely made that I imagine it must have taken an entire year to make for him, but it's his face and the illusion of his body beneath his clothes that holds my attention. I notice again how slight he is, and yet elegant as well. The confidence in his position as King is easy to see. His deep blue eyes are keen, his face thin and narrow, and his moustache is neatly groomed, and I want nothing more than to kiss him.

"Good day," Edgar calls to my father and the sound rings loudly through the day as all eight of the horses begin the journey to the Old Minster. It's not far, and usually, I would have enjoyed the walk, but today, I doubt I'd have been able to do more than fall on my face before the King, muddling my feet with trying to breathe, think and perhaps talk at the same time.

We ride in silence, apart from the puffing of the horses and jangling of their harnesses. My servant was able to do little but tell me where we're going. I don't know why we're going there and feel my tongue stick in my mouth. What should I say to the King that doesn't make me appear foolish and ill-informed?

Luckily, Edgar speaks first, his handsome horse steady at the side of my own. The pair of them complement each other. Both are slight but fit and well used to their work for the King and the fine trappings they must wear to show his royalty.

"I've been speaking with your father, and he tells me of your interest in the Benedictine monks?" Of all the things the King could have said to me, this is perhaps the furthest from my thoughts.

"Indeed, my Lord King, yes. My family and I, my father, in particular, are pleased to see the return of the correct rule at Glastonbury. Archbishop Dunstan is a keen proponent of the idea."

I think the comment is innocuous, but a smirk crosses Edgar's face.

"He didn't tell me you were also a master of the understatement, but it seems that there might be much we don't know about each other."

Those words excite me. It means that we're going to find out more about each other.

"I wish to introduce you to Abbot Æthelwold, another supporter of the Benedictine rule."

I try to place the man, but I only know of Dunstan, not of this Æthelwold, and so I turn a quizzical face to greet the King's blazing eyes. I should perhaps know who the man is, but I've never spared much thought for the King's Court before. Not until now.

"He's Abbot of Abingdon, and like Dunstan at Glastonbury, he's established a Benedictine community there. But he was born and raised in Winchester, and once upon a time, he was my teacher."

The King looks pleased at the surprise that flickers over my face. I think the King is trying to involve me in his policy making and that amazes me. Has his quick thinking mind made similar conclusions to my own? That it is only through the help of the Church that we will gain what we want.

"Abbot Æthelwold will meet with me at the Old Minster. I've need of a new Bishop of Winchester and Dunstan has both recommended him to me and told me I'd be a fool to have him so close to me. I wish to see for myself, and I'd appreciate your opinion on him. It's been a few years since he was my teacher, and it's possible he's changed a great deal, but I fail to see how.

I think Dunstan is trying to put me off because he has other plans for him." The King's eyes look steely as he speaks and I wonder about the relationship between the two men. Certainly, Archbishop Dunstan was an enemy of the King's brother, but I thought the two were close. Or maybe not.

"It would be my honour, my Lord King," I manage to muster. I'm shocked by this abrupt turn of events. It seems we've gone from our frantic meeting before the Hall last night, to the King wishing to be seen with me in public and making far-reaching decisions with my aid. After the evening before, I'm still worried. The King's wife has just made a public appearance in Winchester, proudly showing off her daughter, and yet the King seems to have forgotten she even exists, although he honoured her last night after leaving me. Or at least, I assume he did. What game is he playing?

"I find the advice of a woman on such matters to be important to me. I think it's perhaps because my mother died when I was so young and I have no memory of her. I've always valued the advice of a woman, just as my foster-mother, and grandmothers have always given me."

His illusion to his foster-mother inadvertently reminds me of my dead husband, and with my emotions already running so high I feel the immediate threat of tears behind my eyes.

Why did he have to die and leave me playing this high stakes game that I barely understand?

I think Edgar regrets his choice of words almost as quickly as he's spoken them, but he holds his tongue, and I appreciate his stoical response to his mistake. He will need to get used to the fact that I loved my husband just as much as he did.

"I'd be honoured to speak with the Abbot," I finally manage to mutter, my eyes focused on the delicate stitching around the seat of the saddle, and on the thin reins between my fingers. I pinch the leather tight through my gloves and focus on my breathing and on not crying. The rhythmic nature of the horse's hooves settles me, and in no time at all, I'm able to look at the King without seeing my husband's image superimposed on him.

I sigh deeply. These moments of unimaginable grief still assault me at the most inopportune of times. I fear that my emotions are running too high because of my need for the King, and my desire to have children. It seems that nothing but those twin purposes guides me anymore.

"Is the Abbot an old man?" I think to ask. I'm trying to find something neutral to discuss and Edgar appreciates my efforts, that's clear to see as he begins to speak, with perhaps a little too much forced enthusiasm, but also perhaps his regard for the man is sincere. I don't know the King and his Abbot well enough to say, not yet.

"It depends what you think of as old. Yes, he's older than your father, and mine would have been had he lived, but you wouldn't believe to either look at him or listen to him."

The King's allusion to his dead father is spoken far more pragmatically than the admission about his mother's early death. That surprises me. I would have thought he'd have missed his father more than his mother, but perhaps not. I reflect on my husband's father, Athelstan, known as the Half-King, for his great wealth and power. He was such a powerful man, I assume that Edgar's experiences of a father and a King have perhaps merged, as he was the King's foster-father too. I wonder if when he thinks of his father, even those few fledgeling memories he might have of him, for Edward died when Edgar was no more than a babe, whether they merge too much with those of Athelstan for him to know the difference.

Or perhaps he simply respects his father for giving him his right to claim the English kingdom as his own to rule.

Maybe one day I'll know the answer to these questions.

"The Abbot was my teacher. He's known me for a very long time. But the Abbot is also a serious man. He takes his responsibilities to the spiritual welfare of the English very seriously. I don't know if you're aware, but he and my brother were not allies."

Again, a reference to another close family member who's dead. I think the King must be half surrounded by the souls of his family who died before him. First his mother, then his father, his uncle, and then his brother. I'm glad not to have known such tragedy in my life, well, apart from the death of my husband. But I dismiss the thought. Perhaps the King and I could be well suited to each other because so many of those we love are gone from us.

I've wondered how much Edgar mourned the death of his brother. It was his brother who ruled before him, but he listened to the wrong advisors, banishing holy men such as Archbishop Dunstan, and eventually losing half of his kingdom to his brother. It might almost be a relief to Edgar that his brother's dead. If he'd still lived then, England would still be split between the two of them, with Edgar in the Northern Territories, not in Wessex. If that had happened, our meeting today would never have occurred for Edgar would have needed a Mercian wife or a Northumbrian one, but not one from Wessex itself.

"But my brother was not the most," and here he pauses, trying to search for the right word and a dark cloud seems to mar his face. I think he probably does miss his brother. "Well, he was not the most politically astute individual. A surprise really, when you think of the many advisors he had surrounding him, but he was, unpredictable, always unpredictable and some of his advisors were unscrupulous in pursuing their agendas above that of the Crown."

Abruptly he shakes his head.

"But to the Abbot. He was my teacher but, in his turn, he was taught by Archbishop Dunstan, so they share similar views on the Benedictine movement, and I must confess, that I agree with them. I think those who wish to shut themselves away from the more secular world should be allowed to. We should have those who are dedicated to praying for our souls doing just that. Goodness only knows, but I certainly need someone to intercede on my behalf."

A boyhood smirk covers his face, and I must assume he's thinking of all the women he's alleged to have pursued during his time as King, and beforehand. Scandal appears to follow

Edgar around. Even now, being here with me when his wife is in Winchester with his daughter, will cause unease amongst some. I wonder how the reverent Dunstan handles such matters.

It was, after all, Archbishop Dunstan who caught Edgar's brother frolicking with a mother and a daughter at his Coronation feast when he should have been making great speeches to his nobles, instead of trying to use his divine intervention on two women. I smile at the thought. Dunstan was said to have been in a terrible rage, and even now, maintains that it was worth his fall in favour with the then king, just to force the three naked bodies apart.

Immediately my own thoughts flee back to my dreams of the night before, and whilst Edgar grins, I feel heat flood my face. I can't imagine that Dunstan would approve of my dreams last night.

Luckily, we're nearing the grounds of the Old Minster, and so my quietness goes unnoticed as Edgar and his small troop of warriors escort me almost to the door of the Old Minster.

It's a stately building, in such proximity to the New Minster that actually, they should have only extended the one into the other and done away with the two names. And yet those who work within the Old Minster are fiercely territorial, just as those within the New Minster are. It's almost as though two kings vie for the same kingdom, as once Edgar and his brother did.

The King leaps from his saddle with great haste as my horse slows to an obedient stop along with the other horses, and almost before I've dropped the reins of the horse, his hand's snake beneath my cloak to assist me from the animal. Once more my breath catches with a flare of desire, and only the irritable cough from amongst the small crowd who've come to welcome their King turns my thoughts aside.

The King removes his hands from my side almost too hastily at the noise, as I have to reach for the horse to steady myself. I imagine the sound emanated from Abbot Æthelwold, and that the King didn't wish to be caught quite so openly up to his tricks, but his glancing look assures me that he doesn't much care what the Abbot might think.

"My Lord King," a sprightly voice grates as the horses are escorted away, and then I'm facing Abbot Æthelwold, and I understand Edgar's words to me.

The man looks old. His hair all gone and no need for any monk's tonsure, should he choose to wear one, but apart from that, his face is lively, and I can see, beneath his robes, that he's an active man, far from wiry and clinging on for life as so many men his age are doing.

He has flashing blue eyes, intelligent and searching all at the same time, and while he casts a quick look of censure toward the King, when he looks at me, his face softens, and he reaches out to take my hand.

"Come inside, it's a cold day, my Lady Elfrida," he offers courteously, the manners he must have gained at court remaining with him. "There's a small brazier within the Minster itself, and I've a small room set aside for us to speak more privately within."

I'm surprised that the Abbot has worried himself with such small details, but perhaps this is also his Court manners?

King Edgar walks sedately at our side as we enter the Minster.

It's a large building, well built, completely from stone. It's possible to determine just how important this place has become to the ruling family of Wessex just by looking at the exacting repairs that have been carried out on the building. It's stood for far longer than the New Minster, barely half a century old, and is far more dramatic in its construction.

It has two massive towers, at least nine stories high, a tremendous feat of engineering, and I imagine it could house the entire court of the King, three times over.

Of course, I've been here many times before, but today the splendour of the building imposes itself on my mind, and I honestly consider the implications of the Minster which houses the bones of the King's ancestors, King Alfred amongst them.

More death. I feel as though death stalks the King and I, no matter where we look.

Inside, the building is as cold and drafty as the great churches throughout England are. They were built for visual impact, not for the comfort of their worshippers, and that is no more apparent, than here. This is a shrine, not a place for worship in comfort. It's a shrine to St Swithun, and it elicits more veneration than ease. Our religion is a matter of personal conviction, but it has these massive monoliths to its great cause. They're as much propaganda as the words spoken by the Abbots and the Archbishops on the King's behalf.

My faith is strong and deep, but I'm not fool enough to think that is all Christianity brings to the kingdom of England. It also brings adherence to a given set of principles and also works to guarantee that whatever magnificence we've achieved on this Earth, we continue to receive when we're in heaven.

I shiver a little as I step into the church and at my side, Abbot Æthelwold winces in sympathy. He wears his robes so long that they trail along the floor, but even his face looks pinched with the chill, and I'm grateful when we sweep through the church and enter the small room with the brazier near the front of the church. It's housed beneath one of the towers and so should be cold and sparse, but instead, it benefits from an intricate roof of closely fitting thick slithers of rock, rounded softly on the edges. I know the pattern ensures the structure of the building and if it's dark inside, the merry glow of the burning fire works to dispel the gloom and make the room almost homely.

There are also at least ten candles dotted around, casting light into all the darkest corners of the small room, and there is both a wooden stool and also three chairs with deeply carved backs surrounding a table filled with the paraphernalia of our religion. The room smells of church sermons and incense; at once both reassuringly familiar and also reminding me of the tedious time spent listening to men who possess less passion for their professed faith than the men of the fyrd forced to fight for causes they don't believe in, and lacking all skills. Few truly passionate men follow their faith. This is why the rule of the Benedictines is so needed within England.

"My Lady Elfrida," Abbot Æthelwold escorts me to the chair closest to the brazier, and I'm pleased to feel the warmth through my full skirts. My feet are chill from walking over the uneven stone floor, but I know better than to complain. It seems that Æthelwold shares my discomfort, for without seeing to the King's needs, he helps himself to the next chair and promptly stretches out the bottom of both of his feet towards the welcome heat.

It looks comical and Edgar smirks at the man as he settles himself on the other side of me. He is warmly wrapped in an outer and an inner cloak, and I can't help wishing I'd thought to do the same. He's no stranger to the inhospitable nature of the church.

"I see little changes," Edgar mutters, nodding toward Æthelwold's feet, and a slight grimace crosses the face of the Abbot.

"When one has walked all the way to Rome to kneel before his holiness, it is allowable that one's feet ache a little in the chill." His voice is filled with the warmth lacking from the Minster and Edgar chuckles. I imagine the two men have sparred in this way before. It should surprise me to hear the King speaking so casually, but this is also a part of his intent in bringing me here. He wants me to know that he's a man as well as a King. I don't need reminding of what lies beneath his clothing.

"I would visit Rome if I could," Edgar says, sitting a little straighter and looking dangerous for once. "I would like to speak with the Pope and ask him about such matters that now occupy my mind about the Benedictine's." The King sounds as though he's preaching the sermon, but Æthelwold merely rolls his eyes at the words.

"We all know that's far from the truth. You'd miss the comforts of your women, and wouldn't appreciate it if the Pope directly asked you about your liaisons."

I detect the hint of a warm flush over the King's face and for a moment I think he might berate Æthelwold for speaking so openly before me. I'm certainly sitting straighter, and trying to look meek and obedient as the Abbot censures the King.

"That's as it may be. We came to discuss your plans, not my own, marital arrangements."

"Of course my Lord King," Æthelwold says, bowing his head, but no contrition marks his face. It seems that Æthelwold and Edgar are closer than he at first implied, and also, that Æthelwold is allowed to freely speak his mind before his King, who was once his student. I find the dynamic interesting.

"Tell me how your work progresses at Abingdon," the King asks, recalling Æthelwold to the purpose of their meeting.

"The work has begun well. There was some unease when I removed the canons and their wives, but the monks are keen to see to their duties, and already a quiet sense of sanctuary and purposefulness rings through the church and their lodgings. I feel that the work of worshipping God is now as it should be. As you know, it is only the ravages of the Viking invasions that forced the religious houses to lapse from their adherence to the rule of St Benedictine anyway. The men and women know that I don't blame them for their errors."

I listen with interest to Æthelwold. His words are simply spoken, but even I've heard of the unease about this new movement for monks to live celibate lives within their small communities. In the past, the men who worked in the monasteries were often married and more worldly. Æthelwold's monks, and those at Glastonbury, now follow an older rule, one that calls for more reliance on prayer and meditation.

I find it to be an interesting concept, and one I don't disapprove of, but I also appreciate that these monasteries can only function in such a way when they're wealthy. And that, really, is the heart of the matter. The monasteries must own land, gifted to them by the King or by rich men who wish to be prayed for in perpetuity and that means, or so my father has told me, that men are becoming poorer on this Earth but richer in heaven.

My family is closely linked with the monastery near our home, and my father has richly endowed it, but then, he's a man more likely to see death soon. He must see to his afterlife with some urgency.

"And there was little unrest?" Edgar pushes. When Archbishop Dunstan began his reforms at Glastonbury during the reign of the King's uncle, there was some unhappiness with the sweeping changes being made, but now it is usually only the disgruntled cries of canons, unhappy at being displaced from their homes.

"Any unrest at Abingdon has gone now. The monks are content, and I enjoy my life there. It's one of constant prayer. The scriptorium is filled with the noise of ink scratching over vellum. The copying of the great works goes well, and the men develop new and more elaborate ways of illustrating each and every script."

"So you're content to remain there, then?" there was a challenge in the King's voice, one that neither I or Æthelwold missed.

"There is always work to be done elsewhere. I have trained others to rule the monastery in my absence, just as Archbishop Dunstan once did with me. I am yours to command, my Lord King." There was formality back in the Abbot's voice, and I suddenly appreciated that much of this conversation was being staged. The King and the Abbot know of what they speak. I wonder why the King has decided to include me in the charade?

"Then we'll ensure that the announcement is made as soon as possible. I would appreciate having another supporter in Winchester," the King nods, and Æthelwold meets his gaze with a penetrating glare.

"I am an old man now, my Lord King, don't forget that. I may not have the zeal I once had."

"Your zeal will never leave you, and the people of Winchester will welcome you into our fine town. The twin Minsters are the envy of all who see them."

"And I will not be alone?" the Abbot says, raising his eyebrows once more and something passes between the two men that I don't understand.

"No, Æthelwold, you will never be without supporters. I will always be your firm supporter, and the Lady Elfrida's father is keen to assist your endeavours. He and his sons, and of course, his daughter."

Æthelwold turns to face me then, his feet finally withdrawn from the fire, as he sits more smartly in his chair, no longer an errant child but a dignified man of the church.

"I believe that the kingdom of England can benefit from a strong queen, one who will be more than just the King's wife. One who will work for the good of all, and assist in the dissemination of the Benedictine order. The King's current wife, she is but a little thing at the moment, perhaps not ready for such an important role. I believe she may be happier as a nun, maybe a more secular one than normal, at the royal nunnery of Wilton. I believe she and her daughter would be most comfortable there."

It's clear that this is the purpose of our meeting. My father has committed to support the King, and now Abbot Æthelwold has committed to support me in my desire to become Queen. As such, I must support him as well.

"Your words are kind and well received," I offer. I'm not used to the way of the Court. I'm trying to think how to behave without simply just smiling with pleasure at such an open show of support. "I would welcome you as Archbishop of Winchester. I believe you have the welfare of the King's people at heart."

"My Lady Elfrida," he merely says, bowing once, and stands before me. "I'd like to show you the workings of the Old Minster. I'm sure you know much all ready, but I think it would be well to advise you of how the current arrangements contravene the rule of St Benedictine. Would you escort me, and then," and here he turns to the King for confirmation, "I believe we will be returning to the King's palace for a meal."

"Indeed, yes. I'll go there now and leave you two to your discussion. I wish to check on a few things, and ensure Lady Wulfthryth has left for Wilton."

The King stands smartly and fixes me with a searing glance that no man should be able to produce in a house of God, and then he swirls from the room, a short blast of frigid air reaching its tendrils into the warm sanctuary we've been ensconced within.

I don't want him to leave me, but understand that it's important for Abbot Æthelwold and me to be seen in each other's company. While I slept my night away, it seems that the Abbot and the King have been busy at work. Perhaps I merely fit with plans they'd already drawn up? Only time will tell.

"The King is a gifted man. A quick thinker," Abbot Æthelwold mutters as he reaches for my hand to show me around the Old Minster. "He was always one of my best students. His brother was too quick to boredom, but still, his death was sadness for me. He was such a young man. I sometimes fear that the ruling family of Wessex is cursed with short lives. Kings Athelstan, Edmund, Eadwig. I hope that in the future the Kings will rule for longer and provide stability for our great country."

The Abbot's hand is warm on my own, but not a touch on the heat that Edgar elicits in me. Instead, it's as though my father holds my hand, and I suppose in many ways, that's the truth of the matter. As a widow, I'm protected by the Church, provided I don't remarry before a year has elapsed since my husband's death.

We leave the room as Abbot Æthelwold speaks and make our way back up the narrow stairs that led us to the basement of the tower. I'm shivering a little within my cloak. The Abbot keeps a steady hold on my arm, and I think it must be for his own balance on the uneven stairs that circle the tight space, rather than for my own comfort.

"I understand that your father educated you well," the Abbot says as we enter the main body of the Old Minster, the weight of the lofty towers above my head removed from my consciousness now that we stand to the side of them, and not beneath them. I'm distracted by where I place my feet and answer without too much thought.

"My father saw little difference between my brothers and me when we were small." The Abbot takes a sharp breath, and I wonder if I've spoken inappropriately, but he squeezes my arm at the same time.

"Other fathers would do well to heed his example. Especially when the kingdom is in such need of a clever and well-educated king and queen." His words are barely above a whisper, because there are canons in the church itself, and it seems that much of our recent discussion was a secret.

"Certainly, my husband appreciated my ability to speak with him about the great matters of state and the future of our kingdom, not to mention to discuss points of theology."

"Your husband was the King's greatest friend. Until. Well, I'm sure you've heard the story by now."

I feel ensnared in his gentle conversation and find myself speaking without thinking.

"I understand that the King and my husband fell out over his marriage. I think they both regretted it. Especially. Well, I'm sure you can understand why."

"Men sometimes act irrationally and without thought. Passion is a strong emotion, one that has undone better men than the King, his great-grandfather for instance. Poor King Alfred. A great King, but destroyed by his desire and passion for women when he should have been concentrating on the defence of the kingdom and on spreading the word of God."

It's rare for anyone to criticise King Alfred. He's held in high regard by all and I'm surprised to hear Abbot Æthelwold speak as he does.

"I met his grandson, Athelstan, the King's uncle. He was a truly enlightened monarch, adopting the same celibacy that I think marks the great believers from those who merely try to follow the teachings of the Church. Not all men are built the same, I understand that, and I know that Edgar works hard to absolve himself of the sin of passion and desire."

Abbot Æthelwold has led me to an obscure area of the church, through the main building and outside once more, where I notice that the King and his warriors, and all the horses have gone. It seems I'm to walk to the palace with the Abbot. He takes me to a mostly untended area just within the grounds of the Minster. I recognise it immediately as the shrine of St Swithun, but it is in need of some care and attention.

"Ah, St Swithun. He demanded to be buried here, that people might walk over his grave and that the rain from the eaves of the Minster might forever fall on his head."

There's so much regret in the Abbot's voice that even I begin to feel sorry for the Saint.

"He should have a lavish tomb, far worthier of the miracles that have occurred since then because of his intervention. All churches should have a saint to pray to. I believe very strongly that the intervention of one of God's chosen warriors is a benefit to each and every church."

I almost feel as though Abbot Æthelwold is making a case for himself. He's implied that I should be a Queen, not just the King's wife, and now I think he plans on enrolling me into his scheme. I would do well to listen to what I'm being told here.

"I imagine the King would be keen to assist with any expense." I try hesitantly, but the Abbot merely pats my hand, as though I have much to learn.

"The King would do well to have his nobility do it for him. Winchester is an affluent town, and the Minster must be restored to its grandeur so as to attract pilgrims to it."

"The King should ask his nobility?" I say and then stop. That's not what the Abbot is saying. No, rather he thinks that the information should percolate through the King's assorted nobility without any specific order being given and that men with great wealth should be keen to redistribute it. I remember my husband speaking of such matters. His father, when he retired to the monastery at Glastonbury, was generous to the establishment, as much for the show of the thing, as for the piety it implied.

"The King should never need to command his nobility. They should already know his mind." Abbot Æthelwold's voice is kindly, as though he speaks to a child and not to a woman he's just praised for being well educated. I feel confused by all I've heard and spoken about today.

"But come, we must go and meet with the King. I've still much to discuss with him, and I'm sure you must be hungry by now. We will walk to the palace, as St Swithun once did when he preached to his followers. It will warm us after all our inactivity."

I would like nothing more than to ride to the King's palace, but it isn't that far and so I turn to walk away from the Old Minster, arrested in my steps when the Abbot fails to move, and my arm, linked with his, stretches uncomfortably. He's muttering under his breath, and I hear the words of a prayer and so bow my own head as he speaks. He's offering a blessing to St Swithun, and I can't help thinking that if I can work out how to do it, the Abbot might be one of my greatest supporters, and not only a supporter of the King.

I will need to prove myself to the King's tutor, but that's a challenge I relish.

CHAPTER 6

Winchester – The King's Palace

As the Abbot and I make our way to the King's palace, a small cavalcade of riders almost runs into us, and I'm greeted by the haunted eyes of the King's wife from atop her horse. She rides with her back rigid; her face is fixed in a grimace; her daughter evidently tightly strapped to her chest for she has a bundle under her cloak.

It's no day for a long journey, and yet the presence of chests and pack animals proves that it is to be a long journey. Has the King banished her? I'm unsure as I watch her go. It seems that for all her look is direct, she doesn't recognise me, or even the Abbot.

"The Lady Wulfthryth," the Abbot offers at my side. I know who she is. I don't need him to tell me. "She's a fragile thing. The birth of the child was hard for her, or so the King has said, and I know she quests for a life of contemplation and only female company."

There are stories about the King abducting Lady Wulfthryth from Wilton nunnery. My father thinks they are more likely to be true than not, but to hear the Abbot speak now, I wonder if there's not more to the story. Is the mechanism by which the history of our Kings and our kingdom is rewritten, already underway regarding the details of the King's marriages and affairs with half the women in Winchester?

It wouldn't surprise me. Archbishop Dunstan lost his faith with the King's brother because of his debauchery with a mother and a daughter, and already this is taken as a sign of corruption within the King's brother, as though that immorality accounts for his early death and the elevation of Edgar to the kingdom. Dunstan and Æthelwold appear to understand the potency of the written word. There's nothing like reading something to make it seem truer, as though the effort expended in committing the words to the vellum is all that's needed to show something is true.

"I saw her last night," I half-whisper, and Abbot Æthelwold once more pats my hand as though to offer comfort.

"I hear the King attended the feast. I didn't hear that you did."

"My father asked me to attend and introduced me to the Ealdorman Ælfhere?"

"The ealdorman is a powerful man. He's a friend of the church, sometimes." And that's all he says before lapsing back into silence. Again, his words mean more than they say.

We've walked through the busy market place, and people have respectfully moved out of the way of the Abbot and the woman who escorts him, but even I can hear the muttered curiosity that ripples as we pass. Why has the Abbot so openly allied himself with me already, if indeed, that's what he's done?

Why has the King, to all intents and purposes, sent his wife away, and why does that send a thrill of excitement rippling through my body when I think about it? I can't marry the King yet, not until the first anniversary of my husband's death has passed. I hope he hasn't forgotten that in his haste.

The King's palace quickly comes into view. It is one of the most elaborate buildings I've ever seen that isn't a church or a Minster. It has two levels, joined by stairs, and not by ladders, and the King's nobles can find lodgings within the hall, but right now, the Abbot shows me into the King's hall, where a merry fire glows from the central hearth and where servants and slaves both, rush around the room as though to prepare it for a feast.

I search for the King, hoping to find him close, but instead it's an older woman who comes to greet me, a warm smile for the Abbot on her lips.

"The Lady Æthelflæd," he greets her, and I stop dead in my tracks. This is the King's stepmother, a wealthy and powerful woman in her own right and also through her second marriage to another ealdorman called Athelstan Rota, but more than that, she's one of the few women that Edgar allows himself to be influenced by. Just her, and his foster-mother, my husband's father's wife, and she's been dead for some years.

It seems to me that this situation has been orchestrated but also that the Abbot and the older woman are friends. It's a genuine pleasure for them to see each other again. I can only wonder at my part in the charade.

"Abbot Æthelwold, you look as sprightly as ever," she offers as the Abbot slips his arm from my side and reaches out to exchange a handclasp of friendship with her. I can only hazard a guess as to her age. I'm sure she married young, but she's not someone I've ever thought about let alone met.

For a woman of the same age as my father she wears it just as well as the Abbot wears his own years. I'm beginning to think it might be better to wear the weight of a few years rather than the fresh face of youth. It seems to offer these two an assurance in themselves that I wish I shared.

"And this is Lady Elfrida," the Abbot introduces, and she turns to greet me, and I'm immediately under the influence of the strength of her charisma. I can see why the King listens to her. I almost imagine he has no choice.

"Lady Elfrida," she croons, and without me even realising, the Abbot has disappeared from my side, and the King's stepmother is guiding me to a quiet place within the hall, close to the hearth and around which I notice two wooden chairs have been placed. It seems this conversation has been preplanned by someone other than myself.

I look around for the King, hoping to find some reassurance there, but he's engaged in conversation with the Abbot, and it seems as though everyone else in the hall has melted away. I'm alone with the King's step-mother, and it appears that I'm to have this tête-à-tête whether I want it or not.

"Come, sit," she offers, settling into her own chair and reaching for two goblets that have been left out for us, and offering one to me. Her hands shake slightly as she does so, the first sign of her unease or her age, and politely I take the goblet, ignoring the shaking in her hand.

"My thanks," I mutter, sipping from the cup, noticing that my own hand tremors and not with age.

"I thought it'd be nice if we spoke about a few matters," she says. I don't even want to think about where this conversation might go, and so I nod my head, indicating that she should begin speaking.

"The Abbot said you were a bright woman, and yet I see the same sort of sadness in your eyes that I saw in my own. I don't wish to upset you, but the death of a husband isn't something that a woman ever recovers from."

Whatever I'd thought she might say, this wasn't it. Not at all. I thought she'd come to berate me for my interest in her step-son, or rather, for whatever it is that might be happening. This, I think, is more of a test, and yet it doesn't stop the tears coming to my eyes, unbidden. My emotions are so confused whenever I feel vulnerable.

Her voice is kindly, and I genuinely believe that she's trying to be kind to me.

"The Abbot helped me when my first husband was murdered," she manages to speak without emotion colouring her voice, and yet I hear the pain behind those words. The killing of King Edmund was a terrible thing. He was so young, and so were his sons, Eadwig and Edgar, and their mother had already died.

"But we learn from life's hardships, and as a woman, they make us stronger. Men need women to guide them, in all they do, and I'm afraid that my step-son is never in more need of a good woman than right now. But you need to be strong in this, to get what you deserve."

I feel my head swirl with the implications of our conversation. One moment, tears are leaking from my eyes, and I feel more at ease than I have been since my husband died, content in the company of a woman I genuinely believe does understand how I feel, and the next, I'm being told that I need to be strong to be a strong Queen.

"The Wessex royal family has never accorded their wives the respect that they deserve. I think we should put a stop to that. I should have been a queen, and so should the King's mother. We can set that right with your help."

She's relaxed with her words, and not ashamed at all to be speaking so openly of casting aside the King's current wife.

"Lady Wulfthryth is a quiet thing. She's not happy in the limelight. She'll be happier at Wilton, and so will her daughter. She should never have been forced to leave. The child is only a small thing. I fear for her survival. Perhaps the constant praying of the nuns will ensure she flourishes."

Lady Æthelflæd sounds almost as though she means those words, and yet I sense no affection for the baby. None at all.

"The King and this country need a woman to guide them. I'm old, and my influence with the King can only go so far."

I've still not spoken, and I don't know what to say either. My desire for the King is one thing, but this seems to have become something entirely different. I'd thought to make myself a queen for my own selfish reasons, not those of the people of England.

"Tell me about yourself," she says, a pensive expression on her face. I can see years of political intrigue stored there, and I suddenly wonder who she supported in the brotherly in-fighting that took place between her step-sons? Was she callous enough to just support one of the men? Did she even try and bring them together or did she let them fight it out because she already doubted that King Eadwig had the abilities needed to rule justly?

I think describing myself should be an easy task, but immediately I feel tongue-tied. Should I start with detailing who my husband, my father or my brother is; proving that I could be a decent and politically astute match for the King, or should I talk about myself? Of my hopes and dreams and my loss?

"Just tell me what you enjoy," she offers with a slight smile. She seems to understand my dilemma. But even there, I'm not sure what I do enjoy. I appear to be so little of who I used to be before my husband died. But then I have a flash of inspiration, a memory of when I first met my husband.

"I like to walk through the garden," I offer, hesitantly, saying such a simple thing out loud makes me feel vulnerable. "I enjoy both seasons," I press on, not sure what the expression on Lady Æthelflæd's face means but determined to try and make her understand all the same. "I like to watch the flowers grow, the herbs come to their full growth, to see the bees busy about their work. But equally, I love to see the end of the growing season, the shrivelling of the plants, the death of those that'll not return the following year. I enjoy walking through the falling leaves, the changing colours, the first bite of the frost, all safe in the knowledge that there's an order to my life that is outside of my control. That everything will turn full circle once more." I've been looking away from Lady Æthelflæd, visualising the garden of my childhood, and the garden of my marriage hood, but now I turn back to face whatever the King's stepmother thinks of such foolish thoughts. But she has a faint smile on her face, as though she shares the same images with me.

"I try to dress to reflect the changing seasons, the green and vibrant colours of the summer month, the darker shades of winter. I'm always pleased to cast off my heavy winter under clothes come the warmer weather, but also to put them back on when the weather changes. I enjoy being outdoors, and seeing God's work first hand."

I think I've won her approval, but then her face hardens.

"And what of the poor, and the needy, what of the work that God demands we do to help those less fortunate than ourselves, of our commitment to the future and of preserving the past?"

Her harsh tone makes me feel exposed and vulnerable to having expressed myself so openly and having the words seemingly rebuffed, but I don't snap an angry retort. She asked me what I enjoyed, not what I felt honour bound to do.

"I enjoy worshipping our Lord," I offer sincerely. "The tasks that he's set out for us all I accomplish to the best of my ability although I decry the need to do them. There should be better ways of ensuring that men and women don't descend into the desperation of needing such succour from the Church."

"And what of the past and the future?" she further presses.

"My father's family is old and revered where we live. My father has hopes of raising a renowned monastery near to our ancestral lands. We'll use it to ensure the longevity of our family is remembered."

Whether she's pleased with my words or not, I don't know, for at that moment, I see the Abbot out of the corner of my eye, and he interrupts the Lady Æthelflæd with a wry grin.

"My Lady, I apologise for the interruption," he mutters, and he sounds sincere when he does so, although I doubt it a little. "I believe the King is expecting to dine shortly and asks that the servants be allowed to continue their work."

Lady Æthelflæd gives an irritable shrug of her shoulders but beckons that he should have his way. The Abbot hovers nearby, almost protectively, and I meet his eyes, pleased to see respect there, only then he coughs, and I realise he's waiting for me to stand and escort him somewhere. Am I not to be invited to dine after all? At that moment my stomach gurgles loudly, and Lady Æthelflæd hears the noise, an amused grin on her face.

"Let the girl eat, for goodness sake. The King will need to wait for her."

With those words, all thought of food flees my mind, and yet, I have to sit and wait patiently while food is brought to the tables around the room, and I'm escorted away from the scorching heat of the fire to a more remote location, where other women eat and gossip amongst themselves. The Abbot leaves me there, but without making any introductions and I feel uneasy amongst the women of the court.

Neither is it that they're unfriendly, but I don't know who they are and neither do I know where their loyalties lie. Certainly, they've just seen me in conversation with the King's stepmother, and that could mean that they've made all sort of assumptions and deductions about who I am and why I'm here.

Not that there are many women. No, I get the impression the King's Court is mainly filled with men, probably men who enjoy hunting with the young King. And then I know a moment of deepest dread as I look at the women. Apart from one or two, they're all beautiful and immaculately dressed. I think I might be sitting amongst the sea of women that the King is allowed to dalliance with and shame turns my face to deepest pink. I don't want to be sat with the women, not if they've all shared the King's bed at some point.

But before I can do anything, even seek out the eyes of the Abbot for his assistance, the King reenters the room, and a moment of hush fills the hall as everyone stands to bow to him. He flippantly waves his hand, fully expecting everyone to sit and resume their meal, while he stoops to kiss the cheek of his stepmother. I see her mouth open, and the King glances my way before he takes his seat and begins to eat.

All traces of hunger have vanished from my previously rumbling stomach, but I've not broken my fast yet today, and can feel my head starting to spin a little with the need for food. Wrenching my eyes away from the King, I help myself to some of the food before us, the finely baked bread and the succulent looking venison. I wonder if the King killed the animal himself or whether it was one of the other men within the hall. For the hall is almost full now.

Nearly everyone wears similar clothing, although of differing quality, but there's also a small contingent of monks and holy men, and also some foreign travellers, speaking in a hubbub of duller tones but still comfortable at the King's Court. I also see Æthelwine and Ælfwold, my dead husband's brothers, but they either don't see me, or refuse to meet my gaze. I hope it's that they don't recognise me, or rather, don't expect to see me here.

This is, after all, only my second visit to the King's Hall. Even when I was married to one of the most powerful ealdormen within England, belonging to one of the most powerful dynasties, I was kept away from the King's Hall so that he wouldn't see me, or so the King tells me.

That angers me, and I feel instant remorse. Would I have preferred the King's advances or my short, but happy marriage to my husband?

The food tastes like nothing in my mouth, and I chew without thinking. I need to eat, and I also think I should take the time to try and work out who everyone is, and what their role is within the court.

The ealdormen I have a fair idea about, the bishops as well, but apart from the King's stepmother, I'm unsure who everyone else is. There will be the King's thegns, members of his household guard, servants and slaves, and also some Reeves and Sheriffs who might be visiting the court. There might also be men and women from the Continent, perhaps even from Denmark or from the Pope himself. The court has been cosmopolitan since the days of King Alfred and Athelstan.

I look along the length of the table, but no one meets my eyes. In fact, not until my gaze returns to the King does anyone look at me, and then I'm surprised that I've not felt the heat of his eyes on me before. It seems that he's been staring at me for some time, and doesn't look at all embarrassed when I catch him watching me.

My attention is riveted on him, as the background noise fades away to nothing. If I spoke to him now, I'd expect him to hear me, even though a great distance separates us.

My breath is coming too fast, and no matter the conversation I just had with his step-mother, I want nothing more than to lose myself in his warm arms, to share his bed and to wake with him beside me, his body all hard and ready to pleasure me once more.

I can almost taste him on my lips.

Neither do I think I'm alone in my sudden need for him. The

hunger in his eyes has blackened them, and he looks like a man who's not been fed for days on end.

Abruptly, he looks away, and the wave of sound from the assembled crowd rushes back into my consciousness. I feel naked without the King's eyes on me, bereft without his constant attention.

My chest is rising and falling as I try to catch my breath and I look down toward my lap to hide my burning cheeks and stained lips from the eyes of others. How am I to even be in the king's presence if I can't stop showing my desire so openly. It's not the way of kings and their wives. High profile marriages are arranged for their political value, not for want, desire and lust. It's concubines who show want, desire and passion, and I want more than that. I want to be the queen that Lady Æthelflæd spoke of.

She's been a powerful woman in her own right. And indeed, Edgar's own grandmother, King Edward's third wife, is still a powerful woman as well, although she never earned the title of queen of the English, only of the Anglo-Saxons.

I begin to understand just what it is that the Abbot and Lady Æthelflæd are asking of me. They're prepared to accept that the King wants to bed me, but they're asking me to hold myself chaste and stop him from using me as a concubine. They want England to have a Queen to rival their King. Both of them must have their own reasons for their decision, but I need to honour their commitment to my future, and stay away from the King. No matter how much I wish to be with him, here and now.

A tap on my arm and the Abbot is back with me. He takes in my appearance and tuts softly under his breath.

"The King would see you now," he suggests, but I shake my head, trying to deny the throbbing of my heart at the joy that sentence gives me.

"Please, could you offer my apologies to the King. I'm afraid I feel unwell and must return to my lodgings."

The Abbot's expression flickers in surprise at my words, but then he inclines his head and leans closer.

"Well done, my Lady Elfrida," he says, warm approval in his voice. "I will arrange for a horse to take you home and offer your apologies to the King. Perhaps tomorrow he will call on you again?" he queries, and I hold firm to my recently won resolve and don't capitulate and offer to stay now.

"Perhaps tomorrow. I could send word."

"No," the Abbot says, firmly. "It would be best if the King approached you and not vice versa. Come, we'll leave quickly, while he's distracted by his ealdormen."

I nod in agreement and try not to glance back to the King as I make my escape, for it can't be deemed as anything else, as the Abbot takes my arm firmly and guides me toward the doorway. Just before the door is closed behind us, I catch the anguished face of the King watching me being led away. I almost turn back, forgetting my promise to myself, but the Abbot's hold on my hand is strong, and I allow myself to be led away.

I could sob with my pent up yearning, but it would be unseemly, and instead, I allow the warming day to calm my beating heart and sweaty back.

I don't know how long I'll be able to stay away from the King, but as the Abbot and the Lady Æthelflæd have made their interest in the success of out union so clear to me, I vow to do my best.

I only hope it's enough.

CHAPTER 7

My father asks no questions when I return to my home, and I'm grateful for that as I busy myself with the small tasks a woman must accomplish each day. I see to my clothes from the day before; I tidy my little sleeping space, and I try not to think about the monumental events I've experienced that day.

My father's reticence makes me believe that he knows exactly what's going on. I think his introducing me to Ealdorman Ælfhere last night must be a part of whatever is happening and I'm quickly realising that if I'm to have my way with the King, I'll have an ever increasing number of political allies who will expect something from me in return. Already I have my father, Ealdorman Ælfhere, Abbot Æthelwold, Lady Æthelflæd and whoever else thinks to stand with me as we try and remove the King from his wife and make me his queen instead.

Only exhaustion at the end of the day stops me from my tinkering and my thoughts as I stare into the leaping fire, pleased to be warm and enjoying the simple pleasantries of my life. I know, but try not to think, that such time alone might be denied me soon enough.

Even now, I have little time to myself, as unknown to me, a visitor arrives at the hall, and a warm hand wakes me from my half sleep.

In shock, I look into the haunted eyes of the King and immediately feel all of my determination slip away. My father absents himself from the room, but I don't fail to notice that my servant, and also two of the King's warriors, have made themselves scarce in the dark reaches of the hall. We may never be truly alone in the future I hope we share together.

"My Lady Elfrida," he says in a soft and beguiling voice, and already my heart is beating too fast, and I know that the sweat trickling down my back has nothing to do with the heat and warmth of the room as the summer season fights for dominance.

"King Edgar," I reply, attempting some formality to keep the distance between us. He sits before me, perched on the hearth stones, as though my speaking to him was an invitation to make himself at home and not just an acknowledgement of his unexpected appearance.

I look around a little frantically. I don't wish to be alone with the King. Not yet at least. But there's no one coming to my rescue, and so I school my expression to one of slight interest. He's wearing the same clothes as earlier in the day although his face holds a pinch of chill.

"I missed you after the meal," he continues, as though I've not spoken, and he can't mask the dismay in his voice as he speaks and I feel remorse for upsetting him, even though I needed to.

"I felt unwell," I answer, and it's the honest truth. The thought of being alone with him had made me feel ill. Too hot, too cold, too unsure of myself all at the same time.

"The Abbot told me as such, but I was unsure if he spoke the truth or not, or whether my step-mother had simply warned you off."

This surprises me. It seems that the King might have arranged for me to speak to Lady Æthelflæd but it appears that he had no idea what it was about. This must be another part of the conspiracy that I'm now involved in.

"Not at all, your step-mother is an interesting lady. We spoke, well, we talked about our loss." It seems best, to be honest in this regard, if not in anything else.

A flash of anger crosses his face, although he does his best to hide it with a comforting smile, and I can only assume his anger is directed at events in his life that saw him an orphan before he was three years old.

"Sometimes I forget how linked the Court is, and how much of the past others remember when I was too young to play any part in it." His attempts to sound conciliatory are admirable, in the circumstances.

"Why did you come?" I ask abruptly. The look on his face is making all of my steadfastness melt away and I'd rather he wasn't here, as much as I'm thrilled that he's slipped away from the Court for the very purpose of ensuring that I'm well. The words sound too harsh even to my ears and so I temper them. "You could have sent a messenger or just believed the Abbot."

"I could have done, yes," he accepts, but he's twisting his hands in his lap as he balances on the stone of the hearth and I almost fear to know why he's so nervous.

"But I wanted to ensure you were well, with my own eyes, and that you weren't angry with me for the strange events of the day."

I don't think I could be angry with him if I tried, but his eyes are those of a lost soul, and I suddenly understand that this is the way he entices women to share his bed. He's learnt to use the death of his mother and father as a way of gaining the sympathy of women who might otherwise not be beguiled by his good looks and charm. Perhaps, only I, with my recent losses can understand the need to feel close to someone, no matter how inappropriate.

"The day was beautiful. I enjoyed speaking with Abbot Æthelwold and your step-mother. I found the meal to be a little too long for me, though. And I know so few of the other women who attend the Court.

"Ah, well, if that is all it was, if you come to the Court tomorrow, I can arrange for you to be introduced to some of the other ladies. I could ask Ealdorman Byrthnoth's wife. She's a well-spoken woman, and she knows more about the Court than even I think I do. She's the sister of my step-mother."

He sounds keen as he speaks now and uses it as an opportunity to reach over and hold my hand with his own. My hands have been sitting uselessly on my lap, but now they act as some sort of conduit to my inner being, and I can feel my need for the King taking over my ability to think rationally. At this moment, I genuinely doubt my ability to say no to the King should he ask me to share his bed, before I can convince him that I need to share his crown.

"That would be helpful," I admit, when words are possible again, and I don't miss the flicker of triumph that crosses the King's face at my easy capitulation. Damn. I will need to work harder at this game.

"Should I bring my father with me? It would be advantageous for him to learn more about the Court as well."

The King's expression doesn't change as he considers my request and then he nods.

"Yes, bring your father, and I'll ask Ealdorman Byrthnoth to speak with him, and perhaps Abbot Æthelwold as well. I believe your father is interested in the ways of the Benedictine monks?" There's not really a question in his question and so I only smile, relieved to know that my father will be keeping an eye on me, and that, if I can make a good friend of Ealdorman Byrthnoth's wife, I'll also be able to ensure that I don't have to spend any time alone with the King.

Only, then he releases my hand and instead, runs his hand along the curve of my cheek, as he leans very closely to me.

"I would kiss you now if you'd let me," he says, and it's all I can do to breathe and concentrate on trying to form some words to deny him his request.

He's so close to me, I can feel his breath on my lips, his voice little more than an elongated sigh and I now that I will allow him to kiss me, right now, and hopefully that will be all.

"My Lord King," I try but my words are lost as our lips meet, and the desire of his hand on my own explodes deep within me as I know that this is all I want. I want the feel of this man's lips on my own, forever, and I want never to think of being apart from him.

The attraction I felt to my first husband was like a kindling fire in response to the torrent of heat that rushes through me, and I move my hands to wrap them around the King's head and pull him closer to me, only to hear the faint cough of my servant breaking through the rush of sound in my ears.

Her reminder is a timely one, as the King has moved his hands from my cheek and reaches for my breasts instead.

I pull back, abruptly, and hopefully without upsetting him too much. My face is awash with desire, my back aching for him to take me in his arms and carry me to my bed, but somehow I manage to refrain from dragging his lips back to my own.

I stand abruptly, almost toppling the King to the ground where he's crouched before me, and I look around for some sort of assistance, pleased when my servant is attentively at my side.

"My Lady Elfrida," she says, even her words are breathless, as she too is caught up in the moment.

"Your bath is ready, as requested," she utters, and although it's not true, I'm pleased that she can at least think up a plausible excuse for my abrupt departure from the King.

"My thanks," I say to her, and then turn back to Edgar. His eyes are circles of desire and hunger, and I know that I could easily lead him to my bed and that neither of us would ever have any regrets, but the words of the Abbot and Lady Æthelflæd stops me from even suggesting it.

"I'll be at the Court in the morning," I utter with a bow of my head, and I shuffle past him, where he's almost had me penned into my chair, and follow the servant from the hall, each foot-step away from the King allowing my passion to cool so that when I enter my room and see the intrigued face of my father, I feel almost back in control of myself.

He neither looks angry nor pleased, merely interested and he nods at me with what I believe is approval.

"I'll speak to the King before he leaves and confirm the arrangements for tomorrow."

My father was listening to our conversation! I feel mortified at the knowledge and begin to appreciate that what should be the most intimate and personal of arrangements has become a matter of policy and public debate. I'll need to learn to mask my craving and emotions far better in the future if I'm to survive as an object of such public interest.

"My thanks," I say to my servant, but she's watching my father and the King through the half-open door. I try not to turn and stare myself. I fear that if I saw the King once more today, that would be it. I'd allow him to do almost anything to me. Instead, I listen to my servant's soft words.

"Your father and the King are sharing words and mead," she tells me in a voice that just carries to where I stand, shaking with relief that for tonight, at least, I've managed to evade the King. "I can't see the King's face, but your father is relaxed, almost smiling."

I almost turn again at those words. My father isn't known for being a jovial man. But then, I imagine that any man, honoured by the King in such a way, might be keen to smile a little. If my brothers were here, the hall would no doubt be a riot of drunken young fools, and the King could easily join them. With only an old man to speak to, I assume the King feels a little out of his depth.

"The King and your father have their heads close together. They're speaking quietly of something important." The servant and I both know what they're talking about, but neither of us says anything further.

"Come, help me out of my things," I whisper instead. There might be no bath drawn up for me, but I would appreciate making it appear as though there was, and the call of my bed, where I will be warm and safe and free from everything but my erotic thoughts of the King, is great. I need to sleep to feel renewed for the coming day when I must meet with Lady Æthelflæd's sister. I imagine she'll be as formidable as today's combatant, and that I must also work to gain her support.

The task before me is almost too exhausting to comprehend, and although in-between helping me undress, my servant continues to rush to the slightly open doorway to see if my father still speaks with his King, I find that my interest has waned. I need to sleep, and it's with joy that I finally slide into my bed, and find that, for the first time in many, many months, sleep claims me immediately, dragging me down to a blackness without lust or loss.

CHAPTER 8

I wake early, refreshed from a night without dreams, and immediately, I begin to consider my dilemma from every possible perspective.

I now know that my desire for the King is too potent for me to contain, should I spend time alone with him, and as I'll have to spend time alone with him, to make him my husband, I must think of a way of subduing my passion.

I could pray to my God to show me the way forward, but I believe that in this matter, while religion might further my course, in the long run, it will not bring me the resolve that I need to master.

As I dress carefully, thinking of my meeting with Lady Ælfflæd that day, my mind swirls with the implications of the changes of the last few days.

My father introduced me to Ealdorman Ælfhere; the King made his intentions toward me clear and then himself introduced me to Abbot Æthelwold and Lady Æthelflæd, before coming to visit me personally. Neither have I forgotten that he seems to have banished his wife to the nunnery at Wilton, with his young daughter as well.

It appears that he's trying to clear the way for me, but whether he still means for me to be his concubine or his wife, it seems that others see me as their future Queen. It's a great deal to comprehend and appreciate.

If I become a Queen, I could hope to have as much power as

Lady Æthelflæd, and the King's grandmother as well, the Lady Eadgifu. While King Eadwig was not friendly toward her; I know that King Edgar and she are close, and yet she's also an ancient woman, not often seen at the court. But in her time. Well, she was acknowledged as not quite a queen, but a respected wife of her husband, King Edward, and then in the lifetimes of her sons, King Edmund and Eadred and her step-son, King Athelstan, she was also accorded a great deal of honour and respect, her opinions sought by many, and her patronage favoured by the churches and monasteries she endowed.

Neither does Lady Ælfflæd lack for political acumen at the Court. I've heard my father speak of her in the past. She and her husband are well respected in the land they govern for the King, in Essex. It means that they're both far away from the Court not to be involved in the day-to-day wrangles, but close enough to be with the King at little more than a day's notice. I imagine the two of them know a great deal about the King and events in his Witan and his Court.

I've distracted myself with wondering about the Court, and I've failed to find a solution to my problem. Perhaps I'll have to rely on prayer after all, or indeed a far greater tenacity than I've yet had.

As I emerge from my room, dressed and ready for the day, my father greets me immediately. I'm sure he wears the same clothes as the night before, and I double check the inhabitants of the room just to be certain that the King doesn't keep him company.

"I'd speak with you before you go to the palace," he offers, indicating that we should sit by the fire, over which the kitchen servant is tending to a cauldron of pottage. The smell is tempting, and I realise that I ate very little yesterday.

"Of course, father," I mutter as I kiss his bearded cheek in welcome. He smells of ale and mead, and I wrinkle my nose a little.

"The King can handle his mead far too well for such a young man, and I, far too poorly."

"You drank all night?" I ask horrified, but my father grunts a reply.

"Not I. I fear I feel asleep while the King was still here. I assume he'll forgive me, all things considered."

"Ah," I respond.

"But before I slept, we spoke at some length. I perceive that the King believes his intentions toward you are honourable, but as you feared, and I know you worry, I do not think he means to make you his wife."

"Ah," is all I can say once more. I thought it wouldn't trouble my father, but it seems he too has his eye on a greater prize for his daughter.

"I'll escort you to the court, and stay with you at all times unless you're with one of the great ladies of the court. Lady Æthelflæd, Lady Ælfflæd or even Lady Eadgifu."

A small smile lights my face.

"I see you've decided that I can only be trusted with the most powerful ladies of the land."

I don't know if he appreciates my humour because he doesn't smile, instead rising and issuing a string of instructions to the servants so that he can be dressed and made presentable. I watch him in good humour. Already I feel more confident. I'm pleased I have his support to add to those others who've already pledged to me. Perhaps with the weight of opinion from enough people on my shoulders, my emotions will be contained when I'm in the presence of the King.

My father and I walk to the King's palace, huddled inside our cloaks, in a companionable silence. The day wears a sprinkling of dew over everything, and my feet splash in the occasional puddle formed on the road surface, a soft sound to go with my breathing and the swish of my cloak over the ground.

We gain entry to the Palace with only a few muffled words from my father to the guardsmen, and it seems that our arrival is expected, and looked for, as no sooner have I entered the King's Hall, a little sleepy in the morning light, than both Lady Æthelflæd and Lady Ælfflæd greet my father, and then myself.

The King is once more absent from the hall, but Ealdorman

Bryhtnoth quietly escorts my father away from the conclave of ladies , and I understand that I'm to be at the mercy of the women for the day.

The two sisters look remarkably similar, both a generation older than I, more likely to be my father's age than my own. They both dress impeccably well, and I'm instantly envious of the fine golden thread through their overdresses and the jewels in their hair. They are wealthy women in their right, whereas I once had my father's wealth, and then my husband's, and now my father's once more.

"Lady Elfrida," Ælfflæd greets me, her voice reminds me of the summer, and I hope that she might be easier to speak with than her sister. She might be less concerned with the future of the kingdom than her sister.

"Have you eaten?" she asks politely, and although I have, I still find myself sitting between the two women as they break their fast. I'm surprised to find the fare so similar to my own at home, a bowlful of pottage and some warmed mead. The sisters eat daintily but heartily, and speak pleasantly to the servants who tend to their need.

It seems to me that they are well respected in the hall, as though the servants and the other members of the King's Court, are almost too keen to provide for them. I can only hope that one day I'm accorded the same respect and trust.

"Now, I know my duties to you today are to show you around the King's Court, so that you know those who live here and those who don't, but first, I'd like to visit the Old Minster and pray," Lady Ælfflæd is the one that speaks first, her meal quickly taken away now that she's finished. "Come, we'll walk to my room to retrieve my cloak while my sister finishes her meal."

As soon as we're away from the table, the friendly manner of Lady Ælfflæd evaporates completely.

"My sister tells me that she hopes you'll be the one to take her place as mistress of the King's household. I can't deny we need a woman who can control him and his licentious ways, but I'm yet to be convinced of anything but your beauty. The King is always like a love-sick puppy. But neither is my sister easily swayed by beauty alone."

My ease and confidence feel shaken, but I hold onto them. If I were in her position, what would I think of a young girl trying to steal the King's heart?

"I hope that we can be allies, and also friends," I offer with a wary smile, and respect flashes across her face but she doesn't speak again, instead directing me along a wooden corridor. I pass closed door after closed door, behind which I hear the shuffle of people waking and others snoring, and I understand at that moment just how many people rely on the King for their livelihood.

The room that Lady Ælfflæd steps into is small and yet comfortable. There's a wooden chest for clothing, and a small brazier, lit although the chamber is empty. There's no hearth, but I don't think there needs to be one.

"Age makes you cold," she offers by way of an explanation as she opens her chest and rifles inside for a long cloak.

"Was there a storm this morning?" she asks, and I nod instead of speaking, my attention on the exquisite jewellery I can see safely stored on top of the clothes in her chest.

"They're beautiful," I exclaim, stepping closer to peer at them more intently. There are about ten different items, some newly made, the gold brightly glittering in the sunshine streaming through the open doorway, whereas others must be ancient, their gold almost bronze, and the signs of wear showing in some small scratches and dents on the edges.

"My family is an old one," she offers by way of an explanation. "My father was an ealdorman, and his before him. He died fighting the Viking raiders, but before that, our family had ruled in Essex for many, many centuries. I believe we can trace our ancestors back to the first wave of the Saxons from their homeland."

"My father's family is old and well respected," I almost feel stung into replying but manage to remove the accusation from my voice.

"He's a King's thegn?" she asks, and I swallow back the fear at the back of my throat. I might be the daughter of a King's thegn, but I'm also the widow of an ealdorman. If I could be suitable for an ealdorman then, I can't see how I'm not fit for a king now.

"Yes, he is. But he's capable of much more, my brothers as well."

"I'm sure the men are accomplished." She's swishing the cloak around her shoulders as she speaks so I can't see her face. Neither can she see my own and that's good.

"Come, the Abbot will be waiting for us," she mutters, shooing me from the room and I hope she means Abbot Æthelwold. I know that he thought well of me yesterday. Perhaps he can alleviate any problems Lady Ælfflæd has with my parentage and my past.

We make our way back to the hall, and Lady Æthelflæd is waiting for us, along with a younger woman.

"My daughter," Lady Ælfflæd informs me, "the Lady Leofflæd." The girl must be my age, and she's far prettier than I am. Well, apart from her overly large nose. I fear that men will have to work hard to overlook that problem. Her greeting is warm, though, and I quickly dispel my less than kind thoughts about her appearance. She might prove to be one of my friends at the Court, unlike her mother and her aunt, who only see me as some sort of conduit to the King.

"My Lady Elfrida," Leofflæd says politely, dipping her head, and I mirror her actions. I'm no more worthy of the honorific than she is. And if I want to make her friend it would be good to make a smooth start.

"Come, we should leave. Mother is always late for the Abbot." There's censorship in her voice, as she threads her arm through mine, and I catch a brief look of displeasure on Lady Ælfflæd's face at her daughter's words. I wonder if she'll be berated for that later.

This time the walk to the Minster is quickly accomplished, and I soon see the twin towers of the huge building and feel its icy chill as I step inside the massive wooden door. The clerics inside scuttle away to do their work, and the distracted Abbot Æthelwold greets us.

He leans towards the two older woman and whispers,

"I think I may have hit some impediments to the King's desires here," in a loud enough voice that we all hear it and perhaps one or two of the clerics inside the magnificent Minster.

There's a hint of aggravation in the Abbot's voice, but it's only mild before the two great ladies of the Court.

"But that's no welcome for you all. Please, come, we'll have our short service of prayer, and then we'll retire to the small sanctuary below, where we can talk more."

Together we all walk to the front of the Minster, where the Abbot leaves us and takes his place before us all, as he begins his chants and we kneel and pray. There are elaborately decorated cushions for us to kneel upon that almost stop the chill of the floor from reaching our knees.

Lady Leofflæd fidgets through much of the service and earns herself a rebuke from her mother, but I find her presence heartening. Sometimes I think that the churchmen insist on making their sermons as long as possible just to test the patience of their listeners as if not being able to sit still makes us unworthy of hearing God's words.

The Abbot seems to understand Lady Leofflæd's needs better than her mother, and soon we're once more in the small room I sat in the previous days with the King.

The Abbot is as effusive as he was yesterday and very attentive to the older women and that allows me time to investigate the treasures fully in the room. On the lectern sits a beautifully decorated copy of Bede's 'History of the English People', and I almost reach out to touch it and turn the page, but I stop before I do something I might regret.

The written word is something to be treasured. It's the way our people remember our past, somehow more permanent than the spoken word and the memories of those who lived before our time.

Lady Leofflæd sits with her mother and observes me. She

looks flushed with anger, and I beckon her to my side so that we can examine the manuscript together. Her mother notices my intentions but leaves it to Lady Leofflæd to decide if she should join me or not.

I beg with my eyes, and with a childish jump, she's beside me, exclaiming, as I was, over the decoration and the beautiful gold inlay. The colours are so bright that even in this dull little room, I can fully visualise the twisting creatures on the page as though we stood in brightest daylight.

I've heard of the great monk's writings, but never before have I seen them, and the Abbot, perhaps understanding my desire, stands as well and comes to open another page for me.

"It's a priceless manuscript," he whispers reverentially. "The community from Lindisfarne were destroyed by the first wave of Viking attacks, but luckily, Bede's writings had been copied and so we didn't lose this important part of our history."

I want to ask him to show me more, but Lady Æthelflæd makes a slight coughing noise, as though to remind us of her presence, and the three of us return to the small circle of chairs.

"You spoke of some problems," Lady Ælfflæd immediately asks, and the Abbot bows his head low.

"Yes, my Lady. I feel I'll encounter the same resistance here as I did at Abingdon. It's nothing that I'm unused to, but it's an inconvenience when I'm keen to begin the work immediately. Instead, I'll have to step carefully. I'll have to rely on the support of the King."

"And the nobility as well," Lady Æthelflæd choruses. "We'll ensure that the clerics know it's the will of the King and not just a flight of fancy. They must come to understand that the people of England deserve to be served by monks in their most austere capacity."

"My thanks, My Lady Æthelflæd," the Abbot says, bowing his head to her. Only then his eyes are on my own.

"And you, My Lady Elfrida? What do you think after our discussion yesterday?" I feel uneasy being put on the spot in such a way and I hope this isn't a test that I'm about to fail.

"I think the Minster would benefit from the elevation of St Swithun to a position more fitting of his rank, and I believe that in this way, the clerics will come to appreciate that they can only truly serve their community by reverting to the rule of St Benedictine."

A faint smile passes over the Abbot's face, and somehow I know that I've said exactly what he was hoping I would.

"Already, the King desires that the Old Minster be converted, and he hopes that I'll be placed in such a position to do so. If we present you as a firm proponent of the movement, I believe that we can sway many other members of the nobility and help the King in his wishes."

"I want to serve in any way I can," I reply quickly, but the bark of laughter from Lady Ælfflæd catches me a little off-guard.

"It'll be more than just supporting the King in his quest to install the rule of St Benedictine. You'll have to tease him as well, but give him just enough that he knows he wants you."

My face flushes with embarrassment, and I think that the Abbot may resent our discussion in such a holy place, but instead, he opens his hands wide and watches me with a stern expression.

"The King isn't a complicated man. He likes to think that he is, but he has the same natural desires that all men do, and what he needs is a woman who can tolerate his, whims, or rein them in, whichever comes soonest, and do it all with the light touch of femininity that the Court has lacked for some time."

It seems that almost everyone has an opinion on how I should draw the King in and entice him with my sexuality, while at the same time, keeping him at arm's length.

I feel a sigh escape from my mouth before I can stop it, and the two older women look at me with some sympathy. Suddenly I see them as young women, little different from Lady Leofflæd and myself and I wonder what they had to do to marry a King and an Ealdorman in turn.

"You'll help me?" I ask them both, and the women nod at the same time.

"We know the ways of men, and Lady Leofflæd will help you with the … practicalities of the task," her mother says, and I realise I need to know more about Leofflæd. Is she married? Does she need a good match? Could I perhaps make my first alliance by arranging a marriage between her and my brother, should her mother and father be amenable to the idea?

"And you'll help me as well?" I ask the Abbot, and his face is once more that of the amenable holy man.

"My Lady Elfrida, I'd be honoured, and so will the King."

And that, it seems, is all I need to know from the Abbot for the older women stand and quickly take their leave, Lady Leofflæd trailing in their wake. I wait because I want to speak to the Abbot alone.

When I'm sure that no one can overhear us, I speak.

"You will show me all the manuscripts when I'm Queen?" I demand of him, and his lower lip curls in delight, and he whispers his response as though we are conspirators in a quest.

"I'll show you all you want to see. And more, I'll show you how to make your family strong through the written word. Your family will live on for a long time through the hands of the monks I employ here to sing and write praises about you and your family. You need not fear that you'll fade away such as the Lady Wulfthryth."

"My thanks," I nod and turn to stride away decisively.

"My Lady Elfrida?" he calls to me, and I turn, surprised. I thought our conversation was done.

"The King is a man who thinks of his needs and his wants and only then of whether he should satisfy them. When you're alone with him, remember that he's a man who knows how to charm women into his bed."

It feels strange to take such advice from a holy man, but I understand that Abbot Æthelwold is uniquely placed to understand the King. He has, after all, known him for a very long time.

Back at the King's Palace, I find myself sat with the great ladies of the court, the Lady Ælfflæd to one side, and Lady Æthelflæd in front of me. Lady Leofflæd sits to the other side, and she constantly gossips with a group of women about the same age as myself. I'd love to speak with them, but instead, the sisters are telling me stories of their courtships, and I listen as attentively as I can as I try to imagine the two women with the same heated desire that I have for the King.

"My marriage was arranged for me, very quickly after the King's first wife died. I was not pleased to be singled out in such a way. The King seemed to me to be infected with morose over the death of his wife, and concerned only with pushing back the northern boundaries so that his landholdings rivaled those of King Athelstan's."

"King Athelstan was more monk than King," Ælfflæd interjects with a mischevious smile, and immediately the years peel back from her face and reveal her as the beautiful woman she must once have been.

"My sister was keen to break King Athelstan's vows of celibacy. That she never managed has long been a cause of unhappiness for her."

"I was angry with my father as well when he put you forward for Edmund. I thought I'd have made a better match, but my father promised me another man of equal stature."

"I had a more difficult task than the one you face, for the King wasn't interested in any form of dalliance. He wanted a mother for his children, not a woman to warm his bed."

Lady Æthelflæd sighs deeply as she considers the past.

"I first made friends with the King's older son. Eadwig was a far more pleasant child than the disappointing man he grew to be, and from there, I earned his father's trust and desire. Not that I had long to do so. Every woman at the court was hoping to catch the King's eye after the tragic death of his wife. I only tried so hard because I wished to upset my sister by becoming the wife of the King when I knew she craved the position herself."

Lady Ælfflæd smiles at her sister as she speaks. These two have had twenty long years to confess their deepest secrets to each other, and it seems that they've done so.

"I, however, had a similar problem to your own. Ealdorman

Byrthnoth was a handsome man, well he still is, but he had no idea that he needed a wife as opposed to a concubine. My father tasked me with making him marry me and forbade me to succumb to him before our marriage could be solemnised in a church. It was a very difficult task," Lady Ælfflæd huffs dramatically, and I hear an annoyed grunt from her daughter.

"Must you speak of my father in such a way," Lady Leofflæd admonishes, stressing the 'my father' part. I know how she feels. I wouldn't want to hear of any romance between my mother and father.

"Girl, men need to be captured and shown the right of it sometimes. You'd do well to listen and understand. It's time you were married as well, and yet no man steps forward and shows even the smallest shred of interest in you."

"It is difficult, *mother*," Lady Leofflæd begins, again stressing the word 'mother', "when I'm only ever seen in your company. I can't imagine any of the ealdormen or King's thegns, or Reeves would want to marry a woman who is always flanked by the King's step-mother, and her mother. It might make a man a little wary, a little too unsure of himself when he's trying to win the support of the King, for whatever reason."

I can already tell that the three of them have had this argument too many times before, and yet it eases the tension building in my chest and makes me realize that all women must find themselves a husband, either through their looks, their desires, or by making a man find something in them that he wishes to possess. What I hope to accomplish is no different to their past experiences.

Lady Ælfflæd grumbles something under her breath and continues to reminisce anyway.

"He was a very handsome man, not adverse to taking any woman who came near him. He had no thought of the future. He didn't care about that, and he saw no reason to make a good marriage when all he wanted was sex."

I think the two other women must have heard this story so many times that they're not listening but I find myself leaning forward attentively. The young Byrthnoth sounds very similar to the King.

"My father, bereft of sons and with one daughter already married to a King, was keen to find someone he thought suitable to rule in his stead, and he'd decided that Byrthnoth was that man. He was a man that others followed, and he understood the way of the Court well. Father was prepared to overlook all his slights with women, provided he'd marry me. Not that he told Byrthnoth that. He wanted me to gain him first. But only without expressively breaking any marriage vows."

"Our father expected a great deal from us," Lady Æthelflæd interjected, her voice filled with compassion, but Lady Ælfflæd giggles in response, as Lady Leofflæd purposefully turns away, a loud tut of annoyance remaining after her head spun away.

"Not that I minded. Not at all. Byrthnoth was a man of great passions, and by pretending that my father hated him and had forbidden our union, I excited him enough that he'd do anything to win my affection. And," and here her voice dropped to a conspiratorial whisper, "I don't deny that I enjoyed myself as well."

"Mother," her daughter rejoins, but Lady Ælfflæd touches my arm and drops her voice even lower.

"Ealdorman Byrthnoth followed me everywhere I went with his eyes. I wore my most austere clothing but always ensured that he could clearly see my curving breasts and waist, and always showed just a touch of immodest flesh. When he spoke with me, I either almost ignored him or listened with baited breath, and he never knew which reaction he was going to get. Then one night, when I was almost assured of his good intentions to me, I snuck away from one of the King's feasts and waited for him to follow me into the King's garden."

"It was a warm summer's evening, and I was paddling in the stream near the palace, my dress raised a little too high about my knees, and none of the King's guards anywhere near me. I'd made sure that Ealdorman Byrthnoth had seen me leave the feast, and more importantly, that my father hadn't."

She giggled again.

"He was so keen not to be caught, and also so excited to sneak out against my father's wishes. I pretended I'd not seen him creeping through the evening gloom and when his arms went around my waist from behind, I'd squealed in surprise, and he'd spun me around and kissed me immediately. That was the first time we'd kissed and was no means the last before we married."

"His lips had brushed mine with such tenderness, as though dipping his toe in the water to see if he should have acted so irresponsibly, and I'd responded a little. Given him some indication that I was content to be kissed and held in such an intimate way, but I'd stopped his questing hands from getting their way despite his growl of frustration. I'd giggled at him and tried to push him away, playfully of course, and then I'd allowed him to pull me back into his arms and let him kiss me again and again, as the sound of the King's feast had faded away in the background."

"Your father?" he'd muttered, and I'd looked worried and concerned and made to run away, but he'd held me even tighter.

"I'm not afraid of your father, and I'll prove myself to him," he'd vowed, running his hands through my shoulder length hair, and I'd thought it all a little too easy in the end.

"I helped the situation," Lady Æthelflæd interjected, and now she looks sternly at her sister. "I sent the King after my errant sister and ensured that the pair of them were found together. That made it imperative for the King to preserve my honour, and to heap even more pressure on Ealdorman Byrthnoth to keep his word. The two, had, after all, become friends late in the King's reign.

"Yes, but the King had been in a forgiving mood following his defeat of his enemies."

"Well yes, I can't deny the King was initially amused by Ealdorman Byrthnoth's actions. He told me of what had happened, and I expressed such outrage on my poor sister's behalf, that King Edmund sought out Ealdorman Byrthnoth and told him he must marry to protect the King's name."

The two sisters seem to enjoy telling their story, and I listen, mouth almost agape, at the antics of the two sisters. I wonder if, in twenty years time, I'll amuse other girls with stories of my capture of the King? It would be a fine story to tell, provided I manage to marry the King and become his queen.

"Does Ealdorman Byrthnoth know he was tricked?" I ask Lady Ælfflæd, and she nods, delight in her eyes.

"He likes to think he knew all along, but he didn't. None of it. He was hooked by my antics, and my father was pleased with me when we married, and Ealdorman Byrthnoth settled to a more sedate lifestyle. Not that we haven't had our moments of passion since then."

"Mother," squeals Lady Leofflæd, indignation making her voice high, and we all collapse in laughter, earning stern stares from many others within the room.

Our laughter draws the interest of the King, and I feel his gaze on my own. I'd not seen him enter the hall and I almost wish he hadn't observed me in such an open way. If I'm to believe Lady Æthelflæd and Ælfflæd, I should have shown myself to be a little more reserved.

I sober immediately. The two women have made it appear as though it's simple to snare a husband but faced with the handsome face of the King before me, I know that there's a huge difference between speaking about something, and actually putting it into effect.

"I think the King might spoil our fun," Lady Ælfflæd grumbles as my thoughts run amok in my head, and I realise with half fear and half joy, that the King is making his way toward the table we occupy.

I sit straighter and feel the hands of Lady Ælfflæd smoothing my hair down my back. Her intelligent eyes flicker with mild annoyance, but as the King approaches, Lady Æthelflæd stands and regally faces her step-son.

"King Edgar," she curtsies, fixing him with a stare, but even I can feel his eyes on me as she tries to give me the time to prepare for whatever the King might now ask of me.

"Mother," he responds, a touch of humour in his voice, but

he says nothing else to her, although he acknowledges his step-aunt, and almost cousin, with a sly smile.

But the full force of his smile he saves for me, and it's all I can do to remember to breathe as he turns to face me.

"Lady Elfrida," he greets me, the warmth and desire in his voice impossible to ignore, for all that Lady Ælfflæd tries to return me to the here and now by pinching my leg beneath the table. The sharp pinch barely registers as I stand to meet the King, my food forgotten about and also my resolve not to show the King the effect he has on me.

"I take it my mother and her sister and daughter are treating you well," he asks, and I nod abruptly, before realising that I must speak to the King and not appear as a dumb beast.

"Very well, My Lord King, my thanks for the opportunity to speak with them, and with Abbot Æthelwold again."

"You have more plans for the afternoon," he asks me but luckily Lady Æthelflæd answers on my behalf.

"Of course, My Lord King. We must tour all of the palace, and show Lady Elfrida where the women sit and spend their days, and where the men train and where those who live in the palace spend their nights. There is much that we must still do."

"Indeed," he says abruptly. "Then I'm not to spend any time with the Lady Elfrida today?" It's almost an accusation, and even I can hear the betrayal in his voice.

"Well, you could, of course, join us," she retorts. "You did, after all, ask us to show her the ways of the palace. It's not as if we can whisk her around the place. It is quite large."

"Then I shall join you later this afternoon," he says, but his piercing eyes haven't strayed from my own, and I can feel my heart thumping inside my chest.

"As you wish, My Lord King," she says, as though it would please her as much as it will please him, and then the King sweeps from our presence, and I try to catch my breath as Lady Ælfflæd pats my arm with sympathy.

"Goodness me, you two do have a strong attraction to each other, don't you. Wow, I almost want to rush to Ealdorman Byrthnoth and demand he takes me to his bed."

"Mother," Lady Leofflæd hisses, angrily, and that has us all laughing once more, and even I notice that my laugh is a little too high pitched, and my relief that the King has left me alone, almost makes me feel giddy.

"Come ladies," Lady Ælfflæd scolds, "we must take Lady Elfrida away from here and find some way to cool the heat of this fledgling passion, for if we don't, the King will have his way with her, and she'll never be a Queen, and we'll be stuck with the King's current insipid wife for the rest of our days."

It's her words more than anything that brings me to my senses. I knew she would have a reason for supporting me, but she's blatantly reminded me that nothing within the palace is as it seems and everyone is ultimately working for their goal. The two great ladies have their agenda, and I'm just a part of their plan to gain what they want. I need to think about what I want to gain from the King's interest in me, and how I might ensure my longevity if I am to become Queen. It seems to me that if Abbot Æthelwold, and the Lady Æthelflæd and Ælfflæd are prepared to work to remove the King's wife, then it stands to reason that there must be others who are keen to keep her as his wife.

It would serve me well to work out who those people might be and see if I can make myself impervious to their scheming ways, and ensure that if I do become the Queen, I remain as one.

The two older women sweep through the hall, and I trail in their wake, watching the way they hold themselves, their head, their attentiveness, even the way they match their steps to the other so that it seems that they walk as one.

Neither do I miss that they nod to some of the people they pass, showing their favour for them. I wish I could strain my neck and follow their line of sight so that I know who they look to, but whoever it is, by the time I'm in the correct position, they've all turned back to their original tasks, and I'm left none the wiser. I don't know enough people at the Court to know everyone, and I'm unskilled not to be able to understand anything from people's backs and necks.

I do feel the eyes of others upon me, and I turn when I feel the force of those eyes. A face greets me, an unfamiliar one. I hazard a guess that this must be some relative of the King's wife for in the tilt of her chin, I recognise the mannerisms of Wulfthryth from when I saw her briefly at the feast held in her honour.

I meet the gaze squarely, determined not to be belittled by the woman, yet as I do, I try and decide who she sits with, and who might be her allies. It's a certainty that she won't be at the King's Court alone, not when her relative is currently the mother of the King's daughter and also his wife, albeit an absentee one.

I don't yet know enough people at the Court to know who everyone is so I try and remember the characteristics of those people; the colour of their hair, their stature, whether they're men or women and whom they sit next to. I'm sure that the two older women will know who these people are if I can just describe them in enough detail.

Outside the hall, the day is well advanced, and I can feel the bite of a cold night on the way. I'd much rather be in the warmth, but the sisters have their plans for me, and it appears that not even the King can circumvent them.

"Lady Elfrida," Lady Leofflæd says to me in an undertone, "tell me what it feels like."

I'm not sure what she means and look at her questioningly.

"To want someone as badly as you want the King. I've never felt that, but I can see it. I think everyone can see it."

"I," I don't know what to say. I've been trying not to think about it too much, fearful that if I allow my thoughts to run too deep, I'll be hampered in my quest for the king.

"It feels like. Well, it feels like heat and fire, burning as wildly as the Yule log, leaping from branch to branch, outside my control, volatile and incendiary. I don't like to admit it, but I have no command over it. I can't name it or quantify it. It's just there, all the time."

Her beautiful face is sad as she considers my answer.

"I'd like to feel the same one day," she muses and I want to reassure her that she will, but I know better. I was lucky with my first marriage, and if I should manage to marry the King, I'll have been exceptionally fortunate to find such mutual passion and desire again.

Lady Leofflæd nods as she absorbs my words. The expression on her face makes it clear that she appreciates my efforts not to offer any half-hearted attempts at flattery and false reassurance.

"Lady Elfrida," Lady Ælfflæd calls me to her side, and I leave Lady Leofflæd to consider my words.

"We'll visit the stables first," her eyes twinkle as she speaks, and behind me, I feel an excited squeal from Lady Leofflæd.

"Isn't it too late to see the household warriors training?" she asks, and I understand her delight at her mother's words.

"There's always a few of the more rugged men hanging around," Lady Æthelflæd responds, and I see that all of them are keen to watch the men at their labours. I'd rather be spared the necessity, but it might just be the highlight of the day for the women. First, they've prayed, and then they've eaten, and now they get to watch young men at work. But when we get to the stables, a building much the same as the King's great hall and on almost as vast a scale, I understand that there are other reasons to visit the stable.

It's not only the horses who're here, nor the household warriors. Instead, many people, almost more than were in the King's Hall, have congregated here. The atmosphere is more of a fair than a busy, working yard, and the sisters are greeted by many as they weave their way to where a few of the King's warriors are indeed training, their weapons blunted for training, but their malice clear to see in their precise movements and angry cries as they battle each other.

It's there that I get my first real glimpse of Ealdorman Byrthnoth. He's still a handsome man, with a full head of hair and a neatly groomed moustache. He looks like his daughter, sharing her high forehead and slightly over-large nose, and I can see why he was once an attractive proposition for many of the women of the court. He carries himself well, and although he's middle-aged, with a slight paunch to his stomach, he walks like a warrior and the other men respect him as one, calling to him for his opinion on all matters of their mock battles. It's very easy to see that he is widely respected.

"Come, Lady Elfrida," Lady Ælfflæd gestures irritably, and I rush to her side, and listen as she makes introductions.

"So, you're my wife and her sister's latest project?" the man says, appraising me with appreciative eyes. It seems he might just still like an attractive woman. Men his age are often less interested in women and more in their mead and games, and recounting stories of past conquests, both military and between the furs.

"I can see why " he admits grudgingly and his sister by marriage giggles in girlish delight. She's so different today compared to the woman I met yesterday. Will I need to adopt different personas depending on who I'm with? The thought chills me.

"The King says she's the most beautiful woman in England," I find it strange to hear those words on the lips of another woman, but Lady Æthelflæd winks at me as she speaks. Perhaps that is how others think of me.

"I take it you don't wish to be a nun?" he asks, serious now and I allow a smile to play about my lips. I had, after all, considered the possibility when my husband died.

"I should rather be married to a man who'll love and respect me than serve one who'll never touch me with the same intimacy."

I might have been too candid with my answer, but that is how I feel. I want to be burnt by the man I spend the rest of my days serving. I want to feel lust and excitement.

"But you can resist him?" his pointed reply reminds me that I will struggle in that regard.

"I'll do my best, My Lord." I bow my head a little. "Your wife and sister by marriage have some advice to offer in that regard."

"I imagine they do," he answers with a sour twitch of his mouth. Surely he doesn't still resent his wife's snaring of him?

"Do you have any advice?" I ask him, my eyes a little taunting. It would be good to see how a man reacts to that question.

"Good God girl, no. I look at you, and I want you. God alone knows how you'll keep that rampant beast from trying to mount you at every available opportunity."

Lady Leofflæd gasps in shock at her father's unrestrained words, but I find his honesty compelling, and I laugh in earnest.

"He's that bad?" I ask, but Ealdorman Byrthnoth now has the decency to look a little ashamed of the way he spoke about his King, and I can already see him trying to work out the probable results of his unguarded words.

"He's not always that bad," he attempts to backtrack, but actually, I think his warning is the one I need to hear. I need to know just how determined the King will be when we're finally alone once more.

"I would prefer to know the truth. I'm not above his influence. I feel it whenever I see him."

"Ah, then girl," I do like the fact he's calling me girl. "I suggest you take steps to immure yourself against his particular talents. Men of his age can be very single minded when they want to be. They won't be above trickery and downright lying, even the King."

I almost expect the two great ladies of the kingdom to hush Ealdorman Byrthnoth, but it seems that this discussion between the three of them, with me, now included, is not a new one. I wonder how long they'd been hoping for a candidate they preferred to be shown any great regard for the King.

"And you don't like the King's current wife?" I ask, just to be sure. Ealdorman Byrthnoth shrugs aside the question.

"There's nothing to like or dislike. I don't know who she is. She won't interact with the ealdormen and thegns of the King's Court. She relies wholly on her grandmother's advice, the Lady Wulfhild, and it's Wulfhild who has lots of influence because of who her family is. Wulfthryth is little more than an empty shell put there to serve the interests of her family."

"But who are her family?" I'm not sure, and I need to know.

"She's the daughter of a noble Wessex family. Her father died when she was a baby, in Edmund's wars. Her mother was a mouse, a nun at Wilton after her husband's death, but her grandmother knew that she had a powerful weapon at her disposal, and she kept ensuring that the King saw the girl, for all that she had no interest in him."

"The rumours that he stole her from a nunnery are more than half right. He almost did, only she was no nun, and Archbishop Dunstan forgave him in light of the fact that King Eadwig detested Dunstan and he needed to ensure that he had a King who could shield him and help him with his ideas about the Benedictine monasteries. He's come to regret his decision, although he doesn't seek a way out of the marriage for the King."

"Marriage and politics go hand in hand at the King's Court. The King has tried to give himself strong ealdormen who'll help him rule to the best of his ability, but ultimately, men will become too consumed with their needs and wants, and will pursue their ends instead of the King's."

"I know of why your husband and the King never reconciled after their argument, although you mustn't think that many do, and I know that in his anger he made Ealdorman Ælfhere and his brother, Ælfheah, strong men. The King lost all faith with your husband and his brothers. But since Ealdorman Æthelwald's death, he's been more conciliatory towards them. I'm surprised the brothers don't wish to use you to further their own ends."

This jolts me from considering the intrigue of the Court, to once more considering my husband's instructions to me. I thought he meant to make me secure in the future, but perhaps he was only trying to assist his brothers in his death. That thought fills me with revulsion for the man I've never had anything but a remorseful sorrow for.

But then, if that were the case, his brothers would have been keener to keep me at their side and have me remain a part of their family. Wouldn't they?

I shake my head angrily.

Ealdorman Byrthnoth nods as he sees my frustration.

"The Court is a nest of vipers," he acknowledges. "But it doesn't have to be. King Edgar is much loved by everyone. People wish to serve him and to continue the work of his uncle and his father. He has a lot of sympathy stemming from his father's murder, but he sometimes squanders his chances."

"There's no firm divide between the King's ealdormen and thegns. But there could be if we wanted there to be. I don't think anyone intends to do that, but we do want the King to be stabilised in his passions and his flighty ways. He needs to stop acting as though he only holds the kingdom by default. He was chosen as the King of the Northern Territories long before his brother died, and Wessex might have soon followed suit if his brother hadn't so conveniently died only two years later and made the wooing of Wessex and Kent unnecessary."

My father's told me of the hushed rumours regarding King Eadwig's death. I've chosen to ignore them thus far. I wouldn't want to think that anyone meant the arrogant former King ill-harm. I wouldn't want to believe that Edgar is only King because someone 'saw' to the death of his brother when his conceited ways led to so many problems between the King and his councilors. At one point, he even deprived Lady Æthelflæd of her dower lands and banished her from Court. It was not the kindest of ways to treat his step-mother.

"Who are the King's enemies? Who are his wife's supporters?"

Ealdorman Byrthnoth considers the question carefully.

"It's hard to know. Isn't it. She has her grandmother, and I think that some of the Wessex thegns are keen to support her. Her family is old, almost as old as the king's, but there are few who yet live. It was her Wessex origins that made her suitable for the King. His power base has always been in Mercia, and East Anglia, thanks to Ealdorman Athelstan Half-King and he needs a Wessex-born wife, such as yourself. It's unfortunate that you didn't get to the King first, but Ealdorman Æthelwald found you initially and decided to keep you for himself."

I open my mouth to support my dead husband but then I shut it again. I wouldn't take back those scant few years I shared with him, but Ealdorman Byrthnoth is correct in what he says. It would have been far easier for me, and for everyone concerned, if I'd been presented to the King and allowed to marry him when he was still unattached.

"Not that it's ever that simple," Ealdorman Byrthnoth continues. "Men and women will act in contrary ways just because they can sometimes." He laughs as he says that and I'm reminded that initially he and his wife were open supporters of King Eadwig. I have a vague recollection of my dead husband mentioning that fact. I think they were forced to become allies of King Edgar because their land was within the boundaries of the short-lived Northern Kingdom, when King Eadwig ruled Wessex and Kent alone.

I must take the time to entangle the five years of discord that King Eadwig's reign will forever be known for. I wish that my husband had spent more time at Court during those years, and taken me with him. I feel as though I'm a blind beggar scrabbling around in the muck and filth of the roadway until I find a coin to buy food or find something edible, some shiny treasure to make the way forward clearer for me.

I fall silent as I consider everything Ealdorman Byrthnoth is telling me. He appears to be trying to help me, but he might not be. He might be trying to confuse me and lead me astray. I wish I had someone else to ask, someone who didn't have something to gain from my plans, but even Abbot Æthelwold wishes me to help him achieve something, and that's even when he has the firm support of the King.

Just to add to my confusion, Ealdorman Ælfhere and his brother, Ælfheah, take the opportunity to join Ealdorman Byrthnoth as we stand, talking. In the bright light of day, I can see that Ealdorman Ælfhere is a little older than I thought he was, his brother a scant few years younger than him. It's impossible to doubt their shared parentage. They possess the same sharp eyes, of a dark winter brown, long shaggy hair, and the same build. I could almost think the men were twins if I didn't know that it was so rare for twins to survive their birthing.

"My Lady Ælfflæd," Ealdorman Ælfhere is effusive in his greeting of her, and then he turns the force of his eyes my way.

"My Lady Elfrida?" he questions with a slight inflexion, as though he doubts who I truly am. After all, our meeting was only brief, but I'm alert enough to realise that this is actually some sort of game. He wants me to be grateful that he's remembered me. I want him to be thankful that I remember him. Or rather, that I don't.

"Ealdorman?" I rejoin, the question at the end of my sentence far more pronounced than his gentle one. For a moment his eyes flash furiously but then a sly mark of respect crosses his face.

"Forgive me, my Lady Elfrida," he says, bowing a little now. "I sometimes forget that not everyone has a good memory for names and faces. I am Ealdorman Ælfhere, and this fine fellow is my brother, Ealdorman Ælfheah."

I think he's done an admirable job of recovering from his own bullish behaviour and my rebuffing of him. My respect for him grows just from this little show.

"Good day Ealdormen Ælfhere and Ælfheah," I trill, my voice a slightly too high pitched to my own ears, my triumph at foiling his little game making me feel out of breath and making me believe that I could play court politics after all, and perhaps even enjoy it.

"You're joining the King today?" Ealdorman Ælfhere asks, and suddenly all my poise evaporates as I remember that for all these little jibes and retorts, I still need to face my greatest nemesis, the King.

"Later, I hope," I try to smile, but I feel frozen in terror. I've done little for the past two days but skirt around the issue of the King and try to acquaint myself with the life of the Court. I will, of course, at some point, need to spend more time with the King, or all this will have been for nothing.

With that, Ealdorman Ælfhere begins a conversation with Ealdorman Byrthnoth about some taxes or other, and Lady

Ælfflæd touches my arm and indicates that we should move on. Out of earshot of the men, she grimaces and whispers to me.

"He's a bit of a bore, Ealdorman Ælfhere. He's also not happy unless he's upsetting someone else. Ignore him and his jibes but well done on pretending you'd forgotten him. That's a good tactic. Come on; we should go in for a bit. It's cold today, and I want to show you where the women spend much of their time."

The little trail of women that I've already accumulated in my short time at the palace follows Lady Ælfflæd and me as we walk back toward the main buildings of the palace. I take the time to admire the building work. It's an impressive building, with its multiple floors. Not quite as astounding as the Old Minster with its twin towers, but its size and construction are both enormous and sound. It would be a home I would be proud to live within, and order, to my own desires. If I ever have the opportunity to do so.

Lady Ælfflæd leads me to a building next to the main palace, from which I can see a stream of smoke floating away in the clear sky.

"This is where the women spend much of their time," she explains, opening the door onto a smaller room than the King's Hall, made welcoming by a huge fire at its centre, and by comfortable furnishings around the room. I can see where a crib has been placed near the fire, and think that this must, until yesterday, have been where the King's wife spent much of her time.

The room is almost devoid of all activity and occupants, even though there are servants and slaves on hand to see to the needs of those within the hall. As the door opens, I see sleepy eyes looking my way and notice that some barely look at me, whereas other stare so openly I begin to wonder if my nose has turned bright pink while I've been outside in the chill afternoon.

"Come, let's warm ourselves by the fire," Lady Æthelflæd speaks with relish, and I see that her face is pinched as well. I will need to ensure I dress far more warmly the next time I attend upon the King at his palace, especially if I'm to spend as much time outside.

She also calls for warm drinks and some food as we all discard our cloaks and hand them to the servant near the door. She takes away the four cloaks, looking like a strange furred animal beneath the weight, but I'm pleased to see that she takes them to the other side of the hearth and lays them over some wooden pegs to dry out and be ready for when we leave the small space.

"It's a pleasant room," Lady Æthelflæd continues, as she sips her drink and helps herself to some small pieces of dark brown bread, smeared with a little honey. "I've spent many a day here, seeing to the tasks that women must see to. It's light and airy, and in the summer months, both doors can be thrown wide open, and a pleasant breeze rushes through the room."

What she doesn't say is that this could be mine to command, but she doesn't need to. I can already see it all before me. How I will order the servants, where I will set my loom to work. Where my crib will be placed so that I can keep an eye on my babies.

Subconsciously I rub my hand over my flat stomach, and even though Lady Æthelflæd must see my movement, she remains silent. But I curse myself. I need to be more aware of letting such personal matters show so openly.

"It's silent in here," I comment, as though I've only just noticed.

"The Court has routinely been a place for men, not women. With the King's wife absent, there are even fewer women here."

"The Court would benefit from more women?" I say, both a question and just an observation, and Lady Æthelflæd refrains from answering what seems like a pointless question. Without a doubt, the Court could be a more homely place.

"It's a holdover from the days of King Athelstan. He refrained from marrying, according to his step-mother the position as the head woman in his Court, Lady Eadgifu, then the King's father lost his wife when she was young, and then he died. King Eadred never married, and we all know what happened with the King's brother."

The picture she paints for me is an appealing one. Essentially, if I could become the wife of the King, and then his Queen, this would be my place to hold power. From here I could dispense my patronage at will and help rule the kingdom with my husband. I wonder if Lady Æthelflæd feels regretful that she had so little time to make this place her own and to help her family advance as far as possible.

She leans toward me; her eyes are suddenly hard and very focused.

"You will do this. You will keep the King at arm's length. You will make him marry you, crown you as his queen, and then this will be yours, and I'll help you all I can, and in return, you'll help me, when you can, and you'll support Abbot Æthelwold. We will make you the Queen that England needs to become the great power it's been trying to become ever since King Alfred beat back the Vikings."

My breath catches in my throat at the images she paints for me. I want it. I want it so badly. Only then, there's a commotion at the doorway, and the King walks into the room, bowing respectively to the two noble women, but his eyes are fixed only on my own. Already short of breath, I find myself struggling to remember how to breathe in, and dizziness almost undoes me, there and then.

Only a sharp nip on my leg from Lady Æthelflæd returns me to my senses, and to the reality of the situation.

I smile at the King, a slow smile, a pleased smile, the sort my dead husband would have called seductive.

I stand and curtsy to the King.

"My Lord King," I say slowly, the words forming on my lips as though a caress and the thrill in saying them sends a surge of desire down my legs, and I know that I can do this. I can snare the King, make him marry me, and then I will insist on being crowned his Queen.

CHAPTER 9

The King returns my smile without thought, his eyes brushing my lips and his face lighting up that I seem so happy in his presence. I have, perhaps, been a little nervous over the course of our last few meetings, and I need to ensure that he knows I return his desire as otherwise, he might reverse the action that sent his current wife away and made the way open for me to be with the King as openly as I can be, before he's divorced and we're able to marry once the first year anniversary of my husband's death has passed.

"Lady Elfrida," he replies with delight as he comes to take my hand, and sit beside me.

Lady Æthelflæd has faded away into the background, as though she's merely part of the furnishings, and I try to ignore her presence, and that of her sister and niece and find it remarkably easy.

My world has shrunk so that it is just the King and me in the hall. No one else matters.

"How have you been spending your day?" I ask the King, keen to make small talk with him as he continues to hold my hand. He feels a little too warm, or perhaps I'm a little cold, but either way, his touch burns along my arm, in a delightful reminder of his effect upon me.

"Hampered by people who wish to speak to me about politics and policy while my mind is a little preoccupied with other things."

I look away, a little bashful at his words because he can only be alluding to me. Otherwise, there would have been far less heat in his words, and his hand wouldn't have squeezed my own quite so convulsively.

"But tell me, how has yours been?" I believe he genuinely wants to know what's kept me from him throughout the long day and I smile, a little regretfully, as I speak.

"Informative. Lady Æthelflæd and Ælfflæd have shown me much of the court, and I've spoken with Ealdorman Byrthnoth and Ælfhere, and I met Ælfhere's brother as well. Abbot Æthelwold performed a fitting mass in the Old Minster, and of course, you saw me when we broke our fast."

His eyes flash dangerously as I speak and I wonder what I've said that's so wrong, but he only leans close to me, so close his mouth brushes my ear as he whispers to me, and a shiver of delight creeps down my back.

"I am jealous of all those who you've spoken to today, and who've had the pleasure of gazing upon your beauty, while I've been deprived of your company. Tomorrow we should spend the day together. I'll take you riding into the countryside and show you some of my favourite routes."

The thought of being alone with him should have filled me with fear but instead, I'm thrilled at the suggestion, my breath once more hitching at the thought of being alone with him.

"Surely you must have duties you must fulfill," I whisper back to him, my mouth now brushing his ear. I note with wry amusement that the hair on the back of his neck stands on end at my touch.

"I do," he says, stunned into speaking the truth, and I giggle at his admission.

"But I'm sure that I can find time to be with you, and to have those other events re-arranged." There's a slight whine to his voice, and I giggle again.

"Can I help you with them?" I ask, "as I did with Abbot Æthelwold?" This might be pushing my chances a little, but it's too late, the words are out of my mouth.

Edgar pulls back from his proximity to me and fixes me with an amused smile.

"You're so keen to be with me that you'd sit through a session of my Council, where we talk about policies and points of law, just to be near me."

"I would," I murmur, my two hands entangling with his.

"But I would rather be alone with you?" he says urgently, pulling me closer to him.

"I would as well," I breathe, "but if there is work that must be done, it must be done. Otherwise, I might not have your full attention when we do get to be alone."

His sigh is so heartfelt and dramatic that I almost pity him.

"I have nothing planned for this evening," he concedes, and I nod.

"Then we can eat together, perhaps in here as opposed to your hall. Could you send someone to preside in your place?"

It's usual for the King to eat with his nobles, but it's also not unheard of for someone else to sit in his place.

"Perhaps Ealdorman Byrthnoth or Lady Æthelflæd?"

I try to be as cajoling as possible, without forcing the issue.

He leans back and stares into my eyes for just a moment, and then he stands, quite abruptly, and walks toward his stepmother. She's sitting to the rear of the hearth with her sister and niece, but she stands and moves away to talk to the King.

I think I should try and catch their words, but instead I watch the King. I've not had lots of opportunities just to look at him, but now I do, and my hunger for him grows.

He's an attractive man. Perhaps not the tallest I've ever seen, but he makes up for it with his presence. He seems to fill a room. Even though the hall is only occupied with a few women, all of them watch him, some just with interest, and a few with the hunger I feel for him. If I make him my own, I'll have to ensure that I keep his interest in me.

His eyes are fierce, his face free from lines, and as he almost jumps from foot to foot, I think he has too much energy, and that will need taming as well.

He wears his clothes carelessly. I don't think he'll even appreciate the time and effort that's gone into making them and ensuring the stitching is neat and tidy. Nor the time taken to prepare the clothing for him each day.

But the one thing about him that I find the most attractive is the shape of him. He's as a man should be. His shoulders are broad, his build just bulky enough to show that he's a fit man, and his legs are long and lean. His face is extended and elongated, his chin softly curving and his eyes hold the gaze of anyone he troubles himself to look at for longer than a passing moment.

When he returns to me, he has a smile on the very face I've been examining, and I know that I'm to have my wish. I note that Lady Æthelflæd is watching me with something like admiration on her face. I know she wants me to succeed with the King and will forgive me making silly mistakes, but I want to earn her respect as well. This might be one of those rare occasions.

But just as I'm about to both relax and panic at the same time, the lady I spotted earlier, in the King's hall, walks toward the King. She's older than Lady Æthelflæd and far less deferential in her posture, almost as though she believes she deserves to be in the King's presence, no matter what he might think.

"My Lord King," she says, curtseying low, and showing him lots of respect that she still manages to convey he doesn't deserve.

"Lady Wulfhild," he says deferentially, and I wonder if she notices the slight twitch of annoyance as he says those words, or whether I imagine it because as he says her name, I know who this is.

"I had hoped to speak to you of my granddaughter and great granddaughter." Now she fixes me with a withering stare, and unconsciously, I lean away from the King, only to notice that Lady Æthelflæd is shaking her head at me, telling me not to and that the King, has taken a protective stance in front of me as well. It seems I need to stand up to this woman.

"Another time perhaps. They're only just gone to Wilton," he tries to deflect, but she's having none of it, her stare still fixed on mine, and it takes all of my resolve to stay where I am. I swear the woman could make the statues of our Lord God cry real tears.

"Why is that, My Lord King?" she enquires, her head on one side, as though she can't possibly imagine there being a better time to speak of her granddaughter, but the King must be used to her ways, and he smiles, and bows low, and kisses her old and wrinkled hand, festooned with great golden rings and gleaming stones.

"I'm busy at the moment, but I will make time to speak with you tomorrow, after my council meeting. I'll ensure that Lord Ælfwold is aware of my request, and you would do well to remind him as well, first thing in the morning. And now, I see the other women are leaving for their meal. I suggest you depart with them."

Lady Wulfhild's face is hard as iron as she stands before the King. Even I can see where her pulse throbs angrily at the base of her neck, and I'm amazed at her forbearance when she seemingly meekly turns away to walk to the King's Hall. At the doorway she turns back, anger writ huge on her face, and I know that I've made an enemy without even trying.

This must be what it's like to be close to the King. Some will hate me just for my time spent with him today, for my ability to whisper to him of events I would like to see happen, and of people I would like to see advanced, such as Abbot Æthelwold. It will not matter to these people what my qualities are, or how well I assist the King, they will still see me as an impediment, and in the case of Lady Wulfhild, it will be worse, as she will see me as the woman who supplanted her granddaughter if I succeed in my plan. I wonder how many years she's spent trying to get one of her daughters or granddaughters to become the King's companion.

I wonder how elated she must have felt at her seeming success, and how disappointed she must now be to see it all falling to pieces around her.

I must learn from these examples, but first, well first I must keep the King interested in me, and not give in to his wheedling ways. As soon as the door closes on us, and we're almost wholly alone, apart from Lady Ælfflæd who stands as our chaperone, albeit it, she sits with her back to us and studiously works on her needlecraft, the King grabs both of my hands in his and leads me to the hearth.

"At last," he says, anticipation and hunger on his face.

"My Lord King?"

But he laughs, and moves his hands from my own, to rest on my shoulders, pulling me a little closer to him, one of his hands brushing my cheek.

I can barely breathe, and I know this is a dangerous moment. Should I let him kiss me or should I pull away, and act a little coy?

He watches his thumb on my cheek and then he sighs a little, and drops his hand, sadness in his eyes that I can't understand.

"No," he says, firmly, to himself. "We'll do this the right way. I must win your heart for myself, and then, we shall see what happens after that."

His tone is so reasoned I wonder why I was ever worried about being alone with him. His eyes lose none of their focus, and before I know it, his hand is back on my cheek, his other hand on the back of my neck, and he's pulling me close to him; close enough that I can feel his breath and almost taste him.

I consider pushing away from him, but I think I can manage just one kiss. I think I'll be able to allow just the one, and then we'll be able to talk about our plans for the following day. If not, I'm hoping that Lady Ælfflæd will somehow intercede for me.

His lips on mine are hot and soft, and desire flames inside me, turning my resolve to the molten fluid made by the silversmith in the heat of the charcoal, and it's all I can do not to crush him to my body and demand he lays me down and pleasures me here and now.

My husband has been dead for nearly twelve months now, and before that he was ill for a long time. It's a long time since a man has made me feel like a woman.

The kiss is almost tame by comparison, and I worry that the King's desire is below my own. I pull away from his soft touch, hesitantly, almost fearful of seeing a bored expression on his face.

The fire in his eyes quickly dissuades me of my worries.

"We must be careful," he says through his gasps, and I laugh, a slightly too high sound, one of relief and desire combined.

"We must, My Lord King."

At that moment, and I think we're both pleased of the interruption, a small flurry of servants enters the hall, carrying food for the three of us on golden plates, covered over with a spare piece of linen to try and keep the food warm.

Right now I could eat a slug, and I know I wouldn't taste it, but the King and I must eat, and so must Lady Ælfflæd, and so the King calls her over, and we sit on the side of the hearth and take our time eating and just being together.

Conversation is light between us, and I eat sparingly, unsure if my stomach will take the rich food when it's so tied up in knots from the King's kiss, but needing the sustenance all the same.

I touch my lips, remembering the feel of him there, and Edgar observes the movement, for all he doesn't say anything, other than to offer me a wink.

"Tomorrow, you'll come to the Council. I'm sure that Lady Ælfflæd or Æthelflæd will keep you company, and in the afternoon, we'll ride out, as far as we can in the daylight we'll have, and then we'll race back to the palace and eat like this once more."

He seems delighted with the plan although Lady Ælfflæd looks at me in surprise.

"You wish to attend the Council?"

"No, I don't want to distract the King from his duties, and he wants to be with me tomorrow, so I thought it best to accompany him," I clarify and again, I see respect in her eyes as well. It seems that, for the time being, I'm doing everything right. I'm sure it won't last.

As soon as we've eaten, Lady Ælfflæd meanders away, claiming some duty or other, and I'm pleased to be left alone with the King. We've barely spoken, and I'd like to know the man behind the crown a little better. It seems he has other ideas.

"Tomorrow will be a matter of talking about laws and my hopes for the introduction of more Benedictine monks. Archbishop Dunstan will be attending, and so too will Oswald, Bishop of Worcester. Combined with Abbot Æthelwold the men all share a desire to see a reform of the monasteries, but they all work in different ways to achieve their goals."

I know of Archbishop Dunstan. It was he who once fell out with the King's brother and earned an exile on the Continent. Oswald, I know little about other than that he too is high in the King's regard.

"All three men have their allies, and through them, I can offer some pressure when I'm displeased with something or want something doing. But likewise, they're expected to be able to bend my ear when they want to."

I'm listening to the King, but he's also distracting me. I'm happy to be talking politics, but all I want to do is go back to the moment when we kissed. It was dangerous and exciting, and I want to experience it again.

I want him to hold my hand, to cup my face, to trace my cheek with his thumb. I want to feel his heat and his desire.

"Are you listening to me?" he asks softly, and I know that a flicker of guilt crosses my face.

"My Lord King?"

"You seem a little distracted?" he asks, but there's understanding in his voice.

"Apologies, My Lord King. I was. Well, I was thinking of our kiss."

His eyes fix on my own, and a lopsided smile touches those lips that I want to be kissing me.

"It was a good kiss," he offers, and I grin back at him.

"A very good one." This time it's me who leans forwards, who cups the back of his head with my one hand and strokes his cheek with the other. My hands are steady, I think, but that means that it's the King who shakes under my touch and that gives me the courage I need to lean in close to him. I lick my lips, pleased that they don't feel dry and then once more, we're kissing.

I'm holding the back of his head, and his hands are snaking their way around my head, the one smoothing my long hair behind my ear and the other touching the base of my neck, holding me closer, closer, pulling me to him, just as I was pulling him to me.

I can taste his breath and feel his soft exhalations on my cheek. Our lips move together as one, as though we've been doing this all our lives and this isn't only the third time that we've kissed.

My mouth opens a little and his tongue snakes insides, hesitantly at first, as though Edgar is unsure of his reception, but I pull him closer yet. I want to feel my body crushed against his own, to feel the heat of his flesh through our clothing.

I shuffle forward toward him, just as he does to me. I have to swing my legs to the side, as we sit side by side, and our upper bodies twist and come closer and closer together.

Our kiss deepens, lingers and I drop my hands from his face to his chest, where I rub my hand over the fabric of his clothes, almost desperate to feel nothing there but his skin.

I'd like nothing more than to have him carry me to his bed, tear my clothes from my body and cover me with his naked flesh. But that can't happen. Not yet.

This kiss, this long, lingering kiss is all I can have for the time being.

A polite cough has us both tearing away from each other, not so much embarrassment on our faces, as thwarted desire. We're both breathing as though we've run from the Old Minster to the Palace and I already thrill to know what our lovemaking will be like. It will be frantic and yet slow, all at the same time. With Edgar, provided we marry, I know that I'll be loved each night as thoroughly as my dead husband once loved me.

It's the thought of Æthelwald that finally brings me to my

senses, with a sly smile of intrigue. Edgar is rubbing his hands on his face, as though he can't quite believe what's happened, and for a moment I know fear. What if he doesn't want this? What if he actually wishes to stay with his wife?

He stands, abruptly, as do I, and he looks at Lady Ælfflæd and offers her a curt nod. I think he's thanking her. Then he leans in and takes my unresisting hand in his and brings it to his lips.

"My apologies, My Lady," he whispers. "Until tomorrow," and then he sweeps from the hall, and I stumble back to my seat. I'm still breathing heavily, and I can feel heat flooding my face and turning my legs wooden. My desire for him is almost too high. And so, it appears, is his for me.

"I've never seen him like this," Lady Ælfflæd says, and she's shaking her head from side to side, as she walks toward me.

"Is that a good thing?" I ask, and she looks at me, actually taking in my posture and my response to him.

"It's a splendid thing. He's never shown any restraint before. Never. He takes what he wants, and he thinks about consequences later. When he married his second wife he was fixated on her perceived beauty, but really, it was more that he'd been told she was a good match and then he ravished her beauty. With you it's different. He knows how much trouble this is going to cause him and instead of rushing blindly in, he's already worked out that he needs people to agree with him, to give him their support. The fact that you seem far more able to learn the way of the Court is an added boon for him." She speaks slowly, considering her words.

"No, it's a good thing the King is behaving in this way. A very good thing. But come. We need to get you home and then get you back here in the morning, for your meeting with the Council."

She holds her hand out to me, and I take it gratefully, pleased to feel her firm grip. Somehow her touch grounds me, and I begin to think that I can walk from the room and that I don't need to sit here and spend all night recovering from our intense confrontation.

She leads me to the door, which opens before us, the King returning in a flurry of cloak and chilly air.

He stops before me, somehow not expecting me to be so close. He nods again to Lady Ælfflæd, and she drops my hand and demurely steps away.

He rushes to me, his arms encircling me and his lips finding mine again.

"Just one more," he whispers, and this time when he leaves the hall, I do stumble, only Lady Ælfflæd is ready for me, and catches me, expertly swirling my cloak around me so that we can leave the warm room and step into the night.

"The men will see you home," she says, offering my hand to the warrior standing before a horse.

His hands are gruff on my back as he helps me into the horse's saddle, and his touch is such a stark contrast to the King's, that my head finally clears, and I turn to Lady Ælfflæd.

"My thanks, My Lady," I offer formally, and she smiles at me, a genuine smile of, please.

"Until the morning," she responds, before bustling her way back inside her warm hall.

I huddle into my cloak and feel the horse move beneath me, but I don't see where I'm going. I'm reliving my time with the King, the feel of his lips on mine, the feel of his body pressed against the length of my own.

My dreams that night are the most erotic I've ever experienced.

CHAPTER 10

I t's Lady Æthelflæd who escorts me into the King's Council. She has more right to be there than anyone else, and the King doesn't watch us as we take our seats, but I know that he's aware of my presence. I can tell by his sudden stillness. He's such a twitchy man usually; his tranquility can only mean one thing.

Lady Æthelflæd has apparently been briefed by her sister on the events of the night before, and she's kind to me and reassuring as we settle ourselves before the men.

As the King said, his Council is filled with the holy men he tried to talk to me about, and also his ealdormen. I see my husband's brother, Ealdorman Æthelwine, and his other brother as well, Ælfwold, the King's closest friend, and also Ealdorman Byrthnoth, Lady Ælfflæd's husband, and more men besides. I even catch a glimpse of my father to the rear of the assembly. He's never been much honoured by the King, but I think that his fortune will change with my advancement.

The King sits in the centre of the men, in a small circle. This isn't the Witan. The Council isn't filled to capacity with the thegns and lesser religious men. No, I get the impression that this is where much of the real business of ruling the kingdom is conducted. This is where decisions are made and then presented to the Witan for their agreement so that it appears that the thegns are helping the King to rule his kingdom.

Not that my father has ever complained about King Edgar's

style of government. Not at all, and so I imagine most are happy with the way things are currently being run.

There are some there, though, who despite Lady Æthelflæd and I sitting as inconspicuously as possible, glare at me. I wish I knew who the men were, but I don't recognise them. It seems I'm not to be left without the knowledge for long.

"My Lord King," a large man ambles to his feet, his tone deferential although his gaze on me is anything but that.

"Ealdorman Eadmund?" the King says, his tone is mild, but I think it belies an anger, or perhaps just a wary acceptable that he knew of everyone there it would be he who made trouble.

"Why are we joined by women?" Ealdorman Eadmund asks it in a joking manner now, perhaps wishing he'd not stood so abruptly and spoken his mind, but he has and now he must make the best of it.

"Lady Æthelflæd, my step-mother, is tutoring one of my new councilors daughter's in the workings of my government. It's nothing to fear, and now, we should begin our debates." The words are benign, and yet even I can see how others might find something to worry about in them.

The Ealdorman nods his thanks for the explanation and resumes his seat, but I can feel his gaze returning to me repeatedly as he only half listens to the King and his men discuss the details of a new law code dealing with theft and the calling of the Hundred Courts.

I try to listen carefully, to determine who agrees with the King, who just likes to hear the sound of their own voice, and who genuinely wants to disagree with everything he says just for the sake of it.

Quickly, I appreciate that the three men who labour to bring back the rule of the Benedictines are very different. I think Archbishop Dunstan would argue all day long about the tiny little details; that Abbot Æthelwold is content just to know that new laws will be enacted whereas Bishop Oswald has some points to make about the details, but overall, is just content to be a part of the proceedings.

The same applies to the ealdormen. Ealdorman Byrthnoth is already my ally. Ealdorman Æthelwine refuses to make eye contact with me. He's my dead husband's brother, the man who told me I was no longer a member of their family. I wonder if his opinion of me will change now. Ealdorman Ælfhere and his brother are undecided about me. Ealdorman Athelstan is married to my companion, and he's by far the oldest man there. He doesn't seem to have an opinion of me, and that is fine. And that leaves only Ealdormen Eadmund, Mirdach and Gunnar. Eadmund has made his displeasure known. Mirdach and Gunnar are men I've not met before. I think they must be from the old Northern territories kingdom, probably men who first supported King Edgar when the country was split between him and his brother, because I know nothing about them other than their names.

Eadmund is a tall man, almost so tall that he spills over his chair. Mirdach and Gunnar dress similarly, but the one man is small and rotund, the other taller and skinny as a stick. Their clothes look almost comical on them. I imagine they wished they'd discussed their outfits before entering the King's Council.

Ealdorman Æthelwine looks very much like his brother; almost painfully so. I must be honest and say that I would have happily married him, the mirror image of his brother, if only he'd been interested in me, and the union not prohibited by the Church.

Ealdorman Athelstan is a good-looking man, despite being so much older than me. Ealdorman Byrthnoth is perhaps younger than I think he is. All of this I take in through the corner of my eye, being careful to give my attention to the conversation. I wouldn't want the King to ask me questions later and be unable to answer them.

The meeting drags and I do fear that I'll fidget and disrupt the proceedings, and I try glaring at the King, in the hope that he'll realise I can take no more. I was rash when I told him I would sit here and listen because he had work to do. I should have let him run away with me and then we could have held each other all afternoon long.

Just the thought of being alone with Edgar has my heart racing and a slight sheen of sweat beading my face. And then before I know it, the King is standing before me, a smile on his face and his hand held out to me.

I take it quickly, mindful that the Ealdormen and Churchmen watch how familiar we are with each other, but the King's steady presence enables me to walk from the room with confidence. Quickly we reach the outdoors where our departure has been prepared. There are horses waiting for us, and a few servants and warriors are already mounted and ready to ride out with us.

I allow the King to help me mount, and turn to look at Lady Æthelflæd. She watches me keenly but makes no effort to follow me. It appears that I'm to be trusted with the King. That worries and excites in equal measure. She's said little to me all morning, but her presence has helped me no end. I will have to thank her later.

Even my father watches me sternly, and I hope he doesn't expect too much from me. I've always been a dutiful daughter. I hope I can remain so.

As we ride through the open gateway, out into the crowded market area, I feel a trickle of excitement. It will be good to ride in the open air, to spend time with the King where we're almost alone.

Not that it takes us long to steer the horses through the crowds and exit into the open air, and after that, it only takes a smirk from the King, and I'm kicking my horse to a gallop, the hood of my cloak flying free and my hair streaming behind me. I throw my head back in enjoyment, luxuriating in the view of the clouds scudding across the sky when I look upwards, and the rushing of the sprouting fields beneath the horse.

I don't know where we're racing to, and neither do I much care. It feels relaxing to be free and away from what anyone might think of me. Knowing that Edgar is at my side only adds to the sense of exhilaration.

We could always do this. We could run away and never think of anyone else.

I giggle with delight at the thought, noting that the King's horse is perfectly aligned with my own and that his voice is deeply laughing as well.

This is what it means to be free.

But my rush on the horse only lasts for so long before the King begins to slow his own mount, and I realise that I need to do the same. We're in open country, the warriors accompanying us and the servants' only specks on the horizon. The King leans across to impede my advance, and I encourage the horse to stop as well. As soon as his own horse stops, he slides from his saddle and comes to help me from my own. His hands are warm beneath my cloak, and yet I shiver with delight.

His breath steams in the air, and I lean over and plant a brief kiss on his lips. It was meant only as a bit of fun, but in no time at all, we're clinging to each other, our lips having never parted and his tongue meeting my own.

This is what real passion feels like.

Without realising, we move closer together, our hands exploring each other, almost as though neither of us wears clothes. Our flesh burns through what little we wear, and we could almost be stood naked in the middle of the field. His hands are thorough as they seek out the rounded parts of my body, and I lock my hands around his head to ensure he can't pull away from me. I don't want this moment to end, although I am aware that it mustn't go too far. I can't allow the King everything his questing hands are searching for.

I'm saved by the arrival of the servants and warriors. They ignore the King's actions and instead busy themselves preparing whatever it is that bulges in their saddle packs. The King continues to kiss me, but the ardour of his touch has dimmed. I think that even he must feel strange trying to court me when so many watch us.

In no time at all, I hear the crackle of burning twigs and turn to see that despite the chill summer weather, a picnic of sorts has been arranged for us on the edge of a patch of forest and that a tent has been raised for us to shelter within. The King, gallant now, and with a cheeky smile on his face, leads me to the furs and cushions on the floor while a small fire, and some sort of brazier, bravely tries to warm the inside of the canvas that's been pitched in the clearing.

I almost falter in my steps, thinking that this would be the perfect opportunity for the King to force himself on me, all alone with no one but his servants and his warriors to hear or watch, but as I step under the canvas, I realise my fears are without warrant.

The King hasn't been worrying about satisfying himself, but rather pleasing me. There are candles and a small wooden table, and two small chairs and plates heaped with little delicacies to eat. And more, the entire space is filled with soft purple fabric. Even I don't miss the regal connotations in that.

"My Lady Elfrida," he grins, helping me to my chair, and then taking the plates of food and serving me himself. There's no one else with us now, and the canvas door has been closed so that no one can see us. I almost pity the men standing outside in the chill while we dalliance in the relative warmth.

"My Lord King," I grin, happy to play this small game with the King if it pleases him. Certainly being with him, alone, satisfies me.

I help myself to tit bits as the King fills a golden cup with a glowing wine before filling his own and raising it to his lips.

"To the future," he mutters as he does so and I feel a spurt of surprise at his serious tone. His eyes have grown grave, and I wonder what ails him. But he takes his own seat and begins to eat, all traces of whatever his sudden thought was, seemingly forgotten.

"What did you think of my meeting this morning?" he breaks the silence by asking, and again I'm struck by the discord between our frantic moments of physical contact and his desire that I understand his Court. I always thought the two should be separate; certainly, my first husband kept me at an arms reach where politics were concerned. It's obvious that Edgar has no intention of doing the same.

"The men support you well enough," I offer, feeling a little hesitant. I detected no great malice amongst them all, but whether they have the King's best interests at heart or not, I don't yet know.

"They will as long as I do what they want me to do," he comments, his face curling downwards as though he's eaten a bitter grape.

"You fear they'll turn on you as they did your brother?" I ask. I'm unsure whether the King's brother is openly spoken about. But he nods at my words.

"Yes, I do, and yet there's no one to follow on after me. Not yet. But that's no good thing. I feel as though they accept me because there's no better choice. Not at the moment."

His daughter is too young and also a woman to be a contender for the throne. She will not be able to rule after him. And although Alfred's line of descendants was once widely filled with cousins, nephews, and brothers, few of the old House of Wessex yet remain. There are many families with some small connection to the royal family, not least of which is my first husband's family, but that would no doubt mean civil war if the King were to die.

"The Northern Territories chose you over your brother," I highlight, and that makes his face turn downwards.

"My brother was too young to rule, and the Court was a hotbed of calculating men of politics. My Uncle was ill for too long, and his hold on the Court was too weak."

"Your brother didn't respect his family in the same way you imply you do," I'm thinking of when King Eadwig banished his own grandmother from Court and claimed her lands as his own. She, who'd been the wife of King Edward, had been sourly tried by her grandson's ways. She's an old woman now, but Edgar has ensured she's been compensated for her outrageous treatment by Eadwig.

"My brother wanted his own power base; that was why he married as he did. As much as I am a follower of Archbishop Dunstan, I can't help thinking that his treatment of my brother's marriage was a terrible thing. He had no right to force the divorce, and certainly not on the grounds that he used."

"You miss him?" I ask softly, and the King smiles at me, tears in his eyes.

"No one has ever asked me that before," he says, sadly. "It's as though they all think I wanted my brother's death, as though I resented his life, and yet he was the only real family I had, after my foster family that is."

"And yes, I miss him. He was so young when he died."

There have been rumours that Eadwig's death wasn't natural, but whether it was, or wasn't, I don't believe that Edgar had a part to play in it.

"Young and a fool, but also hemmed in on all sides by men who felt they knew better than him. Our family line isn't as secure as I'd like. It hasn't been ever since Uncle Athelstan chose not to marry, and our grandfather's sons all died too young, even my Uncle. I think that the nobility says one thing and wants another."

"They want a strong royal family, just as your grandfather once provided them with, albeit, it meant three wives and a constant battle for precedence."

"For someone who's spent so little time at the Court, you seem to understand it very well," he offers pointedly, and I almost think it's criticism, only it's not, as he stands and comes to rest his hands on my shoulders. My hand reaches up to hold his own hands, to offer him something that he needs but which I have no name for. I don't know if he wants companionship, or a confidant, a mother, or a mother of his sons. The King is a complicated man after all.

He reaches down and kisses the top of my head, inhaling as he does so.

"I think I could rule far better with you at my side. You'll see events in a different way to me, and the fact that you're the most beautiful woman in England might even distract my allies from their constant attempts to undermine me and have their will imposed on my kingdom."

I squeeze his hand tightly. The vision he has of the future is one in which I will have a significant role, much bigger than just the King's wife, just as Abbot Æthelwold and Lady Æthelflæd implied.

His hands snake down my shoulders, and I smile with mischief as he reaches for my breasts, perhaps all thoughts of politics forgotten about. He's leaning down behind me, his kisses littering my neck as he breathes into my ear, reigniting all of my desire.

I try to turn to meet his lips with my own, but he holds me in place and so I stand, my back still to him, and allow his reach to extend so far that I can step aside from him, a grin on my own face.

"My Lord King," I offer, and I begin to unbutton my overdress, keen to let it puddle on the floor at my feet.

He watches me, his eyes afire with desire. The canvas is warm and inviting. I'm convinced that we could lie almost naked with each other, and not feel the cold air, and this is what I'm inviting him to do now.

I wonder if he'll stop me, but he doesn't. Instead, he stands well back, watching me slowly undress myself.

My overdress pools at my feet, and I step on it. The underdress I wear is of a good make, but it is also light and almost see-through. I need to take nothing else off for the King to see all my body.

I grin at him once more. Inviting him to come closer but instead, he slumps into the chair I've just vacated and beckons me to go to him. I almost don't, but then I reconsider. The King must desire me as a woman as well as someone to talk politics with.

He holds his hand out toward me, and I slip my own hand into his. His grip is firm and warm, and steady. I'd like to think that I'm seducing him. But we're both of a similar age, and this is nothing new to either of us.

He pulls me closer, and I crumble into his lap, our hands still clasped together. He gasps as my weight settles on him and for a moment I feel very conspicuous, but he wiggles his legs, and I realise that part of his seax is sticking into his leg. I jump up from him at his grumble of pain, and he laughs as he pulls his weapons belt free from around his body.

It would be the perfect opportunity for him to take off his own clothes. But he doesn't. I think this is him trying to restrain himself.

If there wasn't a kingdom at stake, I might test that resolve more than I plan on, but instead, I simply slide back onto his lap leaning onto his left shoulder so that I can still see him if I look to the side. His face has lost its humour as his free hand tries to wrench itself free from my own, and I restrain it but move my head so that I can kiss him once more.

He growls at my evasion, and I chuckle through the kiss, a deep throaty sound that even I don't recognise as belonging to me.

He growls again but lets me retain control of his hand, and I bring it into my lap, where it rests softly, and I slowly release it, hoping he'll behave himself, which of course he doesn't do, but this time I let him have his way as he slowly pulls my underdress higher and higher, first over my knee, causing me to shiver a little, and then higher still, until he can hold my inner thigh and all I have in exchange is a hand on his taunt tunic as my other hand is trapped between us.

Now I feel thwarted and want to snarl at him, but I can't, because his hand is exploring its way higher and higher up my thigh, and I can barely contain myself.

If I weren't in the middle of a canvas tent on a cold day. If only…

Slowly, but steadily, his hand lightly along my upper thigh, and I'm kissing him so that our lips never need part and our tongues are playing out the scenario that neither of us can allow to happen until we're married.

I try to shuffle myself on his lap so that I can release him and give myself the same pleasure he's receiving from his exploration, but he refuses to move, and I'm surprised to find him so keen to pleasure me at his own expense.

I surrender then. Our heads are locked together, and I'm not letting him go anywhere while we're so intricately fastened together. I try to stay quiet, keep my passion to myself so that those outside the tent won't have cause to question our time together, but it's been a long time since I felt like a woman, far too long, and as Edgar's hand brushes against me, I know I'm gasping too loudly, desperate to take the pleasure he wants to give me, and he tries to extract himself from my grasp, and tell me to shush, only I won't let him, not until his hand slips from under my dress, and I tear my head away from him, almost in tears at the shock of his betrayal.

But he's laughing as he brings his hand to his lips and mimes that I should be quiet before he reclaims my lips and allows his hand to fall back to its original position.

I find myself rocking against his hand, trying to stay quiet whilst all I can think about is the pleasure I'm about to feel, and then it arrives, and as I arch against his hand, our lips still together, moving as one, his other hand somehow managing to reach my left breast and squeeze it gently, I know that more than anything, this is what I've missed since my husband died.

I moan softly into his mouth when the sensation becomes too much, and he laughs once more, pleased with himself and I suddenly feel utterly naked and laid bare before him, for all that I'm still almost decently dressed.

If he notices my unease, he ignores it.

"My Lady Elfrida," he mutters into my neck, where he's now intent on burying his face. "I believe I might just be falling in love with you" The words are so quiet that I hardly hear them and yet I do, and the bloom of my pleasure is nothing compared to the feeling of rightfulness that those words elicit in me.

"My Lord King, Edgar," I open my mouth to speak, but he quiets me with his mouth, and once more, he loves me thoroughly and leaves me feeling both vulnerable and beautiful. I want to tell him that I love him as well, but it seems he doesn't want to hear that, not yet, barely allowing me anytime when we're not kissing. But I think my failure to reply immediately might have been a terrible mistake.

"Come," he finally says, when our passion seems to have temporarily sated itself, "we must dress you and head back to Winchester. We've much to accomplish if I'm to make you my wife as quickly as I can."

Those few words thrill me, perhaps more than they should. After all, he's not asked me to marry him yet, and I could well refuse, but then I decide I like his confidence. I want to be his wife.

I want to lie naked with him all night long and feel his children grow inside me as a result of our lovemaking. I want to make the King happy, all of the time. Politics will happen around us, but I believe that if we're together, nothing will ever pull us apart.

He lifts me from his lap, and I stand, on shaking legs, and bend to retrieve my overdress and underthings, almost overbalancing as I do so. Instantly, he's at my side, steadying me, and helping me turn my clothing the right way round, and slipping it over my head.

With each item of my clothing returned to my body, he stops and kisses me, a long lingering kiss that leaves little to the imagination, and I regret that this seduction is happening in reverse.

But the King is right. If we're to marry, then it must be done properly, and that means that he needs a divorce from his wife, and for that to happen, he needs to be certain that Archbishop Dunstan will provide the necessary licence, and for that to happen, we mustn't lie together, not yet.

All in a timely manner, I think to myself, and apparently the King shares my hopes for the future, as he lifts me back onto the horse that brought me here, being sure to run his hand over my upper thigh as he does so, reminding me of everything that's just happened between us and tormenting me with what might still occur.

CHAPTER 11

The King doesn't escort me home in the growing gloom but rides onto his palace without a further word of goodbye after a frantic meeting with Lord Ælfwold, my dead husband's younger brother, and as I watch him ride away, I feel abandoned and alone, the exuberance of our almost love-making draining away all my energy. I want nothing more than to cry at his abandonment, and yet I hold myself firm. I wouldn't want any of the household troop or servants who escort me to understand the depth of my new feelings for him.

I replay our time together, our conversations, our silences, but I can see no reason why he's simply ridden away on my account. It must be something to do with the Court. I sleep fitfully and rise the next morning expecting another summons to court, and I dress carefully. I want Lady Æthelflæd and Lady Ælfflæd to approve of how I present myself.

No summons comes, in fact, no one of any importance comes to see me that day, or the next, or even that week, or the week after that, and I grow restless and angry.

Have I erred in some way? Caused the King to change his mind? Did I give too much of myself to him when we were alone? Should I have refused? So many questions circle my mind, and I think I might drive myself quite mad with the worry of what I've done wrong.

My father watches me anxiously. He was pleased to be included in the King's Council, and he too seems confused by this unexpected chain of events.

But for two whole weeks after my meeting, no one seeks me out, not one of the great ladies or their husbands, and I begin to despair of ever seeing the King.

I know I must have done something wrong, and I beg my father to go to Court and find out what's happened, but he refuses as well, vowing he'll not step foot in the place without an invitation. He says he doesn't wish to appear too keen, or too desperate.

On a morning during the third week of my banishment, I dress without any care, listening to my father discussing our return to Tavistock with our host and the servants and handful of household troops he brought with him.

I sit by the hearth, my sewing discarded in my lap as all around me the servants rush to their tasks, whilst all I can do is chew my fingers with worry and recall the touch of the King's hand on my thigh, inside me, and the pleasure his declaration of love gave to me. Perhaps that is where I erred, in not immediately returning his protestation of love? Perhaps he's decided that it would be better to remain with his current wife than take another woman who won't tell him that she loves him?

Only I do love him. I know I do and I wish I'd told him as much. If I'd told him of my love for him, I'd be with him now, weaving my way through Court, and not about to return to Tavistock with my reputation in tatters and my heart broken once more.

I feel listless and lifeless, the spark of joy that had returned to my life is gone, and I find my grief fluctuating between that of a widow once more, and that of an abandoned woman, her lover gone to spend the rest of his life with another women.

I feel powerless to do anything about it. By allowing me to come to Court in the way that I did, the King made his regard for me clear. His subsequent abandonment of me couldn't be more explicit.

The hustle and bustle of the room are so great that I ignore it, completely, oblivious to the furore taking place behind me.

"My Lady Elfrida," a voice, soft and a little hesitant, has me looking up, and I see the searching eyes of Lady Æthelflæd, and know that she's come to tell me of her disappointment in me, and her desire that I never call upon her again as my friend.

I don't even care how distraught I must look as I turn my dull eyes to meet her keen ones. She's dressed for summer; her light cloak still around her shoulders while my father somewhat hops from one foot to another in agitation.

"May I sit?" she asks, indicating the small stall next to the hearth where I sit, not feeling the heat of the fire or the bite in the air.

"Of course, My Lady Æthelflæd," I cough, surprised to hear my voice so rough. I wonder when I last spoke but can't remember.

Instead, she beckons imperiously for my servant to bring me warm mead, and food as well, and sits with me as I try and choke the substances down my parched throat and paper dry lips. The food burns my lips and superheats my stomach. All unpleasant.

She reaches over and runs her hand through my hair before seeking my servant again and whispering something to her. The girl nods quickly and feeling emboldened by the task set before her, quickly gathers three more of the servants of the house to do her work.

"I came as soon as I could," Lady Æthelflæd says kindly, and I feel tears forming in my eyes at the terrible words she's about to say to me. I know I'll weep in front of her. I'll cry, and the great hacking sobs will choke me as they once did when my husband died.

She's pinched from the chill outside, and although her hands are clasped around a cup of warm mead, I see her shiver.

"My thanks for thinking of me at all," I mutter and suddenly her gaze is stern as the sloshing of water behind me, alerts me to the fact that the servant is heating the water. I imagine I need to bathe. I suppose I look terrible.

"You mustn't allow this to happen to you whenever the King becomes distracted. You must be stronger than this." Her words barely register.

"The King is busy. Concerned with discord amongst the Ealdormen. This is nothing to do with you." Her pleasant tone has
evaporated into something that is so sharp I can almost feel the
lash of her tongue.

"The King is busy?" I dumbly repeat. "With his ealdormen and
his ignoring me is all because of that?" My brain is working too
slowly. I can't fathom what I'm hearing.

"Yes, the King is busy with his ealdormen. I've come as soon
as I can get away from the arguments, to ensure you're well and
to bring you back to the Court. Just because the King is busy
doesn't mean that we can't continue our work to make you
popular amongst the thegns and Ealdormen. It will be a welcome distraction from all the arguments and bitterness."

"But you can't go like that. I have a gown for you. My seamstress made it for you, and once you're bathed, you'll wear it
and come to Court with me, and with your father. We'll have a
dinner, in the Women's Hall, and we'll hope that the King hears
of you and comes to greet you, but if not, we'll do the same tomorrow and the next day until he does remember. In the mean-
time, my sister and niece wish to speak to you, as does the King's
grandmother. You've been missed."

She stands quickly and grabs my hands, and before I know
it, she's guiding me to my room where a deep wooden barrel is
filled with steaming water for me to bathe within.

"Make sure you pay attention to her hair," Lady Æthelflæd
commands my servant, who bobs an agreement, as Æthelflæd
returns to my father.

As I lower myself into the steaming mixture, I feel life restored to my stationary limbs, and smell returns to my nos-
trils, and desire to my loins. I can vaguely hear my father and
Lady Æthelflæd speaking through the wooden divide, but their
words are fleeting, mere fragments of what they talk about, and
instead, I dream of the King.

It seems he's not abandoned me. It seems he's only busy.

Lady Æthelflæd is correct in her admonishment to me. I need
something to keep my mind occupied when the King is busy. I'll

need to find a cause or some means of entertainment. Perhaps the garden?

Perhaps I should speak to Abbot Æthelwold if he's still in Winchester. He would know of some good I could do. Perhaps some embroidery for when he becomes Bishop of Winchester, or maybe I could have one of his monks educate me in the Benedictine rule. Or maybe I could just busy myself deciphering the politics of the Court. It would be good to know which of the King's ealdormen were causing problems for him. After all, in the Council meeting, it seemed as though the men were all in agreement.

I rise from the bath, and my servant begins the task of dressing me in the overdress provided by Lady Æthelflæd, and then in the laborious task of drying and finishing my hair. This part of the process we're forced to take into the great hall, so that the roaring fire can dry my damp hair and stop me from gaining a chill.

Still, Lady Æthelflæd and my father talk on, and in the end, tired of trying to listen to their half whispered words, I find my strength of mind returning.

"I'd like to know of what you speak?" I say it with a slight inflexion, but it is more of a command than a question.

My father looks horrified at my tone, but Lady Æthelflæd nods with respect.

"And you should know of what we speak. Come, we'll join her by the fire."

My father amazed that I've not been reproached for my arrogant tone, escorts Lady Æthelflæd to the chair she first sat in, while he finds a small stall for himself.

"We were talking about problems between Ealdorman Ælfhere and his brother, and the King, and the King's foster brothers. It seems that none of the men trusts the other, no doubt because they all share borders with each other, and all wish to claim the same rights from the same monasteries, and all believe that the King owes them the honour of having their requests acceded to."

She pauses and thinks about her next words.

"King Edgar is much loved in Mercia and East Anglia because he's the foster-son of Athelstan the Half-King, but with his death, and sadly your husband's death soon after, I fear the current Ealdorman lacks some of the qualities that the two other men had. Some of the monasteries see him as a threat and look to Ealdorman Ælfhere of Mercia as their saviour. They speak of long discarded boundaries that mean they should be administered by whichever Ealdorman they prefer, and now the bickering has grown too wearisome, and too petulant."

"The King is angry with everyone for their stubbornness, even with Archbishop Dunstan, who tries to calm them all, and to make matters worse, the grandmother of the King's current wife, is crowing to all who will listen of the King's infidelity with you, and how he has no right to divorce her granddaughter, but means to all the same."

"The women of the court are as divided as the men. The King's grandmother speaks for you, the family of King Eadwig's discarded wife are virulently against you. It's a seething mass of discontent, and one that King Edgar is struggling to control. He needs you to be with him, but he doesn't see that yet. But we'll make him realise. My sister and I think that your presence will stop the women from arguing, and that might allow the men to calm down a little. Perhaps without the whining of their wives in their ears, the Ealdormen will realise that they sound much the same as them."

The image that Lady Æthelflæd presents should fill me with dread, but instead, it gives me something to focus on and to take my mind from the King's abandonment of me.

"You make it sound as though they're all a flock of sheep worrying at each other, nipping where they know it will hurt, and being outraged when they're nipped in the same way in return."

"It's a good description of them all," she admits, with a faint hint of a smile on her lips. "You sound like you're almost happy to walk into the mass of attitude and arrogance."

"I almost think I am," I retort, not a little cheekily, and she smiles, and pinches my cheek with her warm hand.

"You look much better. The dress suits you. I knew it would. Now come. It's getting late, and I wish to be back before it's dark. Have your servant send some of your things after you. I think it best if you spend the night at the Palace. There's space in my niece's room. That way you'll be there early in the morning. It would be best to give the King every opportunity to come to you."

The thought of the King floods my face with even more colour, and Lady Æthelflæd notices it wryly.

"It's good that he has such an effect on you whenever I just mention him. I believe he should have a wife who stirs to excitement at the thought of him, and yet who can talk politics in the bedchamber afterwards."

I should feel horrified by her words, but they embolden me even more, as my cloak is thrown around my shoulders, and we ride back to the palace. I thought I'd be riding away from Winchester in disgrace, but it seems I was very wrong, and now I need to show the King that I'm not to be ignored and forgotten about just because some small matter of politics is weighing on his mind.

I ride proudly. Lady Æthelflæd's coming to me has cast my relationship with the King into acceptance. No matter that he yet has a wife and a daughter, it seems that his courtship of me is to be tolerated and openly accepted. At least by Lady Æthelflæd and his grandmother, Lady Eadgifu. For all that the widowed queen is an old woman, with the best of her years behind her, I believe that I should do something for her to show my gratitude. But I don't yet know what that can be. I don't know her well enough to act without consulting her or the King first. Perhaps I'll ask the King, if, or rather when I next see him.

The long summer's day is growing ragged around the edges when I arrive back at the palace. Lady Æthelflæd heads straight for the Women's Hall, as though the King and his worries are of no importance to her, or to me. I find myself hoping for a stray glance of him, and I sit rigidly in my saddle, my face a mask of composure that only drops when we arrive at the Women's Hall, and I've still not seen the King.

I should like him to know that his ignoring me is unacceptable, but also that I don't need him to make me feel complete. The latter would be a lie, but I'm worried that my weakness for him will make him unwilling to continue our alliance. He needs to know that I can survive adequately without him, even if I can't.

I notice my father veering off and heading for the King's Hall, where he's greeted by Ealdorman Byrthnoth. I think the two men might become firm allies, and I admire Lady Æthelflæd's tactics once more. In ensuring my father is where the King is, the King will be reminded of me and will hopefully ask after my wellbeing. I hope my father knows that he must lie and say that I'm well.

The Women's Hall, or Queen's Hall as I tell myself it will soon be known, is sparsely populated by Lady Ælfflæd and Lady Leofflæd, but I also notice someone else within the room, and I'm pleased when the woman turns, and it's Lady Eadgifu.

These four women, well apart from Lady Leofflæd who belongs to my generation, have been members of the King's Court since his father ruled, and his grandfather before him. Their very presence, here with me now, shows that they think I have a right to be here and acknowledged as the King's wife in waiting.

"My Lady Ælfflæd," I greet her with delight, and also her daughter, and they both reach out to grasp my hand or offer me a hug of welcome. Their hospitality assures me that Lady Æthelflæd is right in her encouragement of me. Without waiting for any prompt from the two sisters, I step lightly on the wooden floor to where Lady Eadgifu is enclosed in a deep wooden chair, its back covered with furs and pillows, more of which settle over the old women. For that's what she is; an old lady, but one who still has some time left to her, and seems content to use her influence where she can.

"My Lady Eadgifu," I curtsy to her. Her husband crowned as Queen of the Anglo-Saxons, and during the reign of her step-son, Athelstan, she ruled the Women's Hall for him, and it's her presence that has permeated the years, having far more effect than poor Lady Æthelflæd who was barely married to King Edmund before his murder.

"Ah, good, you're here at last," the woman answers, her gaze taking in my gown and finding it to her taste.

"You were right Lady Æthelflæd; the colour is perfect for her. I'll not argue with you again about the right colour for the Queen-in-waiting." I glance in surprise at Lady Æthelflæd, and she offers me a grim-faced smile. I somehow think that their argument may have been very long and very withdrawn, but it seems that even someone with the history and prestige of Lady Eadgifu is not afraid to apologise when she's wrong, even over something as simple as the colour of a gown.

"Now come, we have much to discuss and much to decide upon. Sit," she commands me, and I do, sitting before her but ensuring I don't block the warmth from the hearth.

"The King is a silly boy," she begins, all the touch of an annoyed grandmother ringing through her voice. "I've tried to speak with him but he leaves the room whenever he hears me, or anyone mentions my name. I'm pleased he fears me as he should his grandmother, but it's frustrating my attempts to offer him my support."

She sounds aggrieved, and from the look on Lady Æthelflæd's face, I think that this is not the first time they've had this conversation in the last three weeks.

"My husband tells me that it's Ealdormen Ælfhere and Ælfheah who cause the most trouble. That doesn't surprise me. Ealdorman Ælfheah does nothing unless his brother commands it of him. But why they're difficult now does surprise me. It's nearly the height of Summer. It would be better to have these discussions come Easter and the King's Easter Feast and Witan, but instead they try to cause problems as Summer covers the land. I wish the damn fools would leave us women alone to ensure the King gets the sort of wife he needs at his side."

"Is this why the King left so abruptly when we were together?" I ask, and the older woman nods.

"Yes, while you spent the afternoon with the King, they spent the afternoon drinking and plotting, and causing problems."

"So what's happened since?" I ask. I don't know all that's befallen the King. No word has come to me from the court since I returned home after our meeting.

"King Edgar decided the best option was to join the men in their drunken stupor and try and settle the matter man to man, over mead and ale, as opposed to seaxs and swords. It was, even I must admit, a good idea. But it didn't work."

"Why?"

"Because all of the bloody fools ended up too drunk to talk and the next day was spent in drunken denial that anything had been discussed. Not one of the Ealdormen had a head for speaking, but still, they tried to talk, and it simply made the situation worse. Ealdorman Ælfhere threatened to leave, and only the intervention of Abbot Æthelwold prevented that. He managed to get all the men to agree to a temporary truce so that they could sleep more, and be able to argue with more clarity the following day."

"Sadly, the next day came, and it seems as though they'd all perhaps had too much sleep. The arguments in the King's Hall, not in his private chambers, were fierce and very, very public. There's no one who doesn't know of the falling out between the King and the Ealdormen."

"Did no other try to intervene?"

"Well, Abbot Æthelwold tried once more, as did Ealdorman Byrthnoth, but the King's foster-brothers stayed silent, much to the King's chagrin, and so another day passed with no resolution and only more unease between all those involved. What had started as a matter of debate and disagreement, has since descended into a series of petty arguments and slights, and now none know who they can trust and who they can't. The King is jumping at shadows, and he's locked himself away from the

Court until he can find a resolution to his problems."

This all makes some sort of twisted sense to me, but Lady Eadgifu hasn't finished in her assessment yet.

"The King doesn't like such discord. He feels he's to blame and he believes that he has to resolve the problems himself otherwise men won't think he's qualified or suitable to be King of England."

This doesn't sound like the confident man who promised me marriage and a crown, and I'm surprised to hear that he can be so easily unbalanced by the bickering of his Ealdormen.

"But there's no one to be King in his place," I reason, and she quirks an amused eyebrow at me.

"The King understands that but argues that just because he's the only option doesn't make him the right choice." She sighs deeply at the words. "I'm an old woman and that bloody boy makes my last years far too difficult. He should be chastised for that if nothing else. I should be able to retire from Court politics after all my years of service without worrying about the future. I've done all I can to secure it for him."

I can feel her frustration and anger, like a strong wind blowing through the room, and I pity King Edgar for a moment until I remember that I'm as angry with him as she is.

"He should be strong enough to understand that the bickering is the way of powerful men and that he'll never be able to stop it. If a great King is meant to stamp out all discord between rivals, then none of the Kings in England has ever managed that." I speak sourly, remembering my lessons about the ancient kings of England, all the way back to the famous battle of Haedfeld and the most recent battle of Brunanburh, which took place just before my birth.

This amuses Lady Eadgifu and a tight smile stretches across her old and lined face.

"You're what the King needs. Someone of his age to provide the clarity of thought he doesn't always believe he possesses. When you're Queen, I'll be able to die knowing that the future is assured." That she speaks so openly about her death jars me a little, until Lady Æthelflæd notices my unease.

"Lady Eadgifu has been speaking of her death for years. Don't let it alarm you. She has her Will all arranged and knows where she'll be buried and who'll pray for her soul. But she won't allow herself to die until the kingdom is secure. She has vowed as much."

Lady Eadgifu pretends she doesn't hear our conversation as she gazes at the hearth.

"Will they never feed us?" she grumbles, and almost on cue, the doors of the Women's Hall open and a stream of servants enters the room, carrying food and drink with them.

"My Ladies," one of the servants says, ensuring she checks all the corners of the chamber as she counts our number. "We bring dinner as you requested. The men still drink and dice in the hall, and we'll feed them when we believe that they might eat the food as opposed to throwing it at each other." The servant is very free with her thoughts, and I almost gasp in surprise, only for Lady Æthelflæd to place a restraining hand on my arm.

"She's been here almost as long as Lady Eadgifu. She's relied upon to keep order by the King and specifically by Lady Eadgifu. She has permission always to speak freely."

"I wish I could chastise the lot of them," Lady Eadgifu speaks acerbically. "If they were my sons I'd have them chopping wood, or mucking out the animals to calm them down. There's nothing like a bit of manual labour to remind men of who they are and how they should be behaving."

I'm sure I've not seen the head serving woman before, and indeed, as she comes to deposit her load on the low table before Lady Eadgifu she stands and fixes me with a stern gaze.

"You must be Lady Elfrida," she conjectures, and I nod and stand at the same time, wanting to make my acquaintance with her. She waves me back to my seat with a wry smile.

"I can see why there's some fuss being made, and I know that I might quite like you as well. My name is Heregyth. If you have need of me, ask anyone for me by name, and they'll know where to find me. Now eat, all of you." She stands as she speaks and runs her hands down her apron as though she's accomplished a good job.

"I would rather the food didn't go entirely to waste. Bloody men," she mutters as she dips her head to none but Lady Eadgifu and hastens from the hall, ensuring she gathers the other handful of servants as she goes.

"A good woman," Lady Eadgifu mutters as Lady Leofflæd offers her a bowlful of stew and some warm bread to go with it. "She knows more than even I do and she's discreet as well. I used to be quite scared of her."

"I am scared of her," Lady Leofflæd replies and this too brings a smile to Lady Eadgifu's lips.

"Young men and young women should be scared of her. Especially when they're unmarried and likely to cause havoc by leaping in and out of the wrong beds."

A faint flush rises along Leofflæd's cheeks, and I feel my own flame as well. I wonder if she knows of what passed between the King and I a few weeks ago. As though hearing my words, and although she eats, Lady Eadgifu winks at me with far more delight than I believe a woman of her age should and speaks again, "She knows everything, I mean everything."

I try not to let my utter astonishment show, but fail and my dignity is only saved by the opening of the hall door and the admittance of someone I'd sooner not see. Lady Wulfhild, the grandmother of the King's current wife. She grumbles almost as much as Lady Eadgifu does as she walks into the hall, and as she drops her cloak on the floor for her personal servant to pick up, she sniffs the air, and an angry look crosses her face.

"It would have been polite to wait," she barks, not noticing my own presence as she hastens to join the group of women. I almost wish I could disappear into the floor but that's not a possibility, and so I sit straighter, waiting for her to notice.

"Bloody fools," she mutters, and I think she must speak of the men as she shakes her head from side to side. "I thought we were eating in the great hall, but Heregyth directed me to here. She says she won't waste good food on men too drunk to taste it. I entirely agree with her."

The two sisters make room for her to sit beside them, and still, she doesn't notice me as Lady Leofflæd serves her with her own bowl and bread, and she settles back to eat hungrily.

We all eat in silence, as though waiting for her to realise who she breaks bread with, and I spend the time deciding how I'll approach her hostility toward me. Should I meet her full on or allow her critical attitude to by-pass me. I wish I were able to ask Lady Eadgifu for advice, but she's settled back in her chair, watching the pair of us with some excitement. I think this is some sort of test of my skills at dealing with awkward individuals, and no one is likely to be more awkward than the grandmother of the King's current wife.

"Why is she here?" I finally hear. Perhaps the woman knew I was there all along.

"The King has made his intentions toward her clear," Lady Eadgifu answers smoothly and with some derision in her voice.

"The King can take any woman he wants as his concubine."

"She will be no concubine." I feel as though the two women have forgotten that I'm there and that I might have my own opinion on the matter.

"And what trumped up reason can the Archbishop possibly have for arranging another divorce? The girl is fertile. The birth of her daughter, a daughter that the King acknowledges as his own, proves that."

There's anger in her voice, but she's doing well to keep it under control.

"The Archbishop will aid the King in his wishes, no matter what they are. We all know how closely aligned their thinking is."

Lady Eadgifu has no intention of revealing any details she might know about how the King will divorce his wife. I must confess that I'm as curious as Lady Wulfhild, but it seems that I'm to be kept as in the dark as everyone else.

"His first divorce was granted because his wife was barren. His second wife is certainly not that, and even if she was, Lady

Elfrida has no children of her own, and she's been married for five years to a man who already had children. It seems to me that he might be divorcing a woman who has far more chance of birthing children than the woman he wishes to marry."

"If only that were true," Lady Eadgifu says sadly. To my ears, it sounds as though the words are genuine, but even I can detect the implied threat in them, and Lady Wulfhild fixes the King's grandmother with an angry glower. I don't know what Lady Eadgifu knows that Lady Wulfhild doesn't want her to know but it seems to be imperative, and something that Lady Wulfhild fears others knowing. No doubt it'll be something that can help my cause. Otherwise, Lady Eadgifu wouldn't speak of it so openly.

"Of course it's true. There's nothing to dread in that regard. The girl is fertile and keen. The birth of her daughter so soon after their marriage speaks of that."

"As you will," Lady Eadgifu mollifies, but there's not one of us who isn't listening to their every word with huge anticipation. "And it was, as you say, very soon after the marriage. If not a little too early."

I feel my eyebrows almost disappearing into my hairline as I listen to the two old matrons talking so openly about matters I'd not expect them to speak of.

Lady Wulfhild offers Lady Eadgifu a forced smile.

"I think we all know of your grandson's amorous ways." She seems to think that's all that needs to be said, but Lady Eadgifu has more to add yet.

"And of course the girl's." The words are a tremendous slight for a woman who wanted to be a nun, and who, was in fact, in her nunnery when the King came to claim her as his bride, and I'm not the only one who hastily stifles their in-drawn breath.

Lady Wulfhild does a lot more than glower at Lady Eadgifu now. I can see where her hands are balled into tight fists in her skirts as she tries to contain her rage. I'm amazed by Lady Eadgifu's forthrightness. She must be very assured of my position with the King, and that whatever she knows will ensure that Lady Wulfthryth won't be the King's wife for much longer. I'd like to know what it was.

"The King has a wife, and a child, as I say, he has no reason for a divorce on this occasion." The old woman finally manages to say with her anger firmly under control.

"We shall have to wait and see, won't we?" Lady Eadgifu rejoins, as the door opens and the servants arrive to take away the remains of our meal. This gives Lady Wulfhild the excuse she's been looking for to remove herself from the awkward conversation, and she takes it with a greater agility than I might have expected in a woman of her age.

I can feel my eyes somewhat bulging in my head at all that I've experienced. Lady Leofflæd meets my gaze with a wry smile, and I realise that she perhaps knew this was about to happen, and more, that she was enjoying it.

"Now, Lady Elfrida, I feel we should maybe talk about how you plan to proceed with the King," I almost quail to be held in Lady Eadgifu's gaze, but it seems that I'm to be saved from her aggressive interrogation for at that moment, the King himself enters the hall.

He looks harassed and forlorn as he strides through the wide-open doorway and I don't think he's come to seek me out, or at least I hope he hasn't. Not with a face like that.

"Grandmother," he calls as the doors close loudly behind him. And I can feel the anger and frustration in his voice. Lady Eadgifu turns to greet him, a smile on her lips, but at that moment his gaze, as always sweeping the room he surveys, lingers upon me, and I see a smile of delight there.

"Grandmother," he says more softly now, as though just the sight of me has calmed him.

"My Lord King and grandson," she bows to him, having first stumbled to her feet in a parody of the old lady I know she's not.

"I would speak with you in private, if possible. But I won't be long," he almost gushes, his eyes reminding me of his touch in his tent, and making me hunger for his hands along my thigh and his tongue in my mouth.

"Very good," she says, taking a step as though to go to him, but he sweeps the rest of the women a look instead, and it's we who move away from the fire. I'm the last to leave, unable to take my eyes from the King, as his eyes return to my own, and hold them there. I wish we were the only people in the hall at that moment.

He only releases me from his look when his grandmother coughs to remind him of his true intentions, and I glide toward the other women. I've been desperate for just one sight of him ever since we last saw each other. It seems that while he might have forgotten about me, that he's keen to be reminded now. I thrill to think of us being alone together. Although the remarks Lady Eadgifu sparred with Lady Wulfhild, bring me up short. I must be above reproach. No one must be able to say that we acted inappropriately before our marriage could take place.

"What did Lady Eadgifu mean about Lady Wulfthryth?" I whisper harshly to Lady Leofflæd, and she responds very quietly.

"The birth was hard. Rumour has it that although the baby is near six months old, that she still doesn't bleed as she should, and neither does she welcome the King to her bed. I think her daughter was too big for her and she's infertile now. At least that's what Lady Eadgifu believes and so too do others. Even before the King saw you, there were rumours that his marriage wouldn't last much longer."

"Oh," I feel my mouth form the shape, as I turn to watch the King, his head bowed low as he speaks urgently to his grand-mother. I wish he'd come to seek me out in such a way, but then, he didn't know I was here. That much was clear to see from his entrance. I wonder if he ever will seek me out in such a way. I would like to hope he would, but the more I learn about the Court, the less and less I feel I know.

It's possible that the King has been planning his marriage to me since my husband's death. That saddens me and also stirs my desire for him once more. I would think it an excellent thing if he's hungered for me all these years.

But then I stop, for if the King had indeed hungered for me all these years, he wouldn't have suggested I became his concubine when we first met. He would have made his intentions clear then. It must only be that he knows his wife will never give him a son that drives him to marry me now. That disappoints me a little.

I need to spend some time with the King, speak to him of his plans so that I know I can provide him with what he wants.

Then it seems I'm to have my wish, for whatever he was speaking to his grandmother about, he turns and beckons for me to join them. I stand abruptly. I feel a little unsteady on my feet, but Lady Leofflæd offers me a grin of support, and I walk calmly to where the two of them sit. Lady Eadgifu meets my eyes, as though trying to tell me something without actually speaking, and I nod primly to her, as she stands and walks slowly away.

"My Lady Elfrida," the King murmurs. His gaze is intense, and sweat beads down my back in the sudden heat from the hearth.

"My Lord King," I respond, dipping a pleasing curtsy and waiting for his next move. He pauses a beat.

"Will you please sit with me?" I can feel the eyes of everyone in that room on me, and it takes all my willpower just to sit sedately.

"I owe you an apology," the King, says, his eyes still on my own. I don't think he feels the attention of everyone else, but then, he's perhaps more used to such constant notice.

"My Lord King?" I say again, feeling stupid that I can't get anything more than those three words through my constricted throat. Looking at him, he seems tired, and it's all I can do not to reach out and run my fingers along the bags that mar his face, and comment on the sad look in his keen eyes.

"My Lady," he smiles, mirroring my short answers, and making me blush with embarrassment. That seems to give him the opportunity he's been waiting for, and now he reaches out and cups my chin with his right hand, rubbing his thumb along my cheek. I wince at his touch, desire turning my legs to leaden lumps, and my breath to a too harsh pant.

"I shouldn't have left you when I did," he continues, amused by my reaction. I wish I'd touched him first, just to see if his reaction would have been the same as my own.

"No, you shouldn't," I manage to gulp, my eyes watching him intently while my mind replays the events of our last encounter. I'd do anything to be alone with him now, but I can't be, not while everyone watches and the King is still married.

I want to sound, angry, aggrieved, but instead, my voice is small and quiet, with no hint of my anger and annoyance.

"I've been much distracted by problems amongst my Ealdormen, and my grandmother tells me that you've been pining for me."

I rather wish she hadn't said that, but it does please the King, and I suppose it's not a lie either.

"I had hoped to hear from you a little sooner," I retort, allowing a haze of anger to cover my words now. It'd be nice if the King didn't think I was just going to sit around and mildly wait for him to remember who I am.

"Yes," is all he says, finally looking away so that he doesn't have to see my angry eyes. "Yes, you're right. I shouldn't have allowed myself to be so easily distracted. If my step-mother hadn't acted in the way that I should have done, this could have ended in a very difficult situation for us. I understand that now. I shan't let it happen again. In fact, I think it would be advisory for you to have permanent rooms within the palace. Perhaps with Lady Leofflæd and with my stepmother and her sister to ensure propriety is kept at all times."

Now I feel cornered. I'd hoped not to give up my freedom just yet.

"If you think that would be wise, my Lord King," I whisper, and now he leans toward me, his lips near my ear, on the right side of my body so no one else in the room can see what he does next, and he gently kisses my ear, as he drops his hand and rests it high on my lap. The reminder of our time together is so intense that his kiss on my ear is almost all it takes.

"I do," he whispers. "I think it would be best if we spend as much time together as possible. Make it clear to people that you'll soon be my wife. You've nearly been widowed for an entire year now; that means that once my own minor problems are resolved, that we'll be free to marry. And, we'll marry," he says, his beard brushing my cheek as he speaks and making me think of all sort of acts we could enjoy on our wedding night.

He leans back and clasps my hand in his.

"But genuinely, I've been remiss. When you're my wife, we'll rule together, and I shan't allow such things to come between us." He sounds rueful of his position, but I think he enjoys being King, most of the time.

"Then we'll need to discuss politics much more than we already have," I answer breathlessly. I'm still thinking of the lover he will be to me, and not the King he must be to everyone else.

"Yes, we must," and a slow smile creeps along his face. "But I think it would be more enjoyable to do just that when we share a bed together when I can pleasure you and then talk politics. I should like to speak about my Ealdormen between kisses, and matters of the church between more intimate knowledge of you. And, I should like to talk about the women of the court, as you sit above me, and remind me of the true place of women in my Court and my heart."

"Then we should bloody well hurry up and do it," I gasp once more, my eyes closing as he portrays a future I wish could start now. I'm so desperate for his touch that I'd forget all manner of decorum just to lie naked with him in our bed.

"We should," he giggles as well, his face once more close to my ear, and then, perhaps daring me to object, he places his lips on my own and the softness of them, the insistence in them, almost makes me undress him here and now, and take from him what it is he's taunting me with.

Yet I manage to hold my emotions in check, to accept the kiss without acting inappropriately, and although I enjoy the long, protracted kiss, giving into the insatiable need he has for me, I know when a polite cough comes from the back of the hall, that it's the King who's being reprimanded and not myself.

Slowly, as though he can't bear to break our contact, he pulls away from me, his lips loosening their hold, his tongue returning to his own mouth. My eyes have opened, watching him once more, but his own are closed, not opening until the kiss has finished and he sits apart from me once more.

"My Lady Elfrida," he stumbles, and I'm pleased I have the same effect on him that he has on me. This is the first time he's allowed his weakness for me to show through. He gasps more than I do, and I can see how great his desire for me is, just by examining his clothing. I think that if the King doesn't resolve the problems with his current wife soon, that I won't be able to spend any time at the Court for fear that we'll surrender to our passion before our marriage can be celebrated.

"My Lord King," I retort, breathlessly. "I see you've lost none of your skills." Fierce resolve meets my comment.

"And this is only the smallest part of it," he rejoins, his own breath still coming in heightened breaths.

I know I need to distill this duel of wills before both of us dare to do something we shouldn't.

"Have you eaten?" I ask him abruptly, reminded of what I was doing before he entered the hall. But he stands quickly, recalled to his tasks.

"I have, My Lady, but even if I hadn't, I have far more urgent matters to attend to. I'll see you, tomorrow, and hopefully, I'll have news of far greater importance for you."

He stands then, all traces of our indiscrete time together forgotten about, and he nods, and strides from the hall. I watch him go, and I know my hunger for him is written all over my body. I can only hope that we won't be kept apart for much longer.

CHAPTER 12

L ady Leofflæd is a pleasant roommate, but I can tell that she's desperate to ask me about the King, but too defer-ential to do so. I wish I had her schooling in keeping my emotions to myself, but I know I don't. Not yet. It's something that I must learn, and quickly if I'm to survive at the Court. As the King has shown these past weeks, he'll not always be there to protect me or offer me his support.

"My Lady," Lady Leofflæd is unfailingly polite in her attitude, and I smile at her, feeling a little mischievous.

"My Lady?" I smirk to her, and the grin falters on her face. "I think that in here you could just call me Elfrida."

"Only if you call me Leofflæd," she retorts cheekily, picking up on my good mood.

"You know there will be people here who'll hate you," she says hesitantly, the good cheer even now forgotten and I'm pleased that already she'll tell me the truth of my future pos-ition.

"I've been warned."

"They'll make your life difficult," she offers, a little sadly, "and you'll not have the opportunity just to leave the Court, as my mother and I do, when the bickering becomes too much."

"No, I suppose I won't, but I imagine I'll get some privacy, some of the time?"

"Very little, and then perhaps even less than you might think. The King is always on display, and his wife with him, and your children."

"Um, but, we'll have the privacy of the bedchamber?" I ask, my eyebrows raised, hoping to lift the sadness in her eyes.

"Well," she stutters, "yes, you'll have that time alone," she stresses 'that' with only the hint of a blush on her cheeks and impresses me again with her ability to be discrete.

"Who'll hate me?" I ask. I'm beginning to think her mother might have demanded she has this discussion with me. I saw the three women deep in conversation when the King left the Women's Hall.

"Aside from the obvious, the current King's wife's family, I think you'll need to be wary of your brother-in-laws."

That surprises me, and also doesn't. There was never any great love between us all, and I'd detected their angry eyes looking my way when I was in the King's Council.

"There will also be the holy men who are adamantly against the Benedictine movement, and there are many of them."

I nod at this as I make myself ready for bed. It's cold in the room despite a brazier, and I'll be pleased to warm up beneath the furs and blankets heaped all over the comfortable looking bed.

"They won't object to the King's divorce?" I ask, "but only to his support of the Benedictine reforms?" The inherent contradiction in that statement overwhelms me. Divorce isn't a matter that the church likes to discuss, although as a whole, our society has no issue with it. It might be rare, but women can divorce their husbands, with no stain upon their character. It's one of the few advantages of being a woman in a society dominated by men, and it's one that we all fiercely guard. The church teaches that divorce is a sin, but our churchmen turn a blind eye to it when they can. It seems that this argument about the Benedictine monks concerns them more.

And that's because, somehow, and I'm unsure how, the King and his holy men, have managed to make the issue about more than following a stricter set of rules about how the monks spend their time. It's become about land. The Benedictine monasteries have become land-hungry. They've become almost too big to manage and the greedy eyes of the Ealdormen and wealthy King's thegns, have started to see them as ripe for being plucked of land they think they shouldn't control.

Neither is that the end of it. The Benedictine reform is something else as well. For a country that has only been a country for a short space of time, when Wessex and Mercia finally managed to reclaim the Danelaw and Northumbria, the Benedictine movement is seen as something more devious than the Viking raids. It's something that's 'foreign', and yet still trying to claim English land.

Many of our greatest churchmen, Dunstan and Bishop Oswald amongst them, might be English, but in their endeavours to ensure the movement is successful, they've taken to bringing men to England from the Continent. The monks in their monasteries praying for the souls of the people of England are often from Frankia or Rome. For all that the King's Court has always been renowned for its welcoming attitude to those from other countries when it comes to a land-grab, it seems their tolerance has disappeared.

Not that I can do anything about that but if I'm associated with the King, and Abbot Æthelwold, and Archbishop Dunstan, I too will be allied with the movement that seems to be making England, unEnglish.

It's a heavy burden when what I want is the King as my lover. Perhaps I would have been wiser to accept his initial offer of becoming his concubine? Perhaps my life would have been easier in the future.

"They'll object to anything if they feel that others are gaining at their expense."

"And the women?" I ask. I've met many of the women at the King's Court already, but I'm sure there must be more of them. I wonder if they stay away while the King's wife is so indisposed to being seen in public. I imagine it must be a boring place for them.

"Well, if you become Queen, I think that more husbands and

brothers will send their wives and sisters to Court, at least for the summer. They will, of course, come with their husbands and brothers presumptions. You'll need to win them to you, or not. It will be vitally important that you know all the family relations so that you don't undo the work of your husband, and he likewise."

I like the sound of the word 'husband' on her lips, especially when it relates to the King. He's right in what he says. It has been almost twelve months to the date that my husband died, and I'll soon be free to marry again, but with that knowledge comes sadness. I'll need to offer my prayers for him when the date comes.

"Your family is loyal to the King?" I ask, just to make sure, and she smiles a secretive little thing, her eyes flaring with darkness.

"Yes, provided the King is sympathetic to our needs and wants. Just because the King's father was married to my aunt, doesn't mean that he always thinks of our interests. Just look at his brother and Lady Eadgifu."

It pains me to think that there will be occasions when I might be out of favour with my family because they might disagree or refuse to acquiesce to the King's wishes, but it was the same with my dead husband's family and my own. Æthelwald's family were the more influential, and yet the marriage had been agreed because my father had something that Æthelwald's family wanted – its influence in Wessex. I imagine that it'll be the same for the King.

"The Court is a complicated place," I sigh heavily, and Leofflæd reaches over and takes my hand and offers it a squeeze.

"I think you'll enjoy it, once you've worked out who everyone is. It's the sort of place that someone with your quick mind will thrive within. And I hope to help you when I can, and if you'll let me."

I want to welcome her with open arms. But she's right. The Court is a complicated place.

"I hope we can be allies," I offer, climbing into the bed and shivering uncontrollably.

"Good," she responds, mirroring my actions and shuffling in between her furs. "There are too few young women at this court, and those that are here, don't want to be."

She giggles as she turns away from me. I know she's thinking of the King's wife. That she sees the humour in her downfall, saddens me a little, but makes me realise that I too will have to see the gain in others distress in the future. The Court can't be one happy sea of people all working for the good of the King and the country. There will be those who see it as nothing but an opportunity to cause problems, and there will be occasion, I don't doubt, that I will have to do the same.

The King is above everyone at his Court, and yet he only rules with the aid of his Ealdormen. As his Queen, I'll be seen as having influence with the King, and some of his allies, but I'll need to choose those people carefully, and first, well first I must ensure the King gets his divorce, can marry me, and that I'm able to provide him with a much-needed son. Until then I'll have to tread carefully, and I'll be entirely dependent on the King and his close family, and that means that I must be an ally to the great ladies who've already shown their support for me, even if at a later date, I'm forced to stand aloft from them.

CHAPTER 13

I'm ushered from my room by an impatient Lady Leofflæd. Our intimate conversation of the night before is all forgotten about, as she fusses with my clothing and hair, and ensures that I look 'correct' for whatever is about to happen. Not that she mentions what that is, and so I'm surprised to find myself back in the women's hall. For all Leofflæd's attention to detail, I'd assumed my summons had come from the King as she didn't mention otherwise.

But that's not the case. Instead, pleased that her task has been accomplished, she rushes from my side as soon I enter the hall and goes to speak with her mother. The King's grandmother greets me, Lady Eadgifu, and she has a stern expression on her face.

"Lady Wynflæd wishes to speak with you," I rack my memory trying to decide who that great person is, as Lady Eadgifu escorts me to the side of the chair she's been sitting in the night before. Still, blank, I turn pleading eyes her way, and she huffs dramatically before taking pity on me.

"The King's other grandmother," she explains and ice leaps down my spine. Of course, Lady Wynflæd. How could I have forgotten who she was? Her reputation is far from dazzling. She's a fierce woman in a world dominated by men. She's the King's maternal grandmother, a woman whose daughter lost her life to birth King Edgar.

She rarely comes to Court, preferring to send her demands

through her son and also directly to the King. King Eadwig rarely allowed her to have her way, treating her as roughly as he did Lady Eadgifu, his other grandmother, but King Edgar is very different to his brother.

This then is yet another test that I have to pass to become the King's wife.

"My Lady Wynflæd," Lady Eadgifu calls as we edge closer, and I can feel my stomach rumbling with hunger and fear combined. I'm beginning to resent all these little tests, especially as they occur with no warning and leave me wondering why I even desire the King and want to be his wife.

"Yes, ah, my thanks," the other woman says as she takes in my appearance, and gives a grim nod of satisfaction.

With a squeeze on my shoulder, I think for support, Lady Eadgifu glides from my side and goes to join the other women. I envy her the ability to move so freely amongst the different parties at the King's Court.

"Lady Elfrida, please sit," the old stateswoman says, and I curtsy and then raise my eyes to look at her. She is even older than Lady Elfrida, perhaps by as much as a further decade, and her skin is wrinkled and sagging around her chin and her cheekbones. Rumour has it that she was never a great beauty, but now she has the look of a willow tree around her, all spindly and overflowing, not being able to discover where the thin branches merge into the even thinner leaves.

I swallow back my fear.

"My Lady Wynflæd," I exclaim, "I'm honoured to meet you." My voice is too high with nerves, but the woman doesn't comment on it.

"Well I can certainly see why he'd want you," she says sourly, as though the truth of my purported beauty is a blow to her. I decide it best not to act all innocent and question those words, and instead wait for her to speak as I make myself comfortable on the small wooden stall I've been asked to sit upon. This show of strength and power in something as simple as seating arrangements is a tactic I must learn to think of more often.

"Lady Wulfhild came to me, very concerned by your presence, and so I've come to court, to see what all the fuss is about myself. Lady Wulfhild is an old friend of mine, and I was very pleased when her granddaughter married the King. It seems that I was premature in my support of the arrangement. The girl has done nothing but produce a girl child, when the King needs a son to rule after him, and now she refuses him her bed."

I open my mouth to say something, although I'm not sure what, but Lady Wynflæd is far from finished.

"My daughter died bringing the King into this world. Her sacrifice was great but also much needed. Even then the ancient house of Wessex was failing. Now its future hangs only on a girl child who's small and weak, and I doubt will live for long. No matter what Lady Wulfhild says, I know that the King needs a new wife. What I don't know, is whether that new wife should be you, or not."

Still, I know not to say anything.

"Lady Wulfthryth is a sick woman. She will doubtless never have another child. I know the rumours are true, even if Lady Wulfhild refuses to accept them. She's gone to the royal nunnery at Wilton, and I doubt we'll see her at Court once more. And that should mean that you have a clear run to the King, but you don't. You do know that, don't you?"

I didn't know that, and it worries me. The King has assured me of his intentions and even Lady Eadgifu seems convinced of my success.

"You never gave your husband a child in nearly five years of marriage. There's no surety that you would now, and so Lady Wulfhild has decided that her other granddaughter should replace Lady Wulfthryth as his wife. She's a bright thing, a pretty thing, and she's robust."

The words startle me and elicit a response I didn't mean to give, not to this cantankerous old crone.

"And what proof is there that she'll birth children for the King?"

"Well there's less evidence that she won't," is her quick retort, and I know that everything hinges on this fact, and it's a deeply personal one, and one I'd hoped never to share, and yet the thought of losing the King is too high for me and so I know that I must.

"I can carry a child," I say slowly, as though the words are pulled from me, as they are.

Lady Wynflæd looks at me fiercely.

"What do you mean?"

"I know I can carry a child, to almost full term, but an accident, a most unfortunate accident when my husband was so desperately ill, led to me losing the baby."

Her sharp intake of breath at my words should draw me to look into her eyes, but remembering that terrible time is too much. First I lost my child in a fall, and then I lost my husband. The past is a truly cruel place and one I try not to inhabit too much.

"What happened," she barks, but I wave her aside. Tears are falling down my face at the memories so fiercely dampened down that have come rushing to the fore. I think the old lady is cruel for making me remember as she does, and for a moment I'm back on that fateful day, watching the colour drain from my husband's face as he was told of the seriousness of his condition, and my own fear, pooling around me, that had become literal as I'd crushed my hand to my swollen belly, only to stumble as I rushed to him and fell down three wooden steps, landing fully on my belly, and feeling the hot tang of blood and water streaming down my legs.

The birth had been beyond painful, so sudden and unexpected, and then crushing when the baby had been born dead, although perfectly formed.

"You have witnesses?" she tries again, and I nod, feeling numb from the centre of my being. For so long I'd hoped for a child, and when I'd realised I was pregnant, I'd done all I could to stay healthy and active, praying every day for a safe delivery, only to have my chances foiled by my twisted feet and the panic on my husband's face.

"Yes, there are many. Perhaps even Ealdorman Æthelwald's brothers will offer witness. They were aware." My voice is dull and lifeless. To lose so much, so soon, is too much for one woman to bear.

"Good," she says, her tone very matter of fact, and I can feel her eyes on me, although I refuse to look at her, staring instead at the hem of my skirt, and twisting a ring around my finger nervously. I'd never thought I'd have to confess to my loss. Not even the King asked me about such matters.

"All the same, people will ask why the child died," she says, and I wish I could spit my rage and anger into her face.

"The child was delivered too soon because of a bad fall. That's all anyone needs to know. It was healthy and hale, but too damn small to survive." My voice reverberates with rage and still the old woman isn't done with me.

"Still, there are those who'll support a younger woman than you in the King's bed. One who hasn't already buried a husband and a child."

"Then they are perfectly welcome to do so," I growl. "I know that the King wants me, and I want him. We'll make beautiful children together and make the House of Wessex strong once more."

"Good," she says and waves her hand at me in dismissal. I struggle to my feet. I've not yet eaten, and I feel weak and ineffectual, the truth just wrung from me a fact I'd hoped to take to my grave with none knowing about it, other than those few who already knew.

"I will do all I can for you, with the other nobles," she mumbles as I finally find my feet. "They're hungry for a powerful woman at the King's side, but with you, I think they may get a woman with too much to gain from power. They might not want that. I know Lady Eadgifu believes the King needs a strong wife, a Queen at his side. But then, she's been a Queen and knows what the position can be used for. It's been many, many long years since there was such a woman, and few may welcome the return of one. After all, Lady Eadgifu and Lady Æthelflæd still meddle in matters of the Court they should leave well alone. I would look to others for your inspiration as well as those two. Much can be accomplished from a distance as well as from up close."

I say nothing to that, but I think her advice might be well intentioned. She might be a hard woman, but she's also warning me, as everyone seems to be, that the future might be a difficult one.

Before I'm fully recovered, the door to the hall opens once more, and this time it's the King who steps inside. His gaze, as always, sweeps the occupants in their entirety and then he ambles toward me, a slow and lazy smile on his face, and I try to summon up some delight at seeing him. I'd rather be alone with my misery.

"My Lady Elfrida," he bows to me, and I curtsy to him, as he greets me. "I've arranged for us to ride this morning. I need to clear my head of the arguments of the men in my Council. You've eaten?" he asks, and I shake my head numbly.

He's no fool, the King, and he soon discerns where I've come from and who's spoken to me, and then he beckons for Lady Leofflæd to take my arm.

"See that the lady eats," he commands her, and then he's striding toward his grandmother, his riding boots resounding on the wooden floor.

"Uh oh," Lady Leofflæd mutters under her breath, but I grab her arm, desirous of her help as she walks toward the small arrangement of items for breakfast. There's bread and a little butter, and also some cheese, and cured meat, and eagerly I eat all I can and drink the warm mead offered to me as well.

In the background, I can hear the raised voice of the King, and his grandmother, but I can't make out the individual words they use, because my head is buzzing with the revelation I just made, and the grief it's reminded me of.

The other ladies in the hall, having already eaten, are obvious in their attempts to listen to the King, and I hear the two sisters providing a running commentary for Lady Eadgifu, who like me, is eating quickly, trying to pretend that a major family argument isn't taking place behind us all.

"Oh my," I hear on Lady Æthelflæd's lips, and "here, here," on Lady Ælfflæd's, but I don't ask them what they agree with, or what shocks them. No doubt the King will tell me soon enough.

I'm pleased he's arranged for us to be alone again. I need the time to assure myself that I actually want to put myself in such a position where I'll always be judged, no matter what I do, from this day forwards. I also need to know if he's made any progress with Abbot Æthelwold and his divorce. Once I know the matter is in hand, I'll be able to concentrate on the first anniversary of my husband's death, safe in the knowledge that soon I'll be married once more, to a husband I desire even more than the first one, and I'll be filled with the hope of a future I couldn't have imagined a year ago.

"Eat," Lady Leofflæd rushes me, as I try to gain back some semblance of myself from when I first woke, "the King is coming this way," she coaxes, but I know the King will wait for me, and despite the heat in his face, the only show of anger from his conversation with his grandmother, it seems he's indeed content to wait, speaking with Lady Eadgifu at length about Court matters and asking her for some idea of how my wedding gown should be designed. The thought thrills me although I think I might quite like to be consulted on it as well as his grandmother.

"My Lady," he finally soothes, just behind my ear and I turn to greet him, my good cheer almost resurfaced, only for it to disappear almost immediately.

"I had hopes you would ride with me for the next few days. I have a desire to visit Ramsey, and pay my respects."

He alludes to my husband, and where he lies buried, and I almost wish he hadn't thought to be quite so supportive of my grief. I had hoped to spend some time alone, perhaps with the Abbot Æthelwold, so that I could console myself to my husband's death.

"You would rather not?" he immediately asks, I can already tell he wishes he'd consulted me first.

"No, My Lord King, I'd be honoured to accompany you. It's just. Well, it's just an awkward time for me, and I was unsure if you'd wish to see me quite so distressed." What I don't say is 'for another man,' but I don't need to. Understanding flashes across his face at my words, but his eyes glint brightly.

"We shall honour the dead, as is right, and we'll do it together, a unified front." He sounds quite convinced that his decision is the correct one. "It will also allow me some time away from the Court. Abbot Æthelwold has my instructions, on important matters, and my grandmother, Lady Eadgifu, is happy to progress with the rest of the arrangements."

"My Lord King," I bow my head low, my mind thinking quickly. It seems to me that the King and I are escaping from the Court for a few days, to make a very public show of our combined grief for my dead husband and that when I return, the divorce might be arranged and the wedding as well. I can hardly argue with his desire to progress quickly.

"I'm afraid I'll need time to pack," I utter a little helplessly, but his smile is infectious, and I return it, entirely.

"No problem. Lady Leofflæd has arranged everything you'll need, and she'll accompany us, as will Ealdorman Æthelwine. It seems only appropriate."

Æthelwine is my dead husband's brother, and Lady Leofflæd will be our chaperone. I wonder if the King has plans for them to marry, or if he just prefers the younger woman to his stepmother and her sister.

"We'll begin our journey at once. I hope it'll take no more than a day or two. The distance isn't too great."

I shiver at the thought of all that time alone with the King. Anything could happen. Anything.

It seems that arrangements have been made and no sooner do I step outside, firmly wrapped in a luxurious fur cloak, than I'm mounted on the same horse as before, and the small party makes ready to move away. My old brother-in-law has said nothing to me, but Lady Eadgifu follows me outside.

"Go with God," she cautions, but in those words, I hear, "keep the King entertained but not too close," and I smile tightly to show I understand. Events at Court are moving very quickly, and this journey gives me the opportunity to undo everything. This trip could prevent me becoming the King's wife and Queen, and I'll only have myself to blame if I err.

CHAPTER 14

The King doesn't test my resolve, perhaps understanding how torn I'll be between my grief and my desire for him. Instead, he and Ealdorman Æthelwine, travel the first day together, their conversation intense and sometimes heated. The strained glances that Ealdorman Æthelwine directs toward me make me think they talk of myself, and that worries me.

I'd not expected Ealdorman Æthelwine to be so adverse to the King's choice of bride, but it seems that he is. He must fear that I'll bring all the benefits of the allegiance of his commended men without needing him as well. It's a stretch to me. My husband kept me out of public view as often as he could, I now know because he feared the King would learn of his deception, and I have few contacts in his household apart from amongst the monastery at Ely and the women who once made up my household. Indeed the King's thegns didn't think I held any sort of power to persuade my husband to do what they wanted.

I ride quietly with Lady Leofflæd while she giggles and chortles her way through conversations with the men escorting their King. I enjoy her as a distraction from my dark thoughts, and although she keeps apologising and promising to stop, I wave her concerns aside. It's nice to hear the sound, and feel joyful on a sombre journey to my husband's grave.

Ealdorman Æthelwald had hopes that he'd build a monastery at Ramsey. I know the building work was barely started when his death took him, but all the same, we conceded to his demands and allowed his body to lie there. I imagine his brother and the rest of his family will have continued his work there, ensured that there is an adequate shrine, so much closer to the family heartlands than Glastonbury, where his father, and mother, are both buried.

We shelter the first night in a grand hall where Ealdorman Æthelwine knows the King's thegn who owns it, and where I sleep well, exhausted by the ride and my grief. I know that tomorrow my sadness will overwhelm me, and it will be difficult to think, let alone be pleasant before the King.

I wish he'd not thought of this as something that I wanted to do. I'd much rather have spent the day remembering my husband kneeling in the Old Minster at Winchester, content to have Abbot Æthelwold pray with me and keeping my distance from the King. I think my grief for Ealdorman Æthelwald might displease the King, no matter what he says.

The journey the next day is conducted in a more peaceful manner. I think Lady Leofflæd has detected my muted mood and she's trying to be sympathetic. I'm not sure if I appreciate it.

The King also stays at arms reach from me, and that, I do appreciate. He rides with Ealdorman Æthelwine still, and the two of them speak quietly and respectfully, and I'm no longer the victim of the ealdorman's pained looks. I hope it means that the King and he have settled their argument from the day before, or perhaps, it's merely a show of respect for his dead brother.

The two were close, no matter how little Ealdorman Æthelwine liked our marriage, the two brothers never fell out about it, unlike the King and Æthelwald. I should respect Ealdorman Æthelwine for that, and indeed, as we ride close to the land where the fledgeling Abbey is being built, I encourage my horse to ride closer to his.

"My Lord Æthelwine," I speak softly. My voice has been little used that day, and I sound croaky, and perhaps worse, make the Ealdorman jump because he was unaware of my approach.

"My Lady Sister," he replies, recovering quickly from his surprise, and even offering me a small, tight smile.

"I, I would have you know that I miss your brother every day, and pray for him."

"I know, sister," he stresses that word, and it's the first time in nearly a year that he seems keen to acknowledge our relationship.

"We all pray for him and wish he were with us now, and you, as well."

"The children," this hurts me to say for the family have stopped my contact with them altogether. "The children are well?" I enquire. This was the only thing that my husband asked me to see to, but his own family have made it impossible.

A look of distaste crosses Ealdorman Æthelwine's face at being reminded of the son and daughter his brother had with his first wife.

"They are well, my thanks for thinking of them, sister." He turns aside as though to stop our conversation, but it's taken me all day to seek him out, and I'll not give up so quickly.

"You will tell them that I ask after them?" I ask, but his face hardens.

"My Lady Sister, the children don't remember their father, much less you. I would think it best if you forgot about the pair of them."

Those words fall like a slap across my face, and tears instantly swell in the corners of my eyes. Whether Ealdorman Æthelwine knows how much those words would hurt, or whether he's just insensitive, I don't know, but I pull my horse back, content to be with Lady Leofflæd again. Only, it's the King I ride beside, and his face shows a spark of fury at the conversation he must have overheard.

I swallow thickly. This day is too hard for him to observe, but he rides more carefully, grabs my horse's rein, to stop the placid animal.

"My Lady Elfrida, you're well?" he asks, his voice rich with understanding, and that kindness almost breaks through my resolve to face this day bravely.

"I will be, My Lord King, I promise, in time," I try, looking at him and feeling such a mixture of emotions that I don't know what to do with myself.

"This was a poor choice, I apologise," he says anger threading his voice, as he looks at me, and then away, to where Ealdorman Æthelwine is now riding with Lady Leofflæd, his back rigid, but his horse's jaunt a little cocky, as though he knew, and planned for this upset to myself.

"Ealdorman Æthelwine was always a mean-spirited boy," he says. "Not like his brothers. I would wish that any of them were ealdorman in his place, but it's not the way these things work."

"My thanks, My Lord King," I manage to sniff, and a small smile tugs at the corners of his mouth.

"Would you hate me very much if I tell you how beautiful you look when you cry?"

His attempt to lighten the mood brings a sad smile to my face, and I shake my head.

"It wouldn't, My Lord King. It would be inappropriate, but it wouldn't make me hate you."

"Ah, you might be right, but all the same, you do look beautiful. Come, we'll ride together. No matter what the good ealdorman does, it's still right that we visit Ealdorman Æthelwald's grave. I only wish we weren't, but then, if we weren't, I'd not be here with you now."

He speaks the truth, and the twisted nature of our burgeoning relationship distracts me for long enough for the half-built monastery to come into view. It seems I was wrong in my assumption. Little of the monastery has been built since Æthelwald's burial, and I wish I could speak my mind to Ealdorman Æthelwine, tell him of my disgust that he's so little adhered to his brother's will. But I think it best if Ealdorman Æthelwine and I stay far away from each other.

Regardless of the small wooden building which houses no more than three monks, and the bare struts of the church under which Ealdorman Æthelwald was buried, I instantly feel a moment of tranquillity. It seems I've been dreading this time for the last year but now that I'm here, and with the King as well, I feel stronger.

I am only doing exactly what my husband asked me to do. If he can see me now, I hope he's proud of my accomplishments.

The monks wait for us. There are no servants, but the younger of them is offering cups of warmed mead, to drive the cold away from the day. I pity them instantly. They have only a pitiful puff of smoke to warm them, and I vow that I'll ensure some of my own wealth is redirected their way. I'll ask Abbot Æthelwold to provide them with what they need. I can't finance the building work, but I can ensure the three men will live through the winter, when, as Queen, I might be more able to exert some influence on Ealdorman Æthelwine to continue the work.

If not, I'll have to approach the King, and also the ealdorman's brothers. I'm sure that they must be unaware of the poverty of the monks.

"My Lord King," the elder monk, exclaims in shock, and for all the serenity of the moment, I stifle a quick smile at the monk's obvious distress at being caught in such an unfortunate position.

"My good man," King Edgar replies, leaping from his horse and going to take one of the mugs from the other monk. "It's a pleasure to be here with you. I wish it were under better circumstances, but I come to pay respects to my brother, and the Lady Elfrida to her husband, and of course, Ealdorman Æthelwine to his brother as well."

The King's tone is smooth and natural, but I think he's angry with Ealdorman Æthelwine, perhaps just as angry as I am.

Lady Leofflæd looks most distressed, and I do share her worry. We thought we'd be spending the night at the monastery, but it's impossible, and we'll need to ride on once our pilgrimage here is made.

I slide from my own horse and hand the reins to one of Edgar's warriors. They are as cold as we are, but I hazard a guess that the monastery only has enough mugs for the monks themselves. I take my own cup and drink quickly.

"Is there more?" I ask the young monk very, very softly. "I think the riders would benefit from something warm to drink."

The man, pinched with cold, and with clothing unsuitable for the summer let alone the coming winter chill settling in the dip of land the building occupies, nods quickly, almost desperate to please, and I watch him disappear back inside the small wooden structure.

I take a deep breath then. I know the way to where my husband lies buried, and I've decided that I don't wish to delay the inevitable.

For all that I'd not expected to visit my husband's grave, I've not been negligent in my duty to him, and I reach back to Lady Leofflæd who hands me the small pouch I've filled with coins, and also the little piece of needlework that I'd made to adorn his grave. I had assumed there would be a roof above the grave but it seems not. I will place it there for now, but will no doubt have to ask the monks to keep the item safe until it can be left with him for all time.

The King walks at my side, flanked by the older monk, who seems content to lead the way, even when it involves the King. He appears to have recovered his composure. After all, there's nothing that they can do now to make the place more hospitable for the King.

As I walk past the younger monk, now carrying the three mugs toward the King's warriors, I stop and press the purse of coins into his hand. I imagine he's the man responsible for providing for this small community. His face, when he feels the weight, breaks into a smile that is far more than just relief. I think I might just have provided him with a lifeline to see them through the imminent long winter season.

The grass has grown long to either side of the small path that leads from the monk's home to the fledgeling monastery. I can see that on any other day when the ground is less than hard baked by the drought of the summer, that this path must be a muddy mess. The very fact that a path is clearly delineated means that while my husband's brother might have been remiss in his duties to the monks, they've not been remiss in their attention to their founder's grave.

Indeed, when we make our way through the skeletal wooden beams, I can see where the men have tried to erect a shelter around Ealdorman Æthelwald's grave, and they've done very well. The harsh wind and rain won't reach the grave slab, and that brings me some comfort. I should have paid more attention to what was happening here, rather than foregoing all my rights to have any say in what was to happen.

The three monks begin to chant as soon as our small party is inside the temporary wooden structure, and the King takes his place beside Ealdorman Æthelwald's grave. I bow my head, content to stand here while we pray for my husband's soul, and I find the chanting and the bleakness of the location actually matches my mood.

This day should be a difficult one for me, and I'm content that it is. My husband might not be happy with my tears, but I feel they are a just reminder of our time together. Next year, and most certainly from the year after, I doubt I'll make this pilgrimage. I hope that by then I'll be a wife once more, with a child on my hip.

The thought of the future, while I think of the past, is a painful reminder of how much my husband lost with his early death. It's not my place to question our God and yet I would if I could.

I stand that way for a while, listening to the undulating chant and when I finally raise my head, I'm alone, with just the monks as the others have all bled away. I step forward, my gift for my husband scrunched in my hand. I'm shaking a little. Flashes from our final day together keep racing through my mind, including his request that I seek out the King.

"My Lord Husband," I whisper softly, bending so that my hand is on the grave slab. It's adorned with biblical images, which I trace through my fingers. This, at least, I ensured was done as my husband had demanded. What's happened since I left his household shortly after the New Year, is for his brother to answer, not I.

I don't know what I expect when I mutter those words, and so I'm not disappointed when nothing happens, and instead I place my offering on the grave slab and stand. I'd felt uneasy being here, somewhat uncomfortable in the presence of the King and my old brother-in-law, but I'm calmer now, assured that I'm excelling in the demands my husband placed on me.

I turn, my shoulders back and my eyes straight ahead. The monks have stilled in their chanting, but they still pray, and I meet the eyes of all three of them; the older one right down to the frozen younger man I gifted with my purse of coins. I hope the King and Ealdorman Æthelwine have thought to do the same, or these men might also meet their death here, and that would be more than unfortunate, it would be no fitting tribute to my dead husband.

But I walk resolutely from the place. There's no need for me to come here again. I've made my peace with Ealdorman Æthelwald, and now I must walk into my future, the future he hoped I'd achieve.

CHAPTER 15

I think I'll ride back to Winchester as the King's wife, finally accepting my place at his side. Edgar seems buoyed by my lifted spirit and we laugh and race our horses as we take our time on our return journey.

Sullen Ealdorman Æthelwine, no doubt in disgrace with the King, doesn't accompany us, having decided to go home instead, and I'm pleased, although Lady Leofflæd is less happy, although she tries to please herself by gossiping and flirting with the King's warriors once more.

I think I should perhaps warn her, but Edgar assures me that the men know that Lady Leofflæd is not a plaything for them.

"They're terrified of her father," he mutters, his eyebrows raised in amusement and I laugh in delight at the image of her father haranguing the men should he ever find out that the men have paid his daughter attention they shouldn't.

"When we return to Winchester, our future should be taken care of," the King says lightly, as we near the end of our first day's journey. That excites me, as does the knowledge that the King has no problem with the mourning I had to do for Ealdorman Æthelwald. In fact, if anything, he seems pleased by it. Perhaps he's been surrounded by so much grief in his life, that it's pleasant to meet someone genuine. I don't know and neither do I need to ask.

"Your divorce will be complete?" I ask. I would have expected it to take longer, but then, he is the King.

"Yes, it will be. Abbot Æthelwold was to meet with Lady Wulfthryth and secure her agreement. Not that there will be any problem with it, but it is only right that I provide for her future and that of the baby. Obviously, there's no longer an impediment to you marrying me as a year has passed since your husband's death."

"Of course, My Lord King," I acknowledge, surprised by the irony that his care for his discarded wife fills me with hope, that should he tire of me, I'll be well cared for, better than when I became a widow. When I was widowed I retained my morning gift, but nothing else, as I should have because there were no children born to our union, but his brother bartered with my father for the land, not happy to lose it from his family's inheritance, and in the end, all I received was a handful of coins, not the rents and tithes I should have obtained.

As a widow, I have far more rights than I'll have as a wife, but it will suit me to be the wife of a King as opposed to the widow of an Ealdorman with rapacious brothers. I feel I will be better off in the long-run even if it means I'll be subject to my husband, as opposed to the Church and my father.

"All I will need to do then is secure the agreement of the Witan, but I hope that too will have been resolved in my favour. There are few who don't wish for me to have a son to follow in my footsteps." He speaks sardonically, too young to appreciate that men always look to the future, and I share his fears and worries.

It seems that our union will be agreed to because of the King's need for a son. I will have to pray fervently that my God provides me with such a son.

As such when we return to Winchester, I'm unsurprised to be met by a glowing Abbot Æthelwold, his task seemingly complete. The King is buoyant as he lifts me from his horse, kissing me as the men and women of the Court look on, some with shock, but others with bemusement. It seems that in the King's absence, and that of Ealdorman Æthelwine, more has been accomplished than in their presence. The divorce has been finalised, and the men of the Court are, to all intents and purposes, keen to make amends with the King.

My father greets me effusively and escorts me to the Women's Hall where the two sisters wait for me, eager to welcome both myself and Lady Leofflæd. They are filled with gossip, and although I long to continue my time alone with the King, I recognise that for the time being, at least, we will have to be apart. The divorce might be finalised, but there are still important matters that need to be dealt with.

"The Lady Wulfthryth is already in Wilton, but she will be ceremoniously escorted into the nunnery in two weeks time. The King will attend, of course, but whether you do or not, is something that others must discuss. I think it best if you don't," Lady Ælfflæd mutters, "but my sister disagrees with me, and I think the King will as well."

"She should stay away," the outraged cry from Lady Wulfhild is unexpected and chilling. I had not seen her in the room, and she sounds as though she's been bewitched, or some such. I'm sure no person should be able to reach such a high tone. She does, and now she rounds on me. Her face is furious, her anger making her spit as she continues to screech in her unearthly tones.

The two ladies look flustered, and even Lady Leofflæd, who I'd taken to be quite unperturbed by most things, seems aghast at the older woman.

"The King has no right to divorce the girl. None at all. And neither do you have the right to take him from his wife, for we all know that's what you've done. Tempted him with your looks and with your tortured soul for the loss of your own husband. But you mark my words, girl," her use of the word is derogatory, and I can't wrench my eyes from the fury on her face, never the prettiest, and now ugly and scrunched up. "This will not go all your way. There are many here far stronger than you, and they would rather see the King unmarried and without an heir, than with you as his wife and the mother of his sons. This is not yet your victory."

With that, she storms from the room, and I'm left shaking and unsure of myself all over again. My hard one equanimity gained on the journey to my dead husband's almost abandoned monastery at Ramsey, has fled, and I stagger to the floor, my legs deserting me as I look around for something to reassure me that the woman doesn't mean her threats, but only Lady Æthelflæd, Ælfflæd and Leofflæd are left within the room, and they all share my look of horror.

My exuberance quashed, I merely tremble where I sit.

CHAPTER 16

For all Lady Wulfhild's threats to me, and my worries, nothing happens over the course of the next week to convince me that her words, although horribly spoken, were anything but a dry threat.

Absenting herself from the Court, I don't miss Lady Wulfhild's presence, and somehow I convince myself that all will be as it should be. I think that Lady Æthelflæd and Ælfflæd try to go along with my desire to forget the unpleasantness, but they must still worry for I often catch them whispering in the corner and Lady Leofflæd is suddenly less keen to share all of her secrets with me. It's as though they want to remain close to me, but fear Lady Wulfhild will somehow manage to accomplish what she's been threatening.

I understand their reticence, but it wearies me. I thought they were my unswerving allies, but it seems not.

Only when I'm with the King does everything become an irrelevance, and my time with him is often and long, my father or I almost constantly attend upon him, and our shared delight in our discussions of our future together make the time between our return from Ramsey and the King's need to set out for Wilton, pass in a quick blur of stolen kisses and other, more intimate moments.

Yet, all too soon, it's time for him to leave, and despite it all, I've made it clear that I don't wish to be in attendance when he formally renounces his marriage union to his wife, and allows her and his daughter, to pass into Wilton, his wife to become a nun, his daughter to become one if she wishes, and if not, to be educated there and remain a member of the dwindling Wessex royal family.

The King seems to accept my words and so we part ways. For the first time in many weeks, I return to the house in Winchester where my father has been staying, and the King makes his way to Wilton. He promises that his journey will be as swift as possible as his kiss lingers on my lips, but I know that this must be done properly.

Neither does the King go alone. For once, Winchester is almost denuded of royal figures of the Court, as the King, his Ealdormen, his churchmen, and the great women of the Court, all trail their way to Wilton. There is some grumbling from the older women, but they know that this needs to be done, just as I do. Only Abbot Æthelwold goes with light steps. This divorce will see him become Bishop of Winchester, a position he's keen to take up so that he'll have the position to make the changes to the Old Minster that he's failed to make while he is only an Abbot.

I chose to spend my time preparing for my marriage, destined to take place with the Christmas feast. The King has also promised to make me his Queen on the same day, and my father, brothers and I, are keen to ensure that everything proceeds as it should do.

My wedding dress has been ordered for me, but my Coronation gown is something that I can organise myself, and I have been. My servant, the girl who's served me so well during this strange time, has proven to be a delicate and careful seamstress, and I've tasked her with working the fine imperial purple, and ensuring that the dress and cloak suit me well. I've already asked my father for permission to take the girl with me when I become Queen, and he's willingly agreed. I don't doubt that he expects her to inform him of events at Court. The fate of the King's last two wives is sobering. He will need to be assured that our marriage is working and fruitful, or else, he might suffer like the families of the two previous wives have.

There's nothing like a daughter becoming the King's wife to make a family powerful, and conversely, nothing like losing that position to return a family to its previous impoverished state. Having experienced the keen loss of a marriage alliance already, when my husband died, I'm sure he wishes to be far better prepared in the future.

The few days I spend apart from the King are long and a little lonely, but I have the future to look forward to, and I fill my days with dreaming of the sons I will birth for him and of the respect I will earn once I'm Queen. Bishop Æthelwold has written the Coronation Oaths I must make, and although they differ to those of my husband's, it little matters. I will be his wife and his Queen, and I have my dead husband to thank for my good fortune.

When I'm finally summoned back to the King's Palace at Winchester, I go impatiently. I'd expected the King to return sooner than he has, and although I'm desperate to see him, I also feel a little angry as I ride through the ageing year. Icicles hang from the trees now, and the fields are almost bare, the rich smell of peat and wood burning mingling with the cold air to make me shiver even in my cloak.

That anger turns to fear when I'm greeted by none other than Lady Eadgifu as I stumble from my horse in the courtyard before the Women's Hall. It is festooned in snow and looks warm and inviting, but the look on Lady Eadgifu's face is anything but.

The palace seems deserted, the sound of my horse's hooves loud in the still and frozen air.

"What is it?" I demand, too fearful to even greet her as I slide from my horse. I'm surprised by my ability to walk and talk. I know, even though she doesn't tell me, that something has gone terribly wrong with my plans.

"It's dreadful," she whispers, as though hundreds might overhear us when really there's no one but us, and of course, Heregyth, standing outside the hall. Quickly, I escort her inside. Under my arm, she's shaking and shivering, and I hope she's not suffering from some affliction.

"Lady Æthelflæd," Eadgifu says, and I look around for the King's step-mother, although I know she's not within the hall. It's as empty and lifeless as the courtyard, and even the crackling logs in the fireplace cause me to jump in the preternatural stillness.

"Not that one," she cautions me, irritably, as though I should know what she talks about when I can't possibly know. "The other one. The one the King married first."

I know of this union, but can't understand why it concerns me. Nothing came of the marriage, and the King divorced her quickly, and she retired to a nunnery so that he could take another wife, just as he's done now, with Lady Wulfthryth.

"What of her?" I ask, wondering if she's died, or if someone has taken her to wife, against the King's wishes and those of her own. She was to be accorded the protection of the church as well as that of once being a member of the royal family. Why that would be so terrible, I don't know.

"She wasn't barren," the woman whispers and I look at her in horror, realisation forming all too soon in my mind.

"She has been raped?" I try to ask, but Lady Eadgifu's hands are soft and warm on my own, as we settle before the fire and she shakes her head from side to side, tears leaking from her eyes with each denial.

"No, she has gifted the King with a son, Edward, all in secret, and no one has ever known." She almost shrieks the words as she speaks them as I shake my head trying to deny the truth of what she tells me, and yet accepting it immediately as well.

She wouldn't lie to me, not the King's grandmother. She looks as though she's spent much of the last few days sobbing, either with relief or despair, it seems I'll never know.

I taste metal in my mouth, conscious that I've bitten my lip as my blood runs cold and my legs threaten to fail underneath me. All this and it will be for nothing. The King, it seems, has a son.

"You've seen the boy?" I ask, and she nods again.

"He is. He is the very image of his grandfather and his father after him. There is no mistaking the likeness. I couldn't lie when they showed him to me. The resemblance was too great. It shocked me to my very core."

"How old is the child?" I think to ask, wondering how such a thing could have happened and without anyone being aware.

"Little older than his sister, but he walks and talks. He is, he is a beautiful boy."

I shudder at her words. I'd been envisaging walking into a palace ready for my wedding, where Abbot Æthelwold would help in the ceremony and would then be raised to the Bishopric of Winchester. It seems neither of us will get what we hoped for.

I've made enemies here and people, perhaps even my husband's brothers, will be pleased to oust me from my tenuous link to the King. Certainly, now that the King has a son and heir there is no legal reason for our marriage to go ahead.

I can't marry the King, not now he has a son.

I can't marry the King when he's taken two wives already and had children with both of them. I imagine he'll reclaim the younger Lady Æthelflæd as his wife if she so wishes it, and that she'll come and manage his Court for him. This room that I thought would be mine, and in which I saw my children being nursed by the hearth, will never belong to me.

Whether she becomes his Queen or not is none of my concern. Nothing at the Court is my concern anymore, not unless I marry one of the ealdormen and why would I do that now. It will only bring me into contact with the King and the women who live here, and that will shatter me.

"Go with God," Lady Eadgifu cautions, and I nod and turn aside, to stumble my way back toward the door. I should say the same to her, for she looks old and wears her years heavily today but my thoughts are all for myself. I can barely speak, let alone think about the correct and politic thing to say.

My time at the King's Court is done, and I can only hope that I never see him again.

CHAPTER 17

Winter shrouds the land in earnest as I retreat to my childhood home at Tavistock. My father is my silent companion. He neither complains nor berates me for what has happened. Some parents might but he's pragmatic enough to know that none of this is my fault.

The King's first wife kept news of her condition to herself. I don't know why, but I can imagine that Lady Wulfhild took great pleasure in discovering the truth, even if it does cast her own granddaughter's marriage to the King into a dubious state. Will the girl, Lady Edith, as she's to be known, keep her position as the King's acknowledged daughter or will she be locked away forever, a stain on the King's first marriage, to be forgotten about in light of the birth and survival of his first son? I note the child has been named after the King's grandfather. Lady Æthelflæd was obviously keen for the child to be accepted by the King, but all in good time, perhaps when he was older.

I try not to think of the King and his wives, of my desolated plans for the future. I try to think only of myself, of what the King has done to me, and yet I know he's as little to blame as I am. A great surge of discontent has arisen to deny us our opportunity for happiness.

I would cry, but all that's happened is that a child has been born and the King has an heir. No one has died, and for that, I try to be grateful. The King might never be mine, but at least he lives and breathes, and for that, I intend to be happy for him.

For myself, I see little in my future but more heartbreak, and yet I try to be pragmatic. It was always a long shot, becoming the King's wife and Queen. I think even the women at Court knew that it was only a pretty dream, but only that.

I don't allow myself to think of his touch on my body. There's no need for me ever to feel such craving and need once more. If I do marry again, the man who shares my bed will do so without any enthusiasm on my part. I'm done with love and passion, loss and hatred. I don't need those emotions in my life.

Tavistock hasn't changed at all in the long summer months that I've been gone. My brothers are unhappy to see my father returned to his place as their Lord, becoming too used to managing affairs as they see fit, but I ignore the discord in the family, content only to spend my time praying and alone.

I overlook the heated arguments my brothers are keen to have with my father about my 'failure' as they term it, and I try not to hate them for seeing me as little more than their conduit to the King, a channel they no longer have.

The weather is harsh as the Christmas season approaches, the snow deep, with storms ravaging the land each night. It turns the land to a blanket of white and I shiver in my bed each night, despite the warmth of the hearth and the layers of furs that cover my body. I know I ache for the body heat of another beside me, but I refuse to think about it, instead shivering myself to sleep. It's a little more comfortable than crying myself to sleep, which is what I did this time last year.

Each day I visit the fledgeling monastery my family has endowed, uncaring of the icy snow that seeps through my leather shoes, and which clumps to the back of my cloak. I seek nothing now but the calmness that I know only God can give me.

I hope never to be intruded upon again by the King or his Court, and I think little of him, even though in effect, his absence coats me just as closely as the snow covers the land. I miss him with every beat of my heart but refuse to accept that it's that which ails me.

Just before the Christmas feast, when the Yule log has been

placed on the fire in my home, I am disturbed at my praying by Abbot Æthelwold.

I know nothing of his coming, and I confess, I am angry to find him in my private space when I visit the monastery. I don't wish to see him or speak with him, and indeed, I don't want to listen to any apologies he makes. It's perhaps good for him that he doesn't offer any to me.

"Lady Elfrida," he touches my head in a blessing as I kneel before the altar, trying to ignore him, despite his best attempts.

"Bishop Æthelwold," I intone. My voice is colder than the air outside, and I shudder to think where such abjection has come from.

"You are missed at Court," he begins, and I lean back on my heels, and glare angrily at him. I don't wish to have this discussion with him. Not here. Not in my monastery.

"The King is bereft without you, the Lady Eadgifu as well."

Hearing those names is like torturing my soul. I don't wish to think of them, and so I stay silent.

"I understand it must have been a shock to you when you discovered the King had another child from his first marriage, but the Court is no longer shocked at the news, instead content to welcome the child amongst them. In all honesty, he will be raised by his mother for some years to come. He is only a small thing."

The thought of the King's son makes my anger erupt, and I stand, abruptly, still not having spoken, and with the express intention of leaving the monastery. It's possible that I will never be able to visit here again without remembering this uncomfortable meeting with the Bishop.

"The King is still in need of a wife," he calls to my retreating back, but I continue to ignore him, instead mounting my horse, and riding it back toward my family home.

I may just have been rude to the King's Bishop, but I don't care. I'm fuming with him for coming to see me, for talking about the King, his son, and the King's need for a wife. What of my needs? Does he think so little of me that he's forgotten that

I'm a person after all, and more, a woman who's husband has only been dead for a little over a year, and who lost a child before it could come to term?

I hope the Bishop doesn't follow me, but outside the monastery, there's a motley collection of horses and members of the King's household troop, and I know that they will no doubt follow me home. At least at home, I can hide away from the Bishop. Here, in the monastery, there's nowhere for me to go.

I kick my horse onwards to home, my servant who's accompanied me, yelping as I set a pace that's too fast for the horses through the high banking snow to either side of the small roadway that is generally cleared of snow. I want to tell her not to rush, to take her time, but I'm already too far away, and I only hope that she and her horse don't have a fatal accident as they try to keep up with me.

I would look behind, to see if Bishop Æthelwold follows me, but I don't want to take my eyes off the road.

If the King was so unhappy, he should have come himself, not sent the Bishop to do his work for him. So I tell myself, but inside I'm hurt that the King has made no effort to reach out to me, to apologise for what happened. It seems that they might all believe there's no impediment to the marriage, but I know differently.

Abandoning my horse in the snowy yard, I stride into my father's home, unsurprised to see him watching me aghast. I must look a fright.

"Abbot Æthelwold accosted me in the monastery," I all but shout and sudden understanding flashes across his face.

"He's coming here?" he asks, quickly gesturing for the servants to make the hall respectable for a visit from a Bishop.

"I don't know, and I don't care. I left him there and hastened home."

My father opens his mouth to speak, but then shuts it again as my servant also rushes through the door, the words of her apology dying on her lips as my father nods to her, and gestures for her to help the other servants and slaves.

"I will entertain him," he offers instead, and I nod myself, and stride to my room. I don't want the Bishop here, not at all, but my father is prepared to speak for me, that much is clear.

In my room, I shrug my cloak from my shoulders, pull my wet boots from my feet, and then I pace, and pace and pace.

I don't know what else to do. I've schooled myself not to think of the King, his son, or his wife, and most especially, not to think of the King and my hunger for him and his touch. I might be angry that he's made no efforts to apologise but I'd also taken it as a sign that he understood that nothing could undo the wrong inflicted on me. I thought he'd accepted what had happened and that was it.

It seems I was wrong, and now I allow my anger and my grief to consume me. And more importantly, my humiliation.

To be widowed once was bad enough. To be cast out of Ealdorman Æthelwald's family was unbearable, to miss the children growing up that I'd come to learn to love as my own, just as Lady Æthelflæd, the King's step-mother, had done with the two princes she was left with when King Edmund was murdered, was one burden that I had to endure. But this. To have Lady Wulfhild purposefully set out to prevent my marriage to the King has been utterly mortifying. I imagine that my old brothers by marriage, have enjoyed watching my very public humiliation. I hate them as much as I do the King and the Bishop.

I hear the arrival of the Bishop and his men as a jangle of harness and breathless calls to each other before I hear my father greeting the Bishop and welcoming him to his home. There is some joviality as the men greet each other, but quickly, their voices drop low, and I can no longer discern what they say to each other.

I trust my father, but I wish I could trust the King and the Bishop as well. I wish I could speak for myself on this matter, but it seems I'm to be ignored.

The short day grows ever darker, and still, I can hear the men speaking and the shuffle of the horses outside. I almost start to pray that the Bishop will leave. I can't stand the thought of him spending the night at my home, knowing that he'll be waiting to pounce on me at any opportunity, but eventually, I hear words of farewell being spoken, and then the sound of the horses leaving. I sigh deeply.

I hope my father has managed to convince the Bishop of my resolve.

A gentle tap on the door of my room has my father gesturing for me to leave my sanctuary.

"They're all gone," he offers unnecessarily, and I note that my brothers are also absent from the main hall. I shiver as the heat of the great hearth reaches me. I'd not appreciated how cold my hands and feet had become. My father even presses into my hand a cup of warm mead, and I hold it gratefully.

"What did he say?" I ask, and my father sits beside me.

"A lot of nothing, in all honesty. He came to summon you back to Court, at the King's orders. I made it clear you wouldn't go. We argued for some time. He tried to convince me that nothing has changed, that the King still needs a Queen, but I assured him that everything has changed and that the King now has an heir and has no need of another unless it is with the same woman."

Here he pauses for breath, and I'm pleased that he's taken my side so clearly in the argument.

"He says that the King will not resume his relationship with Lady Æthelflæd for she is content to be a nun. There's also the difficulty that if he does, it'll mean that Lady Edith's position will be compromised." I'd worked all this out for myself, but I nod anyway. I'm glad I'm not the only one who understands this.

"He said that the King must marry once more as he now has no wife."

And here he takes a deep breath, and I know something I don't wish to hear is coming.

"He says if you don't marry the King, then everyone will support the marriage of the King and Lady Wulfhild's other granddaughter."

If those words were supposed to test my tenacity, they fail, utterly. This too, I've foreseen. The King might need a wife, and he needs a Wessex wife, but I am not the only eligible Wessex woman.

"The King must do as he must," I acknowledge. I will not marry the King, not now. How could I? As brief a time as I've thought that my children will be kings in the future, I have no desire to risk my life birthing a male child who will never be the first in line to the throne. The King has an heir. His need for a wife is no longer important to me. Apart from … but no. I've decided I will not live a life that is dictated by passion and want.

"I told the Abbot as such. He left, unhappily, but I supported your determination."

"My thanks," I offer, reaching for his hand. I know it will have been hard for him. After all, he too must have foreseen royal children in his future, and he could, despite what he's implied, force me to the marriage. I know that my brothers would have done so.

"And you are sure?" and that's all he asks, and I squeeze his hand, tears in the corners of my eyes.

"I am convinced," I whisper, all the fight for the day gone from me. I am sure I can lead a life as frozen as the landscape outside. I must protect myself.

CHAPTER 18

The Yule feast passes in a blur the same as the one the year before when I'd only just returned to my childhood home after my husband's death.

The feast is spectacular but also small and cosy. I speak of inconsequentialities to people and know that they've all been tasked with not speaking to me of the King and his wives and his son. All seems well as the darkest day of the year passes, but then, it appears not to be.

"My Lord," a dishevelled member of the King's household troop staggers through our door, and I turn in shock. It's the middle of the night and the storm howling outside hasn't stopped all day and all night. It's as though my wrath has carpeted the world.

"Come, enter, quickly, food and warm mead," my father calls to my servant, stunned by the appearance of the man. He's someone I recognise. I'm sure he escorted me to Ramsey with the King, and I fear for the King despite my intentions not to.

As he casts aside his snow-shrouded cloak, and removes his helm and boots, before stamping his feet close to the fire, I see some colour return to his blue face. Whatever news the man has, it's paramount for him to have travelled in such atrocious weather.

"What is it?" my father asks, when the man has had the time to eat and drink a little, and warm his frozen digits.

"I came as soon as I could. Lady Ælfflæd set me the task, and I vowed I wouldn't fail."

The use of the name surprises me, as does the rest of his message.

"It's Lady Eadgifu, the King's grandmother, they fear she will soon leave this world for the next life, and before she goes, she's begged to speak to Lady Elfrida. She will be consoled by no one, and every day she becomes weaker and weaker, but refuses to give up until she's had her opportunity to speak to you."

My thoughts immediately turn to the old woman. I knew she was old, but I didn't realise that her death stalked her quite so imminently. She vowed she'd not die until she made me a Queen. I hope this isn't some ploy on her part to get me back to Court.

"She knows that you don't wish to return to Winchester, but she set out, to meet you anyway, despite everyone's worries, and now she is stuck at Sherborne. She's too ill to travel, and Lady Æthelflæd hoped that you would come to be with her, there. As her dying wish."

Immediately, I realise the man's urgency.

"How many days ago did you leave her?" I ask, trying to think about all I will need, and whether I can travel in the dark with the aid of some brands.

"Three, My Lady Elfrida," he bows to me, and I nod my thanks, my mind thinking ferociously. The good lady might already be dead, but I must do all I can to see her before she dies. She was always so kind to me at the Court, and she was determined that I would be a Queen. It's not her fault that her plans came to nothing.

"I will go," I announce, surprising my father and the messenger both.

"We can leave in the morning," my father nods, already assuming that he's coming with me. The household warrior looks concerned at the delay.

"The storm should pass by morning, and our journey will be quicker then," my father explains, and the man, I think his name is Osric, but I don't want to ask him, grudgingly acquiesces to his demand.

"You will sleep, and we will travel at first light."

And so we do. The storm has, as my father thought, blown itself out, but the landscape is unrecognisable every way we turn. My father uses his skills, and also those of his coerls to help us navigate through our land, and then, when we find a road, we keep to its barely defined edges. The snow is so deep it's hard to detect where the trackway ends and the fields begin, some of the hedgerows being completely shrouded in snow.

I feel the pressure of time bearing down on me, although the world is a silent white landscape. With each breath I take, I hope it's not Lady Eadgifu's last one. I can't believe that she would try and travel all the way to Tavistock to see me, but she has always been a formidable woman. She would not have survived the death of her husband, and so many of her children and grandchildren, if she had not been. I'm honoured by her need to see me, and as we travel as quickly as we dare, I genuinely hope that I'm able to see her one more time.

The journey, which could typically be accomplished in little more than a day at the height of summer, stretches into two long days, and we arrive in the pitch black dark, exhausted from two days of travelling and a night sleeping in a mean shelter that we were lucky enough to find. I know I have straw and hay in my hair, and my clothes are damp, but my arrival at Sherborne is greeted warmly by Lady Æthelflæd and her sister.

"On, my thanks for coming," Lady Ælfflæd gushes as she rushes me into the warmth. My father is not far behind me, and neither is Osric. He receives warm thanks from the women, but then, we're away, in a back room where a little brazier burns and the chill of the outdoors completely evaporates.

Lady Eadgifu is nestled in a small wooden cot, perhaps one where a monk would usually sleep, but she's covered in so many furs that the bed looks more comfortable than it has any right to be. She seems small in that tiny bed, and I can see where the ravages of winter have taken the last of her strength.

Lady Leofflæd sits with her, reading softly to her, while a

monk prays at her side. As the door opens, Lady Eadgifu feebly calls my name, and I hear Lady Leofflæd's sigh as she tries to reassure the old woman that I'm on my way. Only I'm there and having discarded my warm layers and heavy boots, I kneel at her side, taking her small hand in my own.

"I am here, Lady Eadgifu," I whisper, and her nose wrinkles at the smell of the outdoors I bring into her warm room.

"No need to whisper my dear," she mutters with annoyance, opening her eyes and fixing me with a steely glare.

"You took your time," she says, and I bite back my angry retort about the weather and poor Osric. Old women with little time to play with are probably likely to be less than patient.

"I am here," I speak regularly, catching an amused grin on Lady Leofflæd's previously serious face.

"About time. Silly boy," she unexpectedly says, and I look at her with annoyance on my previously serene face. Has she dragged me out of my warm home, and herself across half of southern Wessex, so that she can try and reunite the King and me?

"I wished to speak with you. Offer my apologies for what happened. The King is a silly boy, but he suffered from the lack of a father figure to guide him as he needed to be. Ealdorman Athelstan Half-King was too lax on the boy."

I can see that Lady Leofflæd is not alone in her small grin, and I turn to look at Lady Ælfflæd and Æthelflæd in shock. It's only then that I notice that the three women and monk aren't alone in the room. In the corner, his face cast into shadows, is another man, a man I'd hoped never to see again.

The King is in attendance upon his dying grandmother, and it seems she has much that she wishes to say to him, and that it must be done in my presence.

CHAPTER 19

I turn away from the King immediately upon seeing him, but Lady Eadgifu is not as close to death as she appears, neither as unobservant as I might have hoped, and a wicked smile lights her mouth.

I can't honestly believe that she's content to spend her last few days alive meddling in the King's affairs, but then, she was adamant that she'd only die when the King had a Queen, and at the moment, the King has no Queen.

"I've tried my best to see that the boy grew to be a man his father would be proud of, but I seem to have failed, to date, at least. Now I wish to die, and I may not do so until I've settled this matter once and for all. Your grandfather would never forgive me for allowing matters to reach this terrible debacle."

Her voice is so strong as she speaks that I can't believe I thought she was indeed dying, and yet, it might be that her strength has left her body. I can't tell from here, but on account of her age and supposed illness, I say nothing, waiting to see what will happen next.

"I would have preferred your marriage to that of any other, but I now understand that Ealdorman Æthelwald prevented that, just another sign of how ineffectual Ealdorman Athelstan Half-King was at keeping order in his household. It's high time this matter was resolved, to the satisfaction of all. So tell me, Lady Elfrida, why do you refuse my son when you were so keen for the marriage in the first place?"

I rather wish she hadn't decided to include me in this very public rebuttal, but she might be as angry with me as I am with her.

"The King has two wives and two children. He needs to live with one of them."

"Ah," understanding flashes across the woman's face. I know her history. I know she was the third wife of a King who already had many sons. She'll understand my point better than anyone.

"You wish a life of tranquility?" she chortles, spittle flying from her mouth as she does so. "I once wished the same. I don't recommend it."

Her tone is that of a woman who would share all of her history if she had the inclination to, but she must want some secrets to follow her to the grave.

"And you, stupid boy. Why have you not pursued the marriage with the woman you love?"

If I could feel pity for the King, I would do now, but I'm still hurt, angry and outraged, and would wish myself anywhere but here.

"Grandmother," he begins, but she casts him a stern stare.

"I'm your Queen," she mutters, as though he should know that, "I will be until you make another woman your Queen. I am the last bastion of our royal family."

"You were my grandfather's wife," the King mutters but very, very softly. I think the old woman ignores his words, and I don't doubt that it's not the first time she's heard the argument.

"Lady Elfrida has made it clear she doesn't wish to be my wife by absenting herself from Court," he speaks with authority, but a tremor mars his courage, and now I shoot him an angry stare. I left Court to spare him any further embarrassment.

"We know why she left the Court. Why have you not followed her?"

"She repulsed Bishop Æthelwold," he states. I can feel anger in his voice. I almost hazard a guess that he finds this situation as distasteful as I do.

"I would rebuff a Bishop," his grandmother screeches, "I

would not refuse a man I desired, loved and lusted after."

I think she should refrain from saying such things. The ladies in the room are watching the conversation with obvious enjoyment on their faces; only the monk has the good sense to look embarrassed.

"I couldn't leave the Court," the King tries once more, but it sounds pathetic even to my ears.

"You didn't want to risk her rejecting you again; I know the real reason. Stupid boy," she continued, and by now the King's face is almost puce with rage, but I'm starting to lose the edge of my anger and find the situation amusing. Here we are, two young people, being berated by a grandmother for failing to marry and fuck as she wishes us to. I doubt this has ever happened to anyone else before.

"Well, Lady Elfrida, would you have refused me if I'd come to you in person?" I'd not noticed him moving, my eyes too intent on the older woman and her conniving ways, but now I feel the heat of the King's body close to my own. After all, the room is only small, and suddenly all sorts of reactions are taking place inside me. Sweat has broken out on my brow, and I can feel my desire running through me. Damn the older woman. I'd been doing well until now.

"I," I want to say I would have done, but I can't catch my breath. "I might not have done," is the best I can manage and now Lady Eadgifu giggles with delight, erupting into fits of coughing at her apparent success.

My words surely shock the King for his eyes, until now, black with thwarted passion suddenly flare with the reflected fire of the brazier. He can't have been expecting my answer. Neither was I, in all honesty.

He reaches for me, to perhaps take my hand, or caress my face, but he snaps his hand back, as though it's been bitten, a resumption of his anger on his face as his grandmother rails at him.

"See, stupid boy. She would have taken you. Now what will you do? I know about Lady Wulfhild and her other granddaughter. Now you might have to be brave and make a choice and live with that choice. What will it be?" she taunts him, but his eyes are watching my face, and I can't take my own from his. He seems to have aged since I last saw him, the last traces of his youth leaving his face.

"You would marry me still?" he asks, and although I want to deny that question because he's never actually asked me before, I find myself nodding. I want to say, 'only if my sons are king after you,' 'only if the other boy is banished from the Court,' but I already know that I'll rarely see them, and even so, what does it matter what the King did before he married me. It's of little consequence for now. I've not even shared his bed, let alone have a son to show for our union. All those problems can be dealt with in the future, for they will cause problems. But for now, all I see is the man I desire above all others, and who offers me a kingdom to rule as its Queen. Really, what more could I hope for?

I stand abruptly, but he doesn't move away.

"I can't marry you still," I say, and I hear the collective sigh of all four women expelling their held breaths at my words, and it almost makes me smile. The King's face immediately falls, and he glares at his grandmother.

"I can't marry you still, because you've not actually asked me to marry you at all," I say, a quizzical look on my face, and at my words, he actually smiles, a genuine smile and I can see that we will end up together, just as everyone had hoped.

"Then Lady Elfrida, I'll ask you now."

"No you won't," his grandmother interferes, "I've heard all I can take. Now go away both of you, and leave an old woman to die."

She waves her hand at us, dismissing us from her presence, but then she says my name, and I turn to her. She's holding her hand out to me, and I go to her side, hastily vacated by Lady Æthelflæd.

"Come here, girl," she says, and I lean close to her. It seems she has a secret to tell.

"Bishop Æthelwold will ensure your son is King after the King," her words are barely above a sigh of wind, but I hear them and feel her conviction in the strength of her hand squeezing my own.

"Thank you," I utter, just as softly, but she's closed her eyes, and as I watch, Edgar kisses her brow and mutters his love for her but she ignores him, and so he takes my hand and helps me to my feet. Together we stride from the room, our bodies touching, his hand warm in my own.

The old woman has managed what she wanted to achieve, but I will miss her at Court. I can't deny that.

CHAPTER 20

The act of conducting our marriage was a simple thing. An exchange of words and vows, spoken before Bishop Æthelwold. My clothing was simple, but beautiful, the King, my husband now, decked in his finery and as handsome as always. None of this was new to either of us, for him, I am his third wife, for myself, he is my second husband.

There are step-children in their multitudes, but it will be the product of our union that rules after the King. I've been assured of it, and I believe it too. The young boy, the toddler who almost ruined my marriage, is a weak thing, just like his sister. I hope that with the mixture of my own healthy, Wessex blood, to the King's own, apparently inferior lineage, that I'll be able to restore the royal family of Wessex to its previous glory, to a time when there were so many sons, daughters, cousins and half-breeds, that there was a worry about who would claim the kingdom as opposed to who would be gifted it because there was no other.

But now it grows time for our Coronation, and this will be no simple thing. I've not yet had the time to bed my husband, to feel his hot touch on my inflamed skin, but I've already changed my dress since our wedding, from the simple but beautiful dress chosen for me by the Lady Æthelflæd to something far more elaborate and lined with golden thread and purple silk. I feel regal for all that I'm still merely a wife and not a Queen. That will come later.

It is this quick Coronation that Bishop Æthelwold assures me will make my children more worthy of the throne than Edward, the King's recently discovered son. A child born of two royal parents is far more regal than one born from only one parent, and especially one who to this date has only ever been crowned King of the Northern Territories, always waiting for the perfect moment to arrange his coronation as King of England. This was the very fact that prevented King Athelstan from first becoming king on the death of his father, King Edward. He had been born when his father was neither King or married to his mother. Only the death of his half-brother, a man deemed to be born from a crowned King and his wife, a mere few weeks later, allowed him to become the revered King he came to be. It could all have been so different because of the accident of his birth and if his brother had lived.

I will not allow such chance to play a part in the future of my sons. For I plan on having many sons for my King, and one of them, no matter their younger age to Edward, will become King in the event of King Edgar's death. Not that I can think about that at the moment, not when he's so young and virile at my side, and the thought of him brings warm colours to my face and makes my body wish that this Coronation had already happened.

The King, my husband, and Bishop Æthelwold both have warned me that the events of the afternoon will be taxing. They apologised and yet both of them were also fired up, keen to get events under way. I could almost think that they've been planning this event for years and not for the scant few weeks since Lady Eadgifu's death.

I will walk into the Church at Winchester, or rather the Old Minster and Bishop Æthelwold's domain, on the arm of the King. He will be as finely dressed as I am, our clothing making it almost uncomfortable to walk because of the weight, and neither of us will share a smile or a look, too intent on what will be accomplished today.

We will be refined, majestic, and yet assured in our ways.

Lady Æthelflæd, the lady who was once the wife of a King, assures me that little will change with the anointing and the holy oil, but I'm unsure if I believe her. Surely something must happen to make me feel as queenly as I will be? I would have liked to ask the King or even the Bishop, but in doing so I will be questioning their holy ceremony, and I fear to do so.

I've cajoled and schemed to be in this position that I now find myself within and I have no intention of undermining that hard work by questioning it. In time, and only a little time now, I will know the answer to the question. I will have to be patient a bit longer.

For now, my ladies fuss around me. They should already be within the Minster waiting for my arrival, but instead, Lady Æthelflæd eyes me critically, adjusting my thin crown a little so that it sits upon my head correctly. It's not been an easy piece of jewellery to make in such a short space of time, but the King and Bishop Æthelwold were adamant, as was Archbishop Dunstan, that I should have something new to enter into the Church with. They have a heavier crown for me when I become Queen; this is simply to mark me as the King's wife. It seems frivolous to even me. I will only be the King's wife for another half a day at most, and then I'll always be known as the Queen. Still, it is a beautiful piece of craftsmanship.

I'm reminded of the day that I watched Edgar and his previous wife enter the King's Hall. They both looked stately and calm, their clothing and gems adding to the illusion that they were somehow better than everyone else within that hall. I hope to do the same today, only with a little more natural grace. I hope I don't look as awkward as Lady Wulfthryth did.

The gold has been reworked from an earlier royal crown, and its hue is warm and inviting, the three large sapphires that decorate its form, making it appear as though I wear a hot summer's day mingled amongst my hair. Perhaps that's how I will be remembered even on this frigid winter's day.

Lady Leofflæd fusses about my dress. Her own is a beautiful shade of subdued azure and her long blond curls cascade down her back. She is hopeful of a good marriage now that she's so closely associated with me. I only hope I can find her a husband that will be as lively and beautiful as she hopes he will be. I think the Court is a sharp mix between those who are almost too young to rule and those who are old and not far from their graves.

The wars of King Athelstan, King Edmund and King Eadred have stolen many of their generation's lives, and those who've lived to reach old age are the lucky few. Those who are young are more often that not the products of second marriages, or even third marriages, conducted after the death of older children and husbands. It's a daily reminder that even righteous wars can have a damaging effect on the future of a kingdom.

I sigh deeply, perturbed by my grim thoughts on what is my wedding day and Cornonation day combined, and Lady Æthel-flæd meets my eyes with a sombre grin.

"The weight of the Crown can be a heavy burden," she acknowledges, and in those words, I know she means far more than she says. She might not have worn a Crown, but she certainly expected to, and so I think she probably can sympathise with my sudden worries.

"Are you ready?" Ealdorman Byrthnoth hisses through the open doorway of my small room, and we all turn in shock, and then let loose a nervous twitter of laughter. He's been tasked with ensuring that I arrived in time for my Coronation. It's no small task. I was late for my wedding, and he's still fuming about it, although the King found it amusing and even Bishop Æthel-wold afforded me a shy grin of delight. My being late wasn't planned, but it meant that the people of Winchester were able to see me in the late morning sunshine of winter as opposed to seeing little but lamps and torches used to light my path.

But Ealdorman Byrthnoth has vowed, quite stringently, that I'll not be late for the Coronation. He's been busy hissing at us for quite some time now, but I do finally feel ready.

I nod to Lady Æthelflæd and smoothing her face into one of a serious woman, the King's stepmother no less, she leads from the room with a large amount of decorum that I'm instantly envious of. I should like to walk in the way that she does.

Behind me, Lady Leofflæd readies herself to help me with my train. As I said, this dress is far more elaborate than the one I wore for my wedding, and it's heavy as well, for all that I have no cloak to wear, instead wearing as many warm layers as possible beneath my dress, and ensuring that my boots are stuffed with wool so that I stay warm throughout the long service. I am about to be blessed as one of God's chosen, people will not wish to see me shiver as I'm marked.

But to return to the train. It is long and expensive, made from fine silk. I would like to know where it's been hiding, but the King and Lady Æthelflæd are coy when I question them about it. It's clearly been made with a queen in mind; I just don't know which one. It is beautifully perfumed, and so although I should like to think it's been mouldering in a box somewhere for years, it's clear that it either hasn't, or that it's been well cared for.

Bishop Æthelwold has taken me to one side and whispered that he'd ensure I have a brazier close to me. He too is aware of the cold of his Minster and has asked everyone in Winchester to lend his small community any braziers they have. In the cold weather we've been experiencing, I expect there to be few to spare, but I might be wrong. After all, as many of the nobility as can make it have decided to attend the Coronation. They won't wish to shiver their way through the service either and neither will the people of Winchester. It might just be that the Minster is the warmest it's ever been.

I step from my changing room and meet the eye of Ealdorman Byrthnoth with a firm nod. He takes in my appearance and gives a surprised grunt of approval. If I didn't know him so well, and trust him so much, I might be affronted at his surprise, but instead, I wink at him, pleased to have astonished him. Now I must simply do the same to everyone else waiting to cast scorn on the King's choice for his third wife.

The Court is a sea of uneven waves, crashing against the cliff face that my marriage has become. Some have taken the stance that they little mind who the King marries provided he has heirs, and his governance stays stable. For all that my family is old, we are not overly powerful. We can't upset the delicate balance of power that currently infects the Court. We are, to all intents and purposes, the best option for many. But some, such as the King's ex-sister-by-marriage, are happy to cause unease, as is the family of Lady Wulfthryth. I would like to say that I'll have the power to undermine them all and damage their prospects, but as Queen, I must try and let my personal opinions fall by the way-side, and govern with the future in mind.

The Queen's Hall, as it's now known, is quiet. The servants and slaves are standing to attention, ready to begin the work of tidying when I'm gone, only the head woman being given permission to attend the actual Coronation, and even then, I think she'd rather not be in attendance. As I pass her, my skirt rustling over the scrubbed floorboards, I can see her reciting words to herself, perhaps her list of tasks that she must accomplish. I know how she feels.

Outside, a huge selection of the King's household troop, wait to escort me to the Minster and beyond the gates, I can already see that people are waiting to greet me along the route. The people of Winchester, perhaps bribed by the King, but maybe not, are keen to see me for themselves.

The ice of the morning finally touches my face, and I allow myself just one shiver, that spirals from my feet to the crown on my head, and then I mount my horse.

The animal is placid under the gentle hands of Ealdorman Byrthnoth who will lead the animal through the press of people to the Minster. It will not be a long journey, and certainly not if he has anything to do with it. But I will wave to the people I see and greet them as best I can within the time constraints that I have.

Behind me, Lady Leofflæd is helped onto her equally placid beast, and so too is Lady Æthelflæd. These women are being honoured today. Lady Ælfflæd is already at the Minster, ensuring that all is as it should be for my arrival, and we've made an unconscious decision to avoid even talking about the unhappiness of Lady Wulfthryth's grandmother. There is nothing she can do to prevent my Coronation, even if she so desperately wishes she could.

Unlike her granddaughter who opened her legs for the King before she was officially his Queen as well as his wife, I've not made that mistake, although I would have very much liked to. This means that any children born from our union will be considered more worthy of succeeding their father, even if that date lies very far in the future.

The horse is warm beneath my legs, and I take comfort from his heat as Ealdorman Byrthnoth gives the order to move out. It's a cold day, winter in Wessex. Not as cold as the northern kingdoms that were once called Northumbria and Mercia, but all the same, cold for someone such as myself more used to the fair conditions of the Western Provinces.

I snuggle into my cloak. It's as elaborate as the gown I wear beneath it made quickly by the deft hands of all the women I now call my allies, if not quite my friends yet. We've spared no expense in embellishing it with jewels and pieces of silver and gold. I look as noble now as I'll be by God's good grace by the end of the Coronation ceremony.

The journey to the Minster is accomplished quickly, the crowd cheering for me as I ride amongst them. I'm almost a stranger to them all, and yet the rumour mongers have done me a good service, for once, spreading tales of my care for my dead husband and his children, making me appear almost saintly. After the ceremony, I will walk amongst them all and spread largesse as well. I wish to be loved by the general people as much as I am by the King. If I'm to rule as a Queen, I must ensure that I have the goodwill of the people and their support for my actions. I will champion them in the presence of the King and the Ealdormen, and work within the strictures that Bishop Æthelwold believes I should.

I know my first real moment of panic. The monks are chanting inside the Minster, their voices rich and full of meaning, and upon the steps, my husband waits for me. He already wears his crown, a reminder that he's already King of Mercia. He looks blue in the face, and I worry that I'm late. Ealdorman Byrthnoth's muttered comment doesn't relieve me of my fear, but my husband's cold hand in my warm one does.

"I've been waiting for you," he admits, the passion in his eyes undimmed even though we're surrounded by holy men and Ealdormen, and the women who will become my full-time companions now that I'm to become Queen.

"I'm sorry if I tarried too long," I mutter softly, but his eyes are appraising me as I let him assist me from my horse, my body sliding down to settle beside his own. He is cold, and I look at him with some concern as he bends to kiss my cheek in a very public show of our passion.

"You can warm me later, I'm sure of it," he mutters, and I grin at him, forgetting for a moment that this is a sombre ceremony.

"And now we should go in," he concludes, and I hasten to do as he asks, forgetting that my women need to rearrange my dress, and I almost fall backward on the steps as I attempt to walk forward as Lady Leofflæd tries to spread my gown wide to show off the great extravagance of its length and its depth, and more importantly, its decoration.

"My Lady Elfrida," Ealdorman Byrthnoth manages to gasp, and I remember my ally and stop walking before disaster can befall us both.

"What is it?" Edgar asks with some impatience but being taller than I am, he's able to glance over my shoulder and see what nearly happened. He chuckles.

"Well stopped Byrthnoth," he grins, meeting the eyes of the older man with a nod of his head.

I can still hear the chanting inside the Church but abruptly it ceases, and I feel the weight of my dress settle around me. This is it. The King and I will walk together toward the front of the church, preceded by the holy men, Bishop Æthelwold foremost amongst them, and with my supporters to the rear of me. It will take many long moments to reach the front of the church, to then turn and look back at everyone else that my husband rules, and who I will also help to rule.

In silence, apart from the gasps of surprise from those within the church, we make our way toward the altar in a whisper of fabric and a waft of incense. It's my dress that causes such consternation. It sparkles in the hundreds of candles set out to illuminate the ceremony in the gloom of darkest winter, the silver and sparkling gems, reflecting back at the men and women who have been selected to watch the coronation. They will speak of my dress for many years to come, just as we had planned. The first Queen of the English must be presented in the same style she means to continue.

Not that I stand alone in my ceremonial splendour, the King also wears royal purple, his tunic stretching snuggly across his chest and his cloak, inlaid with purple in a careless expression of his wealth and power, sparkles almost as much as my dress does. Even the King must show his wealth conspicuously.

At the front of the Church, there is a small delay as everyone hastens to be in their right place as the King and I stand and wait patiently. There is a sharp blast of chill wind, and then the wooden doors slam gently, and I feel the audience settle to watch. I can feel stray gusts of warmth from the many braziers within the vast space, and the high weight of the tall towers is a reminder that I am merely a part of something much bigger than myself.

I've schooled myself to meet the gaze of those I've already marked as my allies, even Ealdorman Ælfhere amongst them. I try not to meet the eyes of my old brother-in-laws. None of them has done me any great favours, and I wouldn't be surprised to learn at some point in the future that they actively worked against me. I already know that they will be, for some bizarre reason, unhappy at my elevation. A crueller woman than I would make it public knowledge that their brother stole me from the King in the first place, but in light of my own recent difficulties I've decided to let bygones go, provided they try and do the same. Time will tell.

As I said, King Edgar has never yet been crowned officially by his archbishops and bishops, preferring instead to carry on in his office as directed by the people of the Northern Territories when he was first their King, before his brother's unfortunate early death. This means that before my own Coronation I must sit through the King's own.

Whereas before he was known as the King of the Mercians, for brevity, not because he was only their ruler, for he ruled Northumbria and East Anglia as well, he will have his crown taken from him, from his initial coronation at Repton, but he will then have it replaced when the Archbishops have finished their speeches and prayers.

I've never seen a Coronation before. My father was too out of favour with the royal family when Eadred was crowned, and I was no more than a baby when King Eadred fulfilled his Coronation oath. I'm excited to have a front seat position and to be able to sit beside the King as he's once more daubed with the Holy Oil.

We take our places, finally, at the front of the Church, and I settle my expression to one of only passing interest, stifling my impatience and desire for the ceremony to be as brief as possible, but also as official as it needs to be to ensure that the witnesses know they've seen something monumental. Kings might have been crowned King of the English since Athelstan's day, but no woman has yet been crowned as his counterpart, like the Carolingian Queens. No woman has yet been crowned Queen of the English.

The ceremony is conducted by Archbishop Dunstan of Canterbury, the King calling both on his close connection to the man, and also the fact that he holds the foremost religious position within England. It is also a nod to the continuation from his first coronation as King of the Mercians when Archbishop Oda of Canterbury presided.

Not that there is much different in the service itself, or so Edgar assures me.

"They will only change me from King of the Mercians to King of the English," there is sadness when he speaks, but also triumph. His brother's early death has allowed him to reunite England, but before his death, there was bitterness between the two.

I listen to the prayers intoned by the Archbishop, the other bishops and the Abbots and monks of Winchester, joining is as and when they must, the vast audience before us watching with interest and not a little hunger on their faces. For some this will be a new start for them, for others, it will be a reappraisal of all they once held.

That most applies to the families of the Ladies Æthelflæd and Wulfthryth. They will lose much, although the King has been honourable in the treatment of his two children from those alliances. And my father? Well, he beams with pride as he watches me beside the King. This morning he handed me to the King so that he could become my husband and now he watches as my husband makes me his Queen. What more could a father want for his widowed daughter?

But I must follow the service, not my thoughts.

I watch the King's face as Archbishop Dunstan implores his God to grant him the properties that made the Old Testament Kings the men they were, men who were meek, faithful, filled with humility and fortitude, and above all wise. Men who earned the admiration of their God. I know that Edgar will strive to do the same.

And then comes the part of the ceremony where he will be armed with everything he needs to become this wondrous King, raised above everyone else by the use of the Holy Oil. It amuses me slightly to think that in this part of the ceremony the King will also be granted a Queen for his wife, to share his bed and gift him with children. Am I little more than a crown or a sword?

I dismiss the thought. Whatever I will be, I will be unique.

The holy oil dribbles down Edgar's forehead before Archbishop Dunstan can stop it, and the two share a grimace of annoyance that only I can see as they try to halt the oil from dripping onto his clothing. I could laugh, but this moment is one of abject seriousness, and so instead I keep my face clear, turning instead to stare once more at the audience before me.

Ealdorman Byrthnoth stands with his wife and daughter, somehow my allies from the very beginning. They wear clothes almost as richly decorated as my own, for this is their moment of triumph as well. Beside them stands Lady Æthelflæd with her husband, Ealdorman Athelstan Rota. I don't know the man as well as I wish to, but he has been absent for much of the summer months, back on his estates, and ruling for his King as he should.

For all that, he too stands with the family of his sister-in-law. Their honour will reflect well on his as well.

Lady Æthelflæd stands, mouth a little open, as she drinks in the ceremony of watching her step-son crowned King of the English, waiting for my moment of glory. I would pity her, but I know she is happy with the grace God has shown to her in grant-ing her a short, but happy union with my husband's father, and a longer and even more blissful union with her current husband. I can only hope that I am granted the same and that I don't have to forfeit my happiness for the Crown I so crave.

The activity beside me increases, and I turn to watch the King handed a sword, the same one from his initial coronation. He's chosen to keep some continuity, preferring the sword of his foster-father to that of the Royal House of Wessex. It's an old weapon, used in battle, but it suits Edgar well.

The Golden Scepter and Silver Rod, however, are those pos-sessed by the House of Wessex, the items used at his Mercian Coronation now returned to the claw-like hands of the an-cient kings they were once forced to borrow from. I shudder at the thought of touching something that only dead hands have known, but I understand that the needs of the time had to over-ride my squeamishness.

Finally, the weight of his almost everyday gold crown is set-tled on his head, and I see a smirk of satisfaction touch his face. This is the crown from Mercia, made specifically for him, and about as practical as it's possible to make a crown with its crenellations and jewels. It suits him. And to loud cheers, he is acclaimed King of the English by his Archbishop and by his bishops and holy men, the congregation taking up the cheer as soon as they can.

Only then quiet is returned. No one will yet have to pledge their oath to the King, for first I must be crowned, and while the ceremony is far less for myself, the words used less demanding of my status as a woman, they mean a great deal to me.

I am to rule with the same understanding and compassion as Christ's mother, to be as caring and immutable as she was. Specifically, whereas Edgar will have the ultimate care for the holy men of our country, I am to have the same care for the women who spend their lives serving God.

As such my physical symbols of power are less than Edgar's. I have no need for a sword, although I might still appreciate one, one day. But I am to have holy oil dribbled onto my forehead, and a crown placed upon my head.

Just as I watched Edgar when he went through the ceremony, I know he watches me intently, as Archbishop Dunstan, assisted by Bishop Æthelwold, stand before me. I am allowed to sit in the King's presence, whereas everyone else must stand, and I'm grateful now. Even though I sit, I shake with fear as the holy man dips his fingers into the oil and intones a prayer as he places the slick liquid onto my forehead. I can feel it sticking to my skin, no hint of a dribble, and all of us smirk at the other pleased that this time the action has been accomplished without the recourse to a cloth to wipe away the errant spill.

Bishop Æthelwold bows his head once the act is committed, mouthing the same words that Archbishop Dunstan mutters aloud for all to hear. He has accomplished a wondrous thing here today, and I will forever be grateful to him.

Then it's time for the crown to be fitted to my head. I've not been given the opportunity to view the crown before, although it's been made specifically for my head size. No, the King was adamant that this should be a surprise for me, and it is.

As Dunstan leans in he lowers the crown just a little so that I finally get to glimpse it before it sits on my head for everyone else to see.

It is an exact copy of Edgar's crown, complete with its bright gold and plain adornments, only, and here I sense Edgar has had a hand, there are sapphires and diamonds interlaced with the crenellations, which almost blind me with their brightness in the wave of candles that surround me.

Then it's on my head, and I feel its gentle weight, not as a burden but as a promise, and I turn first to my husband, my King and my lover, with a smile of joy on my face.

This crown is a promise of much to come in the future.

CHAPTER 21

The King stands before me, naked, as I've demanded, an impish grin on his face at being so unmasked, but I take my time examining him.

I've waited what feels like an eternity for this, and I plan to savour the moment.

We're now legally married, and I have also been crowned as his Queen, and there is little more to do than ensure that he excites me in our marriage bed as much as I hope he will.

At the moment, it all seems very promising, as I kneel before him on our marriage bed. He's seen me almost naked before, but I've not yet had the opportunity to examine him in any such detail. Just watching him undress has almost undone me, but I hold myself steady.

He smiles at me, a little self-consciously, but I ignore his face, instead tracing the firm muscles of his stomach, and then lower, to where I see he's as keen as I am to perform the act that will seal our marriage.

"My Lady Wife," he exclaims in mock outrage, but I stick my tongue out at him, from my place kneeling upon the bed that will be ours from now on.

We're alone in the room. This isn't new to either of us, and we need none to tell us what needs doing. If anything, we could educate them all. I reach down and pull my underdress over my head, so that in the light of the lit candles and the dance of the brazier he can see me naked as well. It seems only fair.

This he seems to like, but I still don't beckon him any closer. Once we've performed this final act, it will never again be new for us, and although I look forward to a long night of his loving touch, I want to dawdle over these last few moments when we're still strangers to each other.

I plan on Edgar being my second and final husband, just as I plan on being his third and final wife. We might be young, but we've both had our share of wedding nights.

He watches me now, as keenly as I watch him, my chest rising and falling with desire. I sweat a little, even though I'm naked and a winter storm rages outside the walls of the Palace. But suddenly, neither of us can be apart a moment longer, and he takes long strides toward me, as my need for him rises. His lips reach me first, crushing my own, and yet I don't mind, not at all, as his breath hisses through his teeth as I cushion my body against his own. I can feel his strength beneath my hands as I encircle his neck, forcing his mouth to stay on my own, as his tongue presses deep inside my mouth.

I want to nip his tongue with my teeth but refrain from doing so. Our excitement still has a long way to go, and I must be careful. It's been a long time since a man pleasured me in any way.

His hands reach down to encircle my lower back, and we lock our bodies together, one against the other, rocking gently as we feel super-heated skin against super-heated skin.

Certainly, I've been dreaming of this moment ever since we first met, and I plan on enjoying it. Tonight we will be a man and a woman, letting our lust and desire guide our actions. We will love each other thoroughly, and wake with lazy limbs and silly smiles on our face, but first I must touch all of his body, his shoulders, his back, his long legs, his stomach, and a little lower too, and I must have his hands on me as well. I want to feel an imprint of his hand all over my body, to know that he's claimed me as surely as I'm claiming him.

With my hands otherwise engaged, he tries to draw away from my lips, to take his mouth and his lips to my shoulders, my neck, lower still, but I pull him back to my face. I want to kiss him until we breathe the same air, become the same person.

Denied his request to explore further, he lifts me against him, my legs encircling his own, and as his weight slowly settles around me as he lowers me onto the bed, I know that our loving tonight will be long and thorough, all I've ever dreamed it will be.

I gasp in pleasure as we become one.

Tonight we will be lovers, but tomorrow, or perhaps the next day, we will be a King and a Queen, and hopefully, we will have a prince to cement our union.

The First Queen of England Part 2 – now available

CAST OF CHARACTERS

Elfrida, the daughter of Ordgar, a prominent West County thegn
Ordulf and Elfsige, her brothers
Ordgar, her father
Æthelwald, Ealdorman of East Anglia from 956, her first husband, now dead (son of Ealdorman Athelstan the Half-King, and Lady Ælfwynn (King Edgar's foster-mother).

The Court
King Edgar, the son of King Edmund (murdered 946 at Penkelhurst and his first wife, The Lady Ælfgifu who died c.943) Initially King of the Northern Territories after a 'peaceful' revolt against his older brother's rule led to the division of England along the Mercian/Wessex border for a couple of years.
King Eadwig, initially King of England, but then only of Wessex, now dead, the older son of King Edmund and his first wife, The Lady Ælfgifu became King in 956 following his Uncle's death but died himself in 959, allowing Edgar to become King of England. Was briefly married to Lady Ælfgifu before being separated in 958 by Archbishop Dunstan.
King Eadred, the brother of King Edmund (and so Edgar and Eadwig's uncle – allegedly suffered a long illness before his death in 956)
Lady Eadgifu, the third wife of King Edward (mother of King Edmund and King Eadred) and so Edgar's grandmother, dies in 964 (she may have been instrumental in her grandson's fall from power (King Eadwig) and he certainly seems to have punished her by depriving her of her land, or vice versa. She had been a very wealthy woman in her own right and this may be why King

Edward chose to take her as his third wife.

Lady Æthelflæd, the second wife of King Edmund (Edgar's father) and so his step-mother. She didn't raise Edgar, he was raised by his foster mother, Elfwyn, the wife of Athelstan, Half King. Her second husband is Ealdorman Athelstan 'Rota' (a nickname used to differentiate him from Athelstan, Half King).

Lady Ælfflæd, the sister of Lady Æthelflæd. She's married to Ealdorman Byrthnoth of Essex.

Lady Leofflæd, the daughter of Lady Ælfflæd and Ealdorman Byrthnoth

Ealdorman Ælfhere, brother of Ealdorman Ælfheah

Ealdorman Ælfheah, brother of Ealdorman Ælfhere

Lady Æthelflæd, daughter of Ealdorman Ordmaer who dies c.960, King's Edgar's first wife? And proposed mother of his son Edward. (This is a difficult one – no record of Ealdorman Ordmaer survives and this may be a merging of details about Lady Elfrida whose father was called Ordgar). She may have retired to a monastery. She may also have been Elfrida's cousin. But, Edward certainly existed and was acknowledged as the King's son.

Lady Wulfthryth, King Edgar's wife (first or second? – depends on interpretation.) Gave birth to Lady Edith, the King's acknowledged daughter in 963. Retires to a monastery and eventually becomes Abbess of Wilton.

Lady Wulfhild, Lady Wulfthryth's grandmother

Lady Wynflæd, King Edgar's maternal grandmother, associated with Shaftesbury Abbey, where her daughter, Lady Ælfgifu has been married (King's mother).

Ælfwold, Æthelwald's brother (never an Ealdorman but the King's closest friend)

Ealdorman Æthelwine, Æthelwald's brother (of East Anglia)

Ealdorman Eadmund, named on King Edgar's charters

Ealdorman Mirdach, named on King Edgar's charters

Ealdorman Gunnar, names on King Edgar's charters

Heregyth – head serving woman at the King's Court

Holy Men

(Arch)Bishop Dunstan, a firm proponent of Benedictine Monasticism

Abbot (Bishop) Æthelwold, he would become Bishop of Winchester and taught Edgar as a child

Bishop Oswald of Worcester

The House of Wessex Family Tree

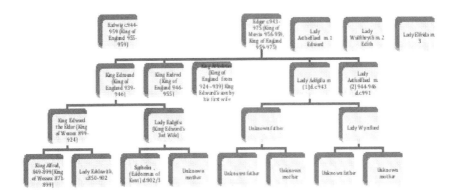

HISTORICAL NOTES

The more I examine this period, the more complicated it becomes, which is both a delight and a hindrance.

The blurring of generations in this brief period is fascinating. As Edgar was an orphan but had a step-mother, a foster-mother, step-brothers, and also his grandmothers, still alive at the time, I almost pity him for having so many family members to appease. It also means that relationships that might not have been close were. It is assumed that Edgar was close to his maternal grandmother, Lady Eadgifu, although she died in 964 (or perhaps 966 as I've now discovered). However, it mustn't be forgotten that she was a tangible link to his predecessors he either never met or died too young to have any recollection of – his father, King Edmund, and also his older half-uncle, King Athelstan, and their father, King Edward the Elder. She was an almost direct link with the accomplishments and religious devotion of his great grandfather, King Alfred, and was herself of noble birth, being the daughter of the Ealdorman of Kent, who she would only have had faint memories of as he dies in 902/3 himself.

This blurring also makes it easy to forget the ages of all the main characters – Edgar was only about 12 years old when his uncle, King Eadred died when his older brother became King. Eadwig too can have been little more than 14 years old. But, there was no one else to become King when Eadred died, certainly not in the West Saxon royal line that descended directly from Alfred (there may have been living descendants from Alfred's nephew, Æthelwold). Whereas when King Edmund was murdered, his brother became King, (Eadred), rather than have a very young king on the throne (a toddler), there wasn't that possibility when Eadred finally died after a long illness. It was one of the two boys, or it was Civil War, or it was gift the family back to the royal line of Æthelwold, if the links are correctly recorded.

It makes it more understandable that so many of Edgar's relatives were still alive, and still keen to interfere in politics.

If Edgar genuinely married three times in almost as many years, with children from those three marriages all being acknowledged, it can only be hazarded at why it was felt necessary for him to marry and divorce so quickly. His older brother had been briefly married, until he was forcibly divorced by ArchArchArchbishop Dunstan, to the daughter of an ealdorman. Edgar's marriages may have worked to 1) shore up his power in Mercia 2) shore up his power base in Wessex 3) enable him to counter any threat from the power of Elfrida's first husband's family, or to piggyback off that power, she was married to her first husband for a number of years before his death. Perhaps the young kings were very vulnerable during this period – the last scions of a once vast royal family that had, by Eadwig's death, probably reduced to Edgar, and his very young son, Edward (although I delay the knowledge of this in the novel to add to Elfrida's difficulties in marrying the King).

Whatever Elfrida had that the other two women didn't have, this third marriage was the one that held throughout Edgar's reign and the difficulties of his two earlier relationships perhaps faded away to be forgotten about, until they resurfaced upon his own, premature death, and the conflict that this caused between the possible heirs to his kingdom, but this, might just be where I find Elfrida once more, about ten years down the line, if I decide to write a sequel.

Elfrida's reputation, and that of her husband's, has greatly suffered through later biases and the efforts to provide some accounting of Edgar's reign, which could almost be called boring because of its lack of fighting and engagements with the Vikings and other enemies that had previously attacked England. I prefer to write my historical fiction using the most contemporary of sources, those from close to her life and death, and as such I have ignored some of the later scandalous traditions, although I did keep the idea that the marriage was one built on passion, and not politics, which is current from the eleventh and twelfth centuries.

If you read my other novels, you will know that I generally only focus on the men in Anglo-Saxon England. This is because few women have any recognisable storyline to develop. I'm pleased to have found a period when so many women are powerful, and I'm very happy to have offered a retelling of their story, even if it's in a slightly less historical manner than normal.

This novel is undoubtedly, the least historical one that I've written to date, and yet it's populated with people who did exist, and who were to play prominent roles in the future of the kingdom, or who already had.

There is no truly accessible biography of King Edgar, although there is one for Lady Elfrida, although it does merge contemporary accounts with later, more fanciful, accounts of her reign and personality.

ABOUT THE AUTHOR

I'm an author of fantasy (viking age/dragon themed) and historical fiction (Anglo-Saxon, Vikings and the British Isles as a whole before the Norman Conquest), born in the old Mercian kingdom at some point since the end of Anglo-Saxon England. I write A LOT. You've been warned! Find me at www.mjporterauthor.com and @coloursofunison on twitter.

Books by M J Porter (in series reading order)

Gods and Kings Series (seventh century Britain)
Pagan Warrior
Pagan King
Warrior King

The Tenth Century

The Lady of Mercia's Daughter

Kingmaker

Chronicles of the English (tenth century Britain)
Brunanburh
Of Kings and Half-Kings
The Second English King

The Mercian Brexit (can be read as a prequel to The First Queen of England)

The First Queen of England (Audiobook now available)
The First Queen of England Part 2 (Audiobook now available)
The First Queen of England Part 3

The King's Mother
The Dowager Queen
Once A Queen

The Earls of Mercia
Viking Sword
Viking Enemy
Swein: The Danish King (side story)
Northman Part 1
Northman Part 2
Cnut: The Conqueror (full length side story)
Wulfstan: An Anglo-Saxon Thegn (side story)
The King's Earl
The Earl of Mercia
The English Earl
The Earl's King

The Dragon of Unison (fantasy)
Hidden Dragon
Dragon Gone
Dragon Alone
Dragon Ally
Dragon Lost
Dragon Bond

As JE Porter
The Innkeeper

THE FIRST QUEEN OF ENGLAND PART 2

Lady Elfrida is Queen of England, her husband enamoured of her, and her supporters many and varied. But the queen finds herself caught up in terse political intrigues, as England is threatened both from external Viking attack and internally from restless factionalism at Court, aggravated by questions about who will rule after the king.

Even when she has accomplished all that she can for the king, a tragedy robs her of her joy and influence, and once more she must toil to retain her position as the first Queen of England and mother to the king's heir.

This is the second part in the continuing story of Lady Elfrida, the first crowned Queen of England.
myBook.to/FirstQueenP2

THE LADY OF MERCIA'S DAUGHTER

Betrayal is a family affair.

12th June 918. Æthelflæd, Lady of the Mercians and daughter of Alfred the Great, is dead.

Ælfwynn, the niece of Edward, King of Wessex, has been bequeathed her mother's power and status by the people of the Mercian Witan but knows she is vulnerable to the North of her kingdom, exposed still to the retreating world of the Viking raiders from her mother's generation.

With her Mercian allies: her cousin Athelstan, Ealdorman Æthelfrith and his sons, Archbishop Plegmund and her band of trusted female warriors, she must act decisively to subvert the threat from the Viking Rognavaldr, grandson of the infamous Viking, Ivarr Ragnarsson of Dublin, as he turns his gaze toward the desolate lands of Northern England, with the jewel of York, seemingly his intended prize.

Inexplicably she is also exposed to the South, where her Cousin and Uncle eye her position covetously, their ambitions clear to see.

This is the unknown story of Ælfwynn, the daughter of the Lady of the Mercians and the startling events of late 918 when family loyalty and betrayal marched hand in hand across lands only recently reclaimed by the Mercians. When kingdoms could be won or lost through treachery and fidelity and when there was little love, and even less honesty, and the words of a sword were likely to be heard far more loudly than those of a king or churchman, noble lady's daughter or Viking rogue.

myBook.to/LadyofMercias

Made in the USA
Middletown, DE
26 July 2020